Secrets Worth Keeping

Secrets Worth Keeping

A Michael Moreland Story

Brad Lussier

RESOURCE *Publications* • Eugene, Oregon

SECRETS WORTH KEEPING
A Michael Moreland Story

Resource Publications
An Imprint of Wipf and Stock Publishers
199 W. 8th Ave., Suite 3
Eugene, OR 97401

www.wipfandstock.com

PAPERBACK ISBN: 979-8-3852-3864-4
HARDCOVER ISBN: 979-8-3852-3865-1
EBOOK ISBN: 979-8-3852-3866-8

VERSION NUMBER 01/22/25

Secrets Worth Keeping is a work of fiction, and any resemblance to actual events or persons, living or dead, is entirely coincidental. While the author enjoyed making some events and locations in the story historically accurate, he made up a lot of things, too. For example, Prohibition on Prince Edward Island was in effect from 1901 until 1948. In this book, however, it ended sometime before 1937.

Chapter 1

Only half awake, Michael felt the explosion before he heard it. He knew it wasn't far away. A prisoner in his chair, he sat with both arms immovable, unable to do anything but wait with his eyes wide open in the gray pre-dawn hours of November 8, 1940, at Highfield on Prince Edward Island. When an acrid odor crept into his nostrils, he sat bolt upright, looking first at his left arm, then at his right, which had fallen asleep under the weight it bore. Heavy and tingling, it was useless when he tried to move it. Desperate and fully awake now, he turned his attention to the dim light creeping under the threshold of the closed door only a few feet before him. The only person within earshot who could answer a plea for mercy stood beyond that door, but Michael's pride kept him from begging. After a second explosion and the arrival of an even more pungent, gaseous odor that threatened to overcome him, he relented, summoned what was left of his voice, and cried out for help.

"Susan?" he called. He waited, but there was no response. "Susan, please, listen," he begged. "Case needs your help," he cried, looking down at the baby lying in his left arm. "I think he's had a blowout, and I'm pretty sure his diaper won't contain the tide."

Just then Michael felt another explosion, but this one originated on his right side. He paused and looked down to where Case's twin, Reed, lay, nestled in Michael's tingling grip, wrapped in his baby blanket, and propped against the arm of the big blue overstuffed corduroy chair.

"Oh, no, Susan!" Michael called. "Reed's in trouble, too! Can you help me?" he pleaded, "*please*?"

Suddenly, the door opened, flooding the room with light so bright that Michael had to close his eyes against its glare. As he opened them to a squint, he watched Susan appear with her hair wrapped in a towel turban.

She was still tying her terrycloth robe as steam from the shower followed her through the bathroom door.

"Michael Moreland," she said in exasperation as she reached for Case, "you are so helpless!" Lifting their son from Michael's left arm, she said, "It's just a soiled diaper, one of many that will need changing today."

"I know," Michael said, "but they ganged up on me. They don't play fair."

"No, they don't," she said, "but the more time you spend with them, the sooner you'll get used to their habits."

"I'm not so sure it's their habits as much as their tactics," Michael smiled. "I'll swear they know when you'll be gone, even for just a minute, and that's when they start playing their tricks on me!"

When Michael finally dared to peek into Reed's diaper a few minutes later, he discovered a second worst-case scenario. Wincing and wrinkling his nose, he rose from his chair and silently approached the changing table where Susan was pinning Case's diaper. Intent on exchanging a very needy Reed for a freshly diapered Case, Michael found Susan one step ahead of him. As he approached, she quickly backed away from the table with Case in her arms.

"Oh, no, you don't," Susan laughed as she shook her head. "These boys need Papa, too." Then, tilting her head to look over an imaginary pair of reading glasses, Michael got a dose of her best school-teacher voice. "I've just taken care of Case. He's all cleaned up, powdered, and freshly diapered. That means Reed is all yours, Michael Moreland." Then she turned her back, walked around her husband toward the overstuffed chair, sat, and prepared to nurse the first of her hungry boys.

The look in her eyes told Michael she meant what she said. At the same moment, Reed began to cry, adding his own opinion about the condition of his diaper. Michael knew he was beaten, but he had to smile. He'd finally worn out the "helpless father" excuse that had worked for the first several weeks after the boys were born. Now, six weeks later, he was on his own. As he looked over his shoulder at Susan, though, he had to remind himself of one great boon. Susan alone took care of all the boys' feedings, a task for which Michael was grateful to remain unequipped. He knew there would be bottles to sterilize and formula to make someday, but, for today, he was happy to leave the future to itself.

With Reed freshly diapered and cooing on his left arm, Michael had only a few minutes to wait before Case finished his breakfast and Reed was ready to begin his. After Michael coaxed a good burp from him, Case was happy to lie swaddled in the bassinet while Michael carried the boys' diaper pail at arm's length to the laundry room downstairs. When he returned a few minutes later, Susan presented Reed to him, well-fed and ready for burping.

Once Reed was comfortable and ready to snuggle in the bassinet beside his brother, Michael busied himself by parting the curtains, raising the blinds, and making the bed. Soon, Susan returned from the bathroom, dressed for the day and with her strawberry blonde locks dried and gathered into a bun. The morning light on Susan's face reminded Michael once more how blessed he was that they were one. One kiss later, which Michael stretched into two, they filled their arms with their sons and started toward the breakfast sounds coming up the stairs from the kitchen. Another new day at Highfield stood ready to greet them.

Chapter 2

A more timely arrival for Sir Richard at Highfield in the summer of 1940 could hardly have been possible. As Prime Minister Churchill had expected, Luftwaffe air attacks on the UK increased dramatically soon after Sir Richard sailed to Halifax from Scotland in a convoy carrying a cargo of gold bullion. Michael remembered his conversation with his father-in-law the evening Sir Richard arrived at Highfield on the first of July.

"Michael," Sir Richard began, "it seems we are all exhausted. However, I can't tell you how wonderful it is to be here on assignment for the foreseeable future. I lack only one thing to make this evening perfect."

"How can I help, then?" Michael asked. "What do you need?"

"I need a cold pint and a few minutes of your time to debrief. There's a great deal I need to discuss with you, and after my six-hour trek from Halifax, I need something cold to slake my thirst. I'm wagering you have what I need close by."

"As close as the kitchen, sir," Michael smiled, "and I can recommend the study for a room where we can relax. I'll prepare the necessities and meet you there in just a moment."

"A man after my own heart, Michael. I'll be waiting," he said.

When he entered the study, Michael's ice bucket held four cold bottles and two glasses. Both men found seats in the overstuffed leather chairs, filled their glasses, and clinked them before Sir Richard related his conversation with the Prime Minister.

"So," Michael asked, "you are on assignment here indefinitely, then?"

"That's correct, Michael," he answered. "For my safety and to ensure that SIS services to Mr. Churchill will not be interrupted by potential Luftwaffe attacks on London, I will fulfill my duties from Highfield."

"Your foresight, sir, continues to amaze me," Michael said. "You predicted this need years ago, and now Highfield is fully equipped to fulfill the mission for which you prepared her."

"It would not have been possible without your help, and for that, I salute you," Sir Richard said as he raised his glass, "and none too soon."

"What do you mean?" Michael asked.

"My first radio transmission from my office at SIS reports that yesterday, the Luftwaffe bombed the village of Wick in Scotland, killing fifteen civilians. Eight of them were children," Sir Richard said.

"What could the Nazis gain from bombing a village like Wick?" Michael asked. "There's no military installation there, no factories to destroy, no worthy target."

"That's correct, Michael. "You see, our strategy would be to destroy our enemy's capability to wage war by bombing military and manufacturing centers. The Nazis, however, are hoping to terrorize the population in the UK as they did those in Poland, Belgium, and France. Indiscriminate bombings turned those civilian victims against their own governments, sending them to beg their leaders to capitulate and surrender. Germany doesn't care how many women and children die in the process. SIS concluded some time ago that the Nazis' long-term intention for Poland had always been to create a nation of slaves. So, the SS closed their universities, killed their professors, sent the brightest and best of Polish society to prison camps, and commandeered the businesses and factories for their own purposes. They'd like to do the same in the UK."

"The newspapers have reported suspected atrocities on the continent," Michael said. "Are those reports true?"

"Not entirely," Sir Richard answered, "because, in truth, the situation is much worse than they dare report. Nazis live by secrets and lies fueled by a disposition of evil no sane mind can comprehend. Eventually, we will learn the depth and extent of the horrors that Jews and other populations in eastern Europe have endured."

"We can't give in to their terrorism," Michael said. "We must determine never to surrender. Otherwise, civilization will cease to be as we know it."

"Correct," Sir Richard said. "Churchill said it best. I can't quote it all, but in essence, he said, 'We shall defend our island, whatever the cost may be; we shall fight on the beaches, the landing grounds, in the fields, the streets, and the hills; we shall never surrender.'"

"But what can we do here, sir? You can continue your work from afar, by radio. But what about someone like me?" Michael asked.

"You've already begun, Michael. You discovered German agents here and turned one of them against the Nazis. There are others. They've already mounted surreptitious attacks on mines and factories in the west of Canada," Sir Richard said. "I have agents pursuing them, but our work is here."

Michael nodded as Sir Richard went on.

"I need you to keep Highfield in readiness so that I can continue to serve SIS undeterred. We must continue our daily life here but with our eyes and ears always open and vigilant."

"It's dark," Michael said, shaking his head. "As you've said, the Nazis live by lies, and, from what I understand, anyone who resists them dies. It's dark."

"Yes, it is," Sir Richard agreed, "but we won't give in and surrender." Then, changing the subject, he said. "Now, Michael, I need your help again on a very present matter."

"Anything," Michael answered.

"First, that second pint in the ice bucket," he said with a smile, "and then I'll need you all day tomorrow to help me set up the office here."

"Done!" Michael said as he opened both bottles. A half-hour later, Michael had a clear list of objectives to accomplish over the following twenty-four hours.

Only a few days after that summer evening in 1940, Luftwaffe bombs began to fall regularly on Great Britain. On July 6, the dockyards at Plymouth and Portsmouth were hit. As the raids continued, civilian casualties grew higher, but the dockyards continued to operate. Churches and homes were not excepted from the Nazi bombs.

Although Germany's primary goal was to eliminate the RAF and establish Luftwaffe air superiority, a secondary goal was to impede overseas shipping to the UK. By blocking food supplies and destroying the British economy, the Nazi hope was to create panic throughout Britain. The Wehrmacht was planning an invasion of ground troops on the United Kingdom, like those that had sown terror across the European continent, forcing governments to capitulate and surrender. Hitler was looking for a similar victory in Britain.

The Brighton Blitz began on July 15, causing evacuations and defensive preparations against a possible German invasion by sea. As the raids continued, civilian deaths rose. At the same time, Hitler looked forward to launching Operation Sea Lion, the Nazi code name for the invasion of Britain from the sea after the Luftwaffe achieved air supremacy. The RAF, however, undeterred by attacks at home, launched their own offensive attacks in night raids at the Krupp armament works at Essen, Bremen, and Hamm in Germany. On July 19, German bombers retaliated in a night raid on the Rolls Royce aero engine factory in Glasgow.

In early August, the Luftwaffe began to target British coastal ports and harbors. They hit Exeter and Birmingham before attacking airfields and coastal radar installations at Kent, Sussex, and the Isle of Wight. On August 15, however, the Luftwaffe began a series of concentrated attacks at RAF installations. Those strikes, however, resulted in Luftwaffe losses of 76 aircraft, while the RAF lost fewer than half that number. On August 18, the Luftwaffe lost another 69 aircraft compared to only 29 British losses. Among the dead that day were 94 German airmen, while the RAF lost only 10. Forty other German airmen were captured. Hitler's goal to disable the RAF before launching Operation Sea Lion was again thwarted. The Luftwaffe boasted over 2,500 aircraft two months earlier, while the RAF had only 750. As a result of Britain's remarkable success against such impossible odds, Churchill praised the RAF before the House of Commons on August 20, saying, "Never in the field of human conflict was so much owed by so many to so few."

Unable to overwhelm the RAF as they had planned, the Luftwaffe turned its eyes toward London at the end of the month. Enraged by successful RAF raids on Berlin, the Luftwaffe began terror raids on London in the early days of September. This strategy gave the RAF time to recover from the August raids on British airfields. When Buckingham Palace suffered a hit from one German bomb on September 10, the RAF answered with a heavy bombing raid at Antwerp four days later. In retaliation, Germany sent two waves of 250 bombers to target London and surrounding residential areas the next day. With the help of Chain Home radar early warnings, the RAF attacked the incoming German air formations and shot down 61 planes while losing only 31 of their own, handing the Luftwaffe another resounding defeat.

Michael knew the skies over London weren't safe yet, and he remained ever thankful for Sir Richard's assignment at Highfield, an ocean away from the bombs and the terror they brought. Well ensconced and equipped at his office in his study, Sir Richard's work for Britain's SIS remained a vital part of the Allies' success in holding back the Nazi dream of total domination in Europe.

Chapter 3

When Canada declared war on Germany after the Wehrmacht invaded Poland in September of 1939, memories of many Canadians went back to the Great War and the cost in Canadian lives the war had meant. More than 650,000 Canadians served in that war, and 66,000 died in Europe. In 1939, many Canadians were not ready to send their men to European battlefields a second time. Nonetheless, recruits swelled the Canadian Active Service Force from 22,000 members to over 58,000 members by the end of September. Following the invasion of France and the Low Countries several months later, the attitudes of many who initially resisted conscription and recruitment began to change dramatically. In 1939, Canada had only two main training bases, one in Quebec and one in Manitoba. By 1940, however, many were under construction, with several not far from PEI in New Brunswick.

Michael was with Jacques Boucher, enjoying a rare Saturday breakfast at the *Home Port*, a diner at the docks in Charlottetown, when Jacques broke the news Michael had been expecting for some time.

"The boys want to enlist together, and the sooner, the better," he said. "They told Doris and me last night after supper."

To a casual observer, the Boucher family might resemble a patchwork quilt. When Jacques met Doris two years ago at Highfield, she was a widowed mother with three children: Luc, Ingrid, and Patrice. Already an integral part of the Highfield family, Doris and her children found a husband and father in Jacques within a few months. They adopted Joseph, a British orphan who had arrived with Susan and her mother from England. Perhaps they were patched together, but no tighter stitches could be found in any quilt on Prince Edward Island.

No parent could have been more proud than Doris and Jacques Boucher, whose two sons, Luc and Joseph, were looking forward to enlisting in the infantry. Nonetheless, they hoped their sons could complete their training close to home before shipping out to the European theater. Fortunately, their recruiting officer was sure both young men could begin their initial training together in New Brunswick.

"Michael," Jacques began as the waitress refilled his coffee, "I have to thank you for what you've done for these two young men. The recruiter was impressed."

"What do you mean?" Michael asked.

"Well, for one," Jacques began, "the rifle training you gave them. Of course, as you know, Luc hopes to train as a sniper and Joseph as a medic. Luc has spent many hours at the rifle range where Francis, the man from Ontario who fought in the Great War, has been schooling him. But, last week, Joseph went with Luc, and both brought back targets signed by Francis, certifying their marksmanship at 300, 400, and 500 yards. Michael, I didn't know Francis was famous for his service, but the recruiter surely did. Our boys already have a leg up, and it started with you."

"Well, I was glad to have some help keeping Highfield's varmint population down and our ovens full of geese in the fall. Your boys were a big help in both departments," Michael answered.

"But that's not all, Michael. Remember that hand-to-hand combat training you gave them? They mentioned it in their interviews, and the recruiter asked them to demonstrate it. He was very impressed with what he saw. That's another reason they'll report for their basic infantry training at the same base," Jacques said. "We have you to thank for that, too."

"Well," Michael began, "I hope you'll always know we're in this together. We consider you, Doris, and your children our family, too. Whatever we have is yours whenever you need it—and that begins with our prayers for our young men readying themselves to defend us during this war. May it end soon."

"Amen," Jacques said, raising his cup to clink Michael's.

"Amen," Michael echoed. "But didn't I also hear from Susan that Ingrid has had some good news from Prince of Wales College in Charlottetown?"

"That's right," Jacques said. "After your Susan began teaching Ingrid and having her help with the younger children at the schoolhouse, Ingrid got curious about Miss Susan's years at Oxford in England. Miss Susan didn't know it yet, but Ingrid was settled on pursuing her own teaching career. They were very impressed at the college when Miss Susan wrote and sent them her university records, and explained the elementary teaching curriculum she had designed and begun with Ingrid. Ingrid has already earned credits at Prince of Wales for what Miss Susan taught her here."

"That's what I heard, Jacques," Michael said, "and Susan is so pleased for Ingrid. Susan believes she may be able to start her formal college coursework in Charlottetown a year or two ahead of other students. I'm also relieved that Patrice doesn't have to make any big plans yet. I hope she enjoys being fifteen for now."

"Oh, she's doing that, Michael. She's doing that quite well," Jacques laughed. "She loves the time she spends attending Lady Moncrieff almost as much as she enjoys the time she spends with the guest children at their chores and keeping the cottages tidy. We're down to only four young folks from London now, isn't that right?"

"Yes, it is. Lois Wilshire, Ingrid's fast friend, has been with us for nine months and is happy to stay. The other three will be leaving for guest homes this week. A new group of seven from London is scheduled to arrive in two weeks," Michael said.

"I'm glad Highfield can provide a safe haven," Jacques said, but I'll be happier when this war is over and all these unfortunates can return to their families. No parent or child should have to bear such a burden."

"Agreed," Michael said, "agreed, Jacques." Then, looking at his watch, he said, "Now, let's get back to Highfield. The *Lady M* will arrive in an hour, and we need to get a few things done so the boatshed is ready to receive her."

With that, the men walked out to Michael's flatbed and were on their way back to Highfield once more.

Chapter 4

She was two weeks beyond her due date, and Michelle Royce had little energy, a meager supply of patience, and only a modicum of civility left. Dr. Andrews, the Royce family physician from New Mills in Derbyshire for more than two generations, had little to offer except, "The baby will come when he is ready. Be patient, my dear." Michelle found his British bedside manner wearisome at best.

It had been six months since Michelle arrived in New Mills from Prince Edward Island, leaving her parents, brother, and the Highfield family with whom she had grown so close over the last two years. Michael and Susan's twins had already arrived, and Michelle knew everyone at home was keenly awaiting her delivery. But home was an ocean away, and although Grayson was only hours away at Kirton in Lindsey, an RAF squadron leader was bound to remain with the men he led into battle. She missed him, especially today when she felt their baby's arrival was imminent.

Of course, her mother-in-law, Mildred, and sister-in-law, Nancy, doted on her and remained very kind, but Michelle was worn from lack of sleep and the constant ache in her back from all that baby she was carrying out front. When she rose a few hours ago, the sun from her bedroom window was busy casting her enormous shadow on the floor beside her bed. Michelle shook her finger toward the sunbeams and said, "So, you think you're funny, do you?" Then, looking back at her silhouette, she said, "Go ahead, but remember, he who laughs last . . . " but she couldn't finish the phrase. Suddenly, a huge cramp possessed her and pitched her forward as she felt her water break. At the same moment, she heard Nancy's knock at the door.

"I have your tea, Michelle. Are you ready?" she called.

"I'm not ready, Nancy," Michelle gasped as Nancy's head appeared around the door, "but Dr. Andrews needs to know the baby *is*. He's ready right now!"

Nancy ran to tell her mother to call the doctor. She returned only a moment later to attend to Michelle, who was already enduring regular labor pains, only two to three minutes apart. Though it was only about twenty minutes, it seemed like hours before the doctor arrived. After a brief examination, he verified that all of Michelle's vital signs were normal, and he reported that the baby's heartbeat was strong and regular. Again, he said, "The baby will come . . . "

"When he is ready," Michelle finished between breaths while Nancy cooled her brow with a compress and Mildred added another cold compress to her wrists.

Dr. Andrews was on the telephone downstairs speaking with another patient when Michelle's baby was finally ready to make his appearance. The doctor hurried up the stairs to confirm what Michelle already knew. The baby's head had crowned, and a few minutes later, Logan Fletcher Royce's voice announced to the world that he had arrived. A big boy weighing more than eight pounds, Logan had his mother's hair, and when he opened his eyes, Michelle was sure she recognized them as Grayson's, eyes she wished were with her to see their son. She had promised Grayson she wouldn't reveal their baby's name, reserving that honor for him, even though Mildred and Nancy were begging to know. Grayson, however, was a hundred miles away with the RAF at Kirton in Lindsey or somewhere in the air facing the Luftwaffe. Even with their healthy newborn in her arms, Michelle couldn't withhold her tears, tears that were strangely mixed with joy but not without fear.

However, there were some circumstances in the skies to which Michelle was not yet privy.

At Kirton in Lindsey earlier that morning, Sqn Ldr Grayson Royce checked the oil temperature gauge as he sat in the cockpit of his Hawker Hurricane Mk 1. He had just reached an altitude of 6,500 feet after taking off and banking with the sun rising behind him. It was unusual to fly west since his squadron was more often used to flying east to meet the Luftwaffe attacking from German-occupied airfields in France, Belgium, or elsewhere on the continent. Today, though, his mission was irregular, for his destination was the RAF airfield at Heywood, a hundred miles west, near Manchester.

Another look at his oil temperature gauge confirmed his expectations. Several of his squadron's Mark 1 Hurricanes regularly suffered from dangerously high oil temperatures that caused the planes to lose power and perform poorly. Unable to reach top speed and altitudes where RAF pilots engaged the enemy, his squadron's airmen remained at perilous risk. The cause of the problem had recently been discovered. Radiator flaps at the exterior of the fuselage sometimes jammed and failed to retract, preventing the cool air flow needed to dissipate engine heat. Hurricane engines relied on a constant flow of cool air to provide the power pilots required to meet the enemy. Grayson's mission this morning had him flying his limping Hurricane to RAF Heywood for repairs. If all went well, he would return with a fully functional fighter and the parts and documentation required to repair two others.

Ordinarily, a flight from Kirton in Lindsey to RAF Heywood would not be considered a dangerous mission. Still, there was nothing ordinary about the skies over northern Britain as long as the Luftwaffe was on the hunt. The flight was only a short hop, but Grayson would be happy to reach Heywood without entertaining a Messerschmitt.

His route took him over some of the best views of the Peak District in Derbyshire. The season's colors came to life in the hills, the valleys, the lakes, streams, and the farms. He flew farther south than his flight plan indicated, and villages he recognized came into view—Buxton, Chapel-en-le-Frith, and Furness Vale. He had eyes for only one village today - New Mills. Just north of Furness Vale, he slowed and descended briefly, trying to catch a glimpse of Fletcher Hall before returning to his course for RAF Heywood.

Upon landing and consulting the repair crew, Grayson learned that the repairs he sought for his Hurricane Mk 1 could not be completed for at least twenty-four hours. The Leading Aircraftman who brought that news was surprised to see a smile emerge on Sqn Ldr Royce's face.

"Begging your pardon, sir," the aircraftman began, "but news like this does not usually elicit a smile. I assure you that we will make every effort to speed the repair."

"I'm sure you will," Grayson said, adopting his most serious demeanor, "but I would rather you engage your most competent staff and take the time required to accomplish a repair of optimal quality. Please be assured that the speed with which you execute and adequately test the repair is not our primary concern. However, its quality is. My mission at RAF Heywood will be complete when I have full documentation of the repair and the parts required for two others at Kirton in Lindsey loaded on this aircraft."

"Certainly, sir," the aircraftman said, "I understand. Will there be anything else, sir?"

"Just one thing," Grayson said. "Would you be kind enough to direct me to the train depot? I must make a short trip to New Mills."

"Of course, sir. We receive supplies via that line regularly. In fact, the parts required for your aircraft are now waiting for us at the depot. I can offer transportation in only a few minutes, sir," the aircraftman replied.

"That would be satisfactory," Grayson smiled. "Thank you."

Grayson was seated on a train bound for New Mills less than an hour later.

At Fletcher Hall in New Mills, with Dr. Andrew's attendance to Logan's needs and Michelle's comfort complete, the doctor left Michelle to Mildred and Nancy's care. Michelle's primary need was rest, but Logan proved to be a hungry boy, ready to attempt nursing earlier than many newborns. He needed no coaxing and seemed somewhat ravenous. Once satisfied, however, he was happy to sleep the sleep of the just and allow his mother the same relief.

It was while Michelle slept that her dreams overcame her. She found herself in a perfect scene with Logan in her arms, Grayson close with her and their son, their new family together for the first time. She could almost detect the scent of Grayson's aftershave in the air as she dared to open her eyes to the afternoon sun and the silhouette in front of her. Only then did she hear his voice.

"Michelle, Darling?" she heard. "We have a son, I'm told. Would you please do me the favor of introducing me?"

Closing her eyes again and returning to her dream, she mumbled, "Of course, Grayson . . . of course," she said as she succumbed once more to her exhaustion.

As she dozed, she felt a kiss on her brow, cheek, and lips, accompanied once more by Grayson's scent, and she opened her eyes wide to find her dream had come true.

"Grayson!" she cried with her tired voice and eyes filled with wonder. "Am I dreaming? Am I?" she asked.

"No, Michelle, no, you are not dreaming. I'm here under the most unbelievable circumstances during war, but assuredly, we were meant to be together at this moment," he said. "Fr. Hunt is a prophet and a wise one at that."

"Fr. Hunt?" Michelle asked.

"Yes," Grayson answered, "but more about that later. For now, I only want to fill my eyes with you and our son and remember this moment forever."

Grayson summoned Nancy for his camera and snapped photo after photo of Michelle and Logan, awake, nursing, and sleeping. Later, Michelle also captured a picture of Logan in Grayson's arms. Mother and Nancy promised to send the film out immediately and to post copies of the photos to him at Kirton in Lindsey. That night, Grayson slept beside Michelle and Logan in a chair, waking for Logan's feedings, learning how to burp his son, and even helping with his diapers. Both he and Michelle awoke at first light, knowing that Grayson's exit was imminent.

"I don't want to let you go," Michelle said through sad eyes.

"And I don't want to go, Darling," he replied.

"We've had a miracle moment, Grayson, and I have to believe there will be more," Michelle said.

"Oh, yes," Grayson answered, "many more. So, for now, let us rehearse these twenty-four hours and look forward to those to come."

"Done, my darling, done," Michelle replied.

When Grayson left with Nancy for the train station that morning, Michelle hid her tears until the car disappeared beyond the hedge on the street. The miracle and timing of his visit did not elude her, but her heart ached nonetheless. Perhaps Logan recognized her sudden burden, for he began to cry for no apparent reason. As she comforted him, she vowed to celebrate the miracle their family had enjoyed and look forward to the day another miracle would surprise them by grace.

Chapter 5

"Case and Reed are fed, dry, and happily sleeping, Patrice," Susan said as she turned to leave the nursery and return to her bedroom. "I'll be downstairs after I shower, so if they get cranky, you know where to find me, OK?"

"Yes, Miss Susan," Patrice answered. "I'm working on an inventory of the root cellars and the larder for my mom, so I'll stay busy until they call for you."

"Thank you, Patrice," Susan said, "I never worry about the boys when they're with you."

Susan had to smile. "Miss Susan," she said to herself. That's how the Boucher children addressed her when she arrived at Highfield years ago. Now, she was Mrs. Moreland, but to them, she'd always be "Miss Susan," which was fine with everyone. Already at Highfield, a history was budding, and it felt right.

Susan had two letters to write this morning, one to Nigel and one to Boyd. She knew how important it was for her brothers to hear from home when they were living in battle conditions far, far away. While the seas rolled beneath their ships, they needed to remember that solid ground awaited them with their family at home. She needed to help provide that ground.

When she and her brothers grew up together at Clifton Manor, Nigel and Boyd proved to be the imps with which every younger sister learns to contend. Although merciless in their teasing even into her teenage years, they proved to be heroes when heroes were required. She still remembered a garden party at Somerleyton Hall when she was fifteen. Perhaps a bit naive, she walked with a boy named Rodney into the yew hedge maze, a walk she'd taken several times before with family and friends. Rodney, however, a guest she had just met, had a goal beyond walking. At first, she could laugh and brush off his familiarities, but deeper into the maze, he grew persistent in his intentions, and she began to panic. When she finally had to shout, "No, Rodney, no!" Nigel appeared from beyond the next turn in the maze as Boyd approached from behind. Boyd took her hand and escorted her back to the open gardens while Nigel took some time to converse with Rodney about his manners. Later that afternoon, Susan learned that Rodney had tripped and fallen into one of the granite garden walls, leaving him with a well-bruised face and a loose tooth. He found it best to leave the party early that day.

Susan's years as the daughter of a retired Rear-Admiral and sister of two Royal Navy officers helped her make educated assumptions concerning her brothers' whereabouts at sea. Although her father kept military secrets and intelligence to himself, general principles of naval strategy sometimes fell out of his mouth in conversation. Coupled with newspaper reports, however delayed and incomplete they might be, she regularly gathered enough information to help her follow her brothers from Canada, even though they were at sea as far away as India or Norway. The names and classes of many British warships, from battlecruisers, battleships, aircraft carriers, and destroyers, had become common vocabulary at Clifton Manor.

Susan's best information led her to conclude that Nigel had been transferred from the HMS *Furious* and was now serving in the Fleet Air Arm aboard the HMS *Ark Royal*. She gathered that the *Furious* had been deployed with other home fleet units in the North Sea, searching for submarines and protecting commercial shipping. She reasoned that Nigel's transfer to the *Ark Royal* might keep him in the same theatre, flying reconnaissance missions and making torpedo attacks on German ships.

Susan knew Boyd's service on the HMS *Revenge* had kept him escorting convoys across the North Atlantic and back to the UK several times. Perhaps his duty there continued. For Susan, even the slightest information helped to guide her prayers, for beyond her letters, she was helpless to do more to comfort and encourage the brothers she dearly loved.

Today, she wrote to them about her boys, noting that Case and Reed were already developing their own personalities despite being twins. She was happy to tell them about how fatherhood was challenging Michael, too. She was sure they would understand Michael's point of view.

After another page about daily life at Highfield, she added a note or two about their father and mother, telling them how good it was that they were together after so many years apart while Father worked in London. Despite the war, never had she seen them closer or more content. As she finished her final paragraph and prepared to add her signature, she heard Michael's truck arrive. After she heard the thump of his steps on the porch when he came through the back door, she heard him call, "Susan, have I got news for you! A telegram from a place called 'New Mills.'"

He held the telegram high in the air and, with a swashbuckling sweep, placed it on the table before her and watched her face carefully as she read.

Her eyes lit up as she asked him with a gasp, "Logan Fletcher Royce? Eight pounds four ounces?" she gasped a second time. "And Grayson arrived just hours after the birth?" she laughed. "Oh, Michael, how could it have been better?"

"It couldn't," Michael said. "And they're sending photos and asking us to tell everyone, especially Fr. Hunt," he said as he pointed to the last two lines of the telegram.

"Fr. Hunt will be so pleased, Michael. He's been such a help to them, and I know they are always in his prayers," she said.

"That's why I'm driving back to Charlottetown now," Michael said. "I stopped at St. Peter's after I left the telegraph office, but Fr. Hunt was busy at a meeting with his deacon. He should be available now, though. I'll tell you about his reaction when I return, OK?"

"Of course," she said, "and will you post these two letters for me as well? They're for Nigel and Boyd."

"On my way, Darling," he said as he wrapped his arms around her with a hug that took her off her feet. With a quick kiss, he was out the door.

Michelle sat quietly, shaking her head. "All they wanted was to be together when the baby was born, knowing their hopes were probably impossible. And then it happened. They couldn't plan it or make it happen, but someone could," she said, looking upward. "Almost like Case and Reed arriving as they did."

Chapter 6

As he drove toward Charlottetown, Michael recalled Case and Reed's arrival as if it were yesterday. It was a day he would never forget.

September 8, 1940, had brought warmer temperatures than usual, and Michael was perched at the top of Highfield's abandoned fire tower, making connections for a new antenna. The fire tower had become the hub for SIS communications with London, and Sir Richard had just taken delivery of some new radio consoles and antennas designed to ensure the most dependable signals on Prince Edward Island. With Armand Verrier's expert help, an all-day installation atop the tower was completed just before noon. During testing, though, Michael was surprised to hear a different voice coming from the console at Highfield. It was no longer Sir Richard's routine "Testing, testing, 1,2,3." No, it was Susan's voice, and it was arriving with a sense of urgency, bringing Michael down from the top of the tower at double time.

"It's time, Michael," she said with broken breath, laboring with each syllable. "We need to go to the hospital, and we need to go *now*!" she said.

Michael had never descended from the tower so quickly. Armand had overheard Susan's voice on the radio and smiled as he watched Michael's flight down the one hundred narrow steps to the flatbed parked on the path below. He heard the engine roar and watched through the tree branches as the truck disappeared down the North Path toward Highfield.

Simon, Michael's springer spaniel, had been asleep on the seat when Michael leapt into the truck. Still sleepy-eyed, he looked at Michael as if to ask for an explanation.

"Sorry, boy," Michael said as he shifted gears, "but Susan needs me at home now. We've got a baby on the way, and when babies decide to arrive, they just won't wait."

Simon's eyes bore a confused look as they left the shadows of the rutted path in the woods and drove into the brightness of the open pasture. There, the road evened out enough so he could stick his head out the window and enjoy the warm air, rich with scents. When Michael stopped the truck at the kitchen door, Simon was content to return to his nap again. Michael, however, sprinted from the truck to the garage and returned driving the Ford sedan. He parked at the front door before running into the house to find Susan.

Susan's water had broken, and the labor pains were beginning to become regular. Attended by her mother, Doris Boucher, and Alida Henault, Susan was wrapped in fresh linens and a plaid blanket for the short walk to the car, but Michael carefully swept her into his arms, kissed her cheek, and placed her gently on the front seat.

"Sorry for the rush, but our baby is rather insistent that this is the day and the time," Susan smiled through the grimace on her face.

"I couldn't be more proud of you, my darling," Michael said as he helped her settle into the seat.

Over his shoulder, Michael heard Doris say, "I called the hospital, and Dr. MacMillan and Nurse Emily are expecting you. Don't worry about anything here, but please call Lady Moncrieff as soon as you have news. I know she'll be anxious to hear."

Tucking the blanket around Susan's feet and closing the car door, Michael assured Doris, "I'll call you as soon as we have news."

When they arrived at the Accident Room entrance, Susan's contractions were coming at four to six-minute intervals, but once she was safely in a hospital bed, they slowed, arriving every eight minutes. Soon, however, they began to speed up again. Michael had been remanded to the Waiting Room, where he sat and paced alternately for what seemed like hours.

In the Delivery Room, a surprise awaited. Amidst the contractions, Dr. MacMillan had some difficulty hearing the baby's heartbeat with his stethoscope. Though the heartbeat sounded normal initially, now it appeared rapid and irregular. He feared the baby might be under stress until Nurse Emily offered her help. Her experience while training in London included over a year in a maternity home for the indigent and another year serving in a maternity ward in a hospital. Her trained ear heard what Dr. Macmillan's could not.

"Dr. MacMillan," she said, "I believe that there are *two* heartbeats present."

"Two?" the doctor asked.

"Yes," Emily said, "which would be completely consistent with Mrs. Moreland's weight gain during these past several months and the confusion we're finding in our stethoscopes. Please listen again to confirm or correct my conclusion."

A moment later, Dr. MacMillan agreed, "I believe you are correct, Nurse Langdon. Please prepare the staff for the arrival of two babies."

Seeing the surprise on Susan's exhausted face and a sudden look of fear in her eyes, Emily said, "Oh, how wonderful, Mrs. Moreland, to deliver not one, but two babies today for your husband, who is waiting without." Smiling, she continued, "I assure you that the second will arrive as easily as the first, and a strong, healthy woman like you will have no difficulty bringing both into the world. Dr. MacMillan and I will have it no other way."

Susan needed to hear those confident, comforting words. Her contractions began arriving more regularly now, and before thirty minutes could pass, Case found his way into the world. While the nurses were still attending him, Dr. MacMillan found that his brother, Reed, was not far behind. It was only another quarter-hour before Reed joined Case in a chorus of healthy cries. Exhausted, Susan held her boys only briefly before releasing them to Nurse Emily and the rest of the attending staff. Together, they kept attentive eyes on both newborn boys. Susan relaxed into her pillows and was dozing a moment later. It was nearly noon now, almost four hours since she arrived at the hospital.

Meanwhile, Dr. MacMillan found Michael at the waiting room door, eager to hear how Susan was doing.

"Michael," the doctor said, "I want to assure you that all is well with Susan. Please sit with me for a moment while I ask you a question."

Not expecting questions instead of news about their baby's birth, a confused Michael returned to his chair while the doctor joined him.

"Michael," Dr. MacMillan began, "I need to ask if you and Susan have chosen a boy's name."

"A boy? We have a boy?" Michael asked as he leapt to his feet, heading for the Delivery Room door, laughing and crying at the same time. "Yes," the doctor said, taking Michael's arm and leading him back to his seat. Still standing, Michael said, "We chose 'Case,' named for my grandfather."

"Wonderful," Dr. MacMillan smiled. "But let me ask you another question. Did you have a second name in mind for a son?"

Puzzled, Michael answered, "Well, yes. We had considered 'Reed,' named for Susan's grandfather."

"Excellent," Dr. MacMillan said, "because I am pleased to inform you that you will need both names. Congratulations, Mr. Moreland. Your wife has borne you twin boys, Case and Reed."

Michael stood transfixed. For a moment, time stood still before he said, "My dear, little wife, my sweet Susan has borne twins?" Yielding to his weak knees, he sat down in surprise. "And all are well, yes?" he asked intently, looking into Dr. MacMillan's eyes. "No complications of any kind?"

Leaving his professional demeanor behind, Andrew put his hand on Michael's shoulder and said, "None, Michael. Emily is attending them now. They'll be ready for you to see them shortly. I'll come back to find you then."

With his mind awhirl, Michael sat distracted, eventually remembering to call Highfield with the news. Sir Richard and Lady Moncrieff were surprised, of course, but clearly overjoyed. Michael was just hanging up the telephone when Andrew came to guide him to Susan's bed in the maternity ward.

Susan looked weary as she lay spent and fully surrendered to her hospital bed, too tired to move. When she opened her eyes and saw Michael's face, her eyes lit up, and her smile returned. As he kissed her forehead, she said, "Well, Father, how much more blessed could we be than to have two healthy sons?"

Before he could answer, Emily arrived and carefully placed Case in Susan's waiting arms while another nurse placed Reed in Michael's.

Both boys were sleeping, but Michael, utterly inexperienced in caring for a newborn, was suddenly overwhelmed. He responded with a rapid succession of questions.

"Am I doing this right? Is he supposed to be just sleeping like this? Susan, is this Case or Reed? How will I know?"

Susan had to laugh. "Michael, they don't come with labels or instruction manuals. We'll learn many things as we go. For now, we only have to love them and welcome them. But, one answer I do have. Case has a small birthmark on his right ankle. See?" she said as she unwrapped Case's blanket. Reed does not. When in doubt, we can always check right ankles."

"Got it," Michael said as he began to relax. "You know, though, I'm thinking of another way."

"And what is that? Susan asked.

Michael leaned over to kiss Susan and said, “I might just kiss their mom and ask her. She’ll know. After all, that’s how these boys got here in the first place, isn’t it? It all began with kisses.”

Susan rolled her eyes but had to smile. “I suppose it did begin that way, but now their mother needs to sleep.”

“And sleep you shall,” Michael said. “Andrew wants you here for at least the next week, and Emily promises she will attend you regularly. The entire nursing staff is elated. Most have never seen twins before. You and our boys will lack for nothing!”

“But, what about you?” she asked quietly.

“Oh, I’ll be back to visit each day, but remember, now we need another crib, a bigger bassinet, and a few other things. I’ll be busy in the workshop for a few hours every day getting furniture for the nursery ready for you and the boys to come home,” Michael said.

“Of course,” Susan answered. “I hadn’t thought of that. I never considered twins, but after holding them, feeding them, looking into their tiny faces, and seeing your eyes, I don’t know how I could ever live without them.”

“I can’t say I understand, but I understand,” he said, “as much as a father can. I didn’t carry them or birth them, but I couldn’t be happier now that they are ours. Now,” he said, looking into her tired eyes, “you need to rest. You’ve had a big day, Mother!”

Susan nodded as Michael added, “Oh, I nearly forgot to tell you. The Boucher’s red setter, Duchess, gave birth to six puppies yesterday. They have Simon’s dark ears and some spaniel spots here and there. I asked Simon what he could tell me, but he didn’t seem ready to discuss it.”

Susan smiled through her tired eyes. “Well, God bless Duchess,” she said. “I’m perfectly satisfied with our two.”

With one last kiss, Michael had turned toward the door, looking back with a final wave as the happiest of fathers headed home to Highfield, but not before stopping to spend some time at a kneeler in the nave at St. Peter’s to offer his thanks.

Chapter 7

September yielded to October and then November, and now Michael and Susan could hardly remember when Case and Reed had not been with them. Highfield had never been more full of life. While always buzzing with activity, the entire house enjoyed the new family focus these two newborns brought to their parents and grandparents. Still, though, no one forgot that the world remained at war.

The summer had been especially busy as Highfield's expanded gardens yielded bumper crops of vegetables. The livestock had their own banner year, with the births of lambs, pigs, and beef calves. The smokehouse stores of ham and bacon were full. The larders would soon overflow with canned vegetables, while the fields assured Michael that the root cellars would soon be well-supplied with root crops—potatoes, carrots, beets, and turnips. Sir Richard's dream of making Highfield self-sufficient kept him busy as his ideas became a reality. With the ice in the icehouse nearly depleted for the season, he furnished Highfield's basement with two additional refrigerator-freezers for the beef, lamb, pork, and poultry the family would consume during the winter. One problem remained. Throughout the summer, Highfield's gardens yielded more vegetables than Highfield, the Boucher, and the Henault households could use. All of the guest children enjoyed fresh produce, and when they moved to their guest homes, their new families returned regularly for all the fresh vegetables they needed. Even then, a surplus of summer crops remained, and the early fall crops would be ready for harvest soon.

Michael had an idea that he shared with Sir Richard.

"I'd like to build a farm stand at the end of the driveway on Suffolk Road where we can offer our bounty to anyone who needs it," Michael said. "There are still families here who have never recovered from the hard times the depression brought. They could use our help. Jacques and his boys will lend a hand, and we have all the lumber we need at the sawmill. We could have it done in a weekend."

"A capital idea, Michael," Sir Richard agreed. "Keep me posted on the progress."

As Michael predicted, the farm stand, a simple structure measuring about twelve feet by fourteen feet with a saltbox roof, was framed and ready to open within a few days. Highfield's young people stocked the stand with fresh produce daily—green beans, wax beans, sweet corn, squash, and tomatoes. They posted a sign that said "Farm Fresh Vegetables—Free" and waited for the shelves to empty.

Michael was surprised and disappointed that most shelves were still full after three days. The weekend brought a few more visitors, but something was wrong. After the service at St. Peter's on Sunday, though, Michael had a new thought and found time to talk with Jacques and Phillipe in the afternoon. Together, they decided to add another sign. It was larger and read, "Take All You Need - Leave What You Can."

The response over the next week was remarkable. More and more folks began stopping to pick up vegetables to fill their tables. Michael realized he had failed to consider the character of the people he hoped to help. He had to stifle a laugh in his pew at St. Peter's when he listened long enough to remember that the people of PEI were like him—proud, hard-working people who didn't like the idea of taking handouts. However, when they read "Leave What You Can," everything changed.

The next day, an older woman filled her basket with green beans and summer squash and hurried away after leaving a gift box on the counter. Inside, Patrice discovered a charming lady's handkerchief, hand-embroidered with roses. Patrice placed the handkerchief in its open gift box on a shelf near the tomatoes. The next day, a man on a bicycle filled his basket with sweet corn and tomatoes and left a hand-made fishing lure, saying, "It'll catch bass, y'know." On another day, an older couple left two new tightly woven handmade baskets, perfect for gathering eggs from the henhouse. These fine people were not afraid to give of themselves and to give the best they had. But there were more surprises yet in store.

Each day of the following week seemed to bring fresh instances of generosity as Highfield's neighbors began to care for each other, enjoying fresh vegetables and leaving whatever they could spare for others in need. Some brought honey from their hives and fruit from their orchards, while others supplied fresh fish straight from their boats.

News of the little farm stand in Suffolk spread, and eventually, folks were driving from Charlottetown and beyond to give much more than they took. Merchants from stores downtown began to return regularly, delivering clothing, shoes, and boots. From time to time, a businessman's truck would stop and unload household necessities, like linens, dishes, and even pots and pans. Others left cases of motor oil and fanbelts, spark plugs, tires, and inner tubes. Whatever hard-working people might need, from garden tools to house paint, began to arrive almost daily.

Eventually, Michael and Jacques had to double the size of the structure to accommodate all the donations. When the harvest of summer crops ended, Highfield was ready to share her fall crops. Michael decided to add eggs, milk, and meat in the winter when cooler temperatures would keep them fresh in the little farm stand beside the road.

Michael knew that Highfield could take no credit for the success that began with a few vegetables at a little farm stand in Suffolk. No, the open hearts of the good people of Prince Edward Island made Highfield's farm stand a haven of goodwill and a godsend to many. Now that it was here, Michael suspected it was here to stay.

Chapter 8

He had to smile. It had been too easy, but he couldn't spend time reveling in his victory. There were only so many hours of darkness left, and he had some business to accomplish. Still, for Ernest Duncan, the fresh air, the stars over his head he hadn't seen for months and months, the wet streets of Halifax under his feet, and the sounds coming out of the pubs at the waterfront remained immensely invigorating.

When they secured him at Pier 21 at the port of Halifax over a year ago, they insisted on calling him Ernst Hoffman instead of his legal name, Ernest Duncan. The name "Hoffman" made it easier for those guarding him to remember that he was born in Germany and had served as a Nazi Oberleutnant before he became a naturalized US citizen more than six years ago. Although he had abandoned the name Ernst Hoffman for Ernest Duncan then, he was a German POW to them now. Over the last few months, however, the hatred so many at Pier 21 had felt toward this captured German spy had abated. His cooperation and talent in protecting the Allied convoys that sailed in and out of Halifax Harbor made him a uniquely respected ally, despite his German heritage and former Nazi allegiance. He had become somewhat of a hero to the RCN colleagues with whom he worked daily. That hard-earned familiarity and respect had helped him escape his imprisonment tonight.

Four weeks ago, his jailers released him from his cell's iron bars and concrete walls. They moved him to their new "Secure Residential Quarters" in a basement corner, a short walk from the office where he worked each day. The walls and floor were still concrete, but a single steel door replaced the iron bars that secured him previously. His quarters were within a hundred steps of his radio station, not the quarter mile requiring an armed escort twice daily. Still their prisoner, though, two RCN officers escorted him to his radio console before 7:45 each morning and returned him to his quarters promptly at 6:15 each night. All day, every day, two RCN officers, clipboards in hand, monitored his work.

But that was over now that he was free. Scheduling shipping in and out of the harbor at Halifax, following incoming and outgoing convoys, anticipating and documenting inbound and outbound local shipping, and delivering accurate reports to RCN officials while sending misleading data to the Kriegsmarine as a double agent for the RCN during wartime—all that was behind him now. He had only a few hours of darkness to secure the prize essential to make his getaway. He needed little, but what he needed was specific.

His escape had been simple. His quarters were down a single hallway where Able Seaman Warren Driscoll remained the only guard. Four weeks of familiarity and daily small talk had earned Duncan a relationship with Driscoll that had become only too casual. When the usual pair of RCN officers delivered Duncan to Driscoll's care overnight, Driscoll saluted, initialed their clipboard, and saluted again as the officers left Duncan in his care. However, bored with his routine duty, Driscoll didn't immediately remand the prisoner to his quarters and lock him behind the cold steel door at the end of the fifty-foot-long concrete hallway. Instead, he wanted to hear every detail about Duncan's day on the radio, how many ships he had saved from German U-boats, and any other news the prisoner might have about the war's progress. They talked for almost half an hour before a seaman from the officer's mess delivered Duncan's supper tray while Driscoll answered a simultaneous telephone call. Duncan excused himself with a wave and a yawn and headed toward his quarters, leaving his tray behind on Driscoll's desk.

Duncan was waiting when Driscoll appeared at his door to deliver the tray. No match for Duncan's hand-to-hand combat skills, Driscoll lay unbruised on the floor in seconds, the victim of Duncan's sleeper hold around his neck. Once Duncan squeezed hard enough to block the blood flow through Driscoll's carotid arteries, the guard fell unconscious, leaving Duncan all the time he needed to make his escape. Taking Driscoll's key-ring, he locked Driscoll in his cell and hurried to the long row of officers' lockers in the outer hall. Locker after locker surrendered its treasures, but cash and a spare uniform were all that Duncan needed.

The single object he needed to procure tonight was nothing an RCN officer possessed. The treasure he sought was a US Merchant Seaman Z-card, the ticket required to sign on with the crew of a cargo vessel at the harbor and find his way quietly to a port in the US. He needed to find a US Merchant Seaman who was about his height, weight, and age and had light hair and complexion. He was sure the bars at the local pubs would have several from whom he could choose. Though that seaman didn't know it yet, he was going to supply Ernest Duncan with the papers he needed to make his escape.

The first bar Duncan entered catered to an older crowd, and one look around led him back out the door. The second pub, noisier and overflowing with younger patrons, offered more opportunity. He found his mark almost immediately.

An American seaman at the bar, recognizable by his accent and attitude, was already well-oiled by the looks of the nearly-empty whiskey bottle in his hand. Duncan bought the drinks for the next hour before suggesting they take a break outside for some fresh air. A few minutes later, Duncan relieved the seaman of his Z-card, left him unconscious in the shadows behind the bar and hurried to the docks to find a likely ship. Before nine o'clock the next morning, Duncan had filled a seabag for his journey and signed on to a ship already loaded and ready to sail south to the ports of Providence, New York, and Baltimore.

For the moment, Duncan was safe from RCN pursuit. Sailing as Thomas Enright, an Apprentice Seaman from Scarsdale, New York, he jumped ship when it docked in Providence a few days later and began his trek north toward Prince Edward Island. He had unfinished business there with Michael Moreland, the superintendent of an estate called Highfield.

The news of Duncan's escape reached Highfield within twenty-four hours. In his study, Sir Richard left the radio console to find Michael in the paddock with Abe and Billie.

"A word, Michael?" Sir Richard called, motioning Michael toward the stable.

Once the men were inside and the doors were closed, Sir Richard said quietly, "We have an issue, Michael. Ernest Duncan has escaped RCN custody in Halifax."

"Escaped?" Michael asked. "But, how could that happen? I've seen his cell."

"He was moved out of the cellblock to a minimum security 'secure residence' in the building where he worked. One too-familiar guard was all it took," Sir Richard said.

"Do they have any idea where he is now?" Michael asked.

"They have nothing solid but suspect he may have found his way onto a merchant ship. An American merchant seaman reported that his papers had been stolen overnight."

"So Duncan could be sailing anywhere right now?" Michael asked.

"Yes, anywhere, but I suspect he would choose a close destination to avoid discovery. He'll want to board only once and leave the ship as soon as he reaches the next port. I suspect Boston, Providence, or New York would be among his preferred destinations. After all, the fewer times he has to produce his papers, the less likely he'll be discovered," Sir Richard answered.

"I don't know what to think," Michael said. "My last impression was that he had rescinded his allegiance to Germany. I don't know if he is a threat to us any longer or not."

"Nevertheless," Sir Richard began, "for the time being, we have to assume that he remains a danger to Highfield. SIS sources will be scouring port arrivals for any evidence they can find. Meanwhile, we must stay vigilant here at home."

"Absolutely," Michael said, "absolutely."

Chapter 9

A comforting security to be found in the village of Suffolk was one of familiarity. Here, everyone knew everyone. Visitors and strangers didn't remain unnoticed in Suffolk as they might in Charlottetown. There, travelers and vacationers came and went regularly. No, in the village of Suffolk, everyone truly knew everyone else. Of course, there was also an unspoken pride among a particular population of full-time residents on PEI—the ones who could name generations of ancestors on the island. Those with deep roots knew who they were and who everyone else wasn't.

The security that Highfield's neighbors provided was palpable. With the Boucher home a quarter mile to the south on Suffolk Road and the Henault's home a half mile to the north, few vehicles passed Highfield's driveway without being noticed. The daily neighborhood traffic at the farm stand also kept folks from several miles away commenting on anything unusual they might have seen on any given day. The wonder was that no one had to prompt them to report what they had observed. They simply cared, and when they cared, they spoke. That openness provided genuine comfort to their neighbors.

Michael could testify that several of Highfield's neighbors had become close and fast friends over the last few years. Some, like Doris and Jacques Boucher and Alida and Phillipe Henault, came to work only part-time at Highfield. When Highfield's needs grew, however, they were happy to fill those needs, but not just as full-time employees. Highfield had become family to them, with resources she was ready to share should a need arise. Even young people hired to help with seasonal planting and harvesting found a familiar comfort among the Moncrieffs and the Morelands. Others who witnessed the provision the farm stand provided for Highfield's neighbors quickly discovered that whatever bounty Highfield enjoyed, Highfield shared.

Only Sir Richard, Michael, and Armand Verrier were privy to the news about Ernest Duncan's escape. Memories still lingered since the attack he perpetrated at the sawmill last winter. Although Joseph had made a remarkable recovery, no one could forget the extent of his injuries nor the threat the attack left behind. No one outside the immediate Moncrieff and Moreland families and SIS personnel knew the name of the man who had attacked Highfield. Rather than incite fear at home a year later, the details of his escape remained a secret while Highfield re-doubled her security procedures.

Little changed for Sir Richard, who habitually maintained a low profile and was rarely seen in public. As a high-level administrator of Britain's Secret Intelligence Service, he remained ever aware that he was a prime target for Britain's enemies. Michael, Highfield's primary representative to the local community, remained her regular liaison with neighbors, friends, and the merchants and local administrators in Charlottetown. Lady Moncrieff enjoyed her association with the local Canadian Red Cross Society efforts but did not extend herself far beyond those portals. With Case and Reed as her primary concern, Susan spent most of her time at home. Though all worshipped regularly at St. Peter's in Charlottetown, they limited any further public exposure. Instead, they maintained a polite social distance, hoping to preserve their security, given possible threats they could not yet identify.

It was about a week after the escape that a letter arrived. The handwritten envelope addressed to Michael carried a postmark from a town named Woonsocket in the state of Rhode Island, more than seven hundred miles away. Michael knew no one from Rhode Island and didn't recognize the hand, but he was impressed by the order and precision he saw in the script. There was no return address, but Michael knew who had written the letter. He left the post office in Charlottetown with some haste and drove to the Soldier's Monument on Grafton Street to find a private place to park and open the envelope. He read,

Dear Mr. Moreland,

By now, I am sure you have been informed that I am at large. Let me assure you that I pose no threat to you and yours. During my escape and flight from Halifax, I injured no one. Even now, I carry no weapons. I bear no malice or ill will toward anyone, though I know I am regarded by many as a monster.

To you, I owe a debt of gratitude. You authored a plan that offered me freedom at the war's end in exchange for my cooperation in protecting shipping vital to the Allied forces. Though I cooperated for a season, I have abandoned my pledge by my escape. Please forgive me. I could not have been convinced to help protect shipping until you visited with me and offered your counsel, counsel you granted even after I attacked your home and gravely injured a young boy in your care. Please know that our conversations and your care for me have changed my life, making this letter possible. You cared for me, Mr. Moreland, as no other man has.

"So, why?" you may ask. "Why did you leave the security of a program that protected your future? Why risk pursuit as a criminal now?"

The answer is age-old and neither reasonable nor logical. I learned about incarceration as a young boy. My jail was the basement of my family's four-room flat. It was damp, cold, and smelled of mildew, but mostly, the odor was one of terror and hopelessness. I was terrified by the sound of my father's drunken voice when he came home each day. When he walked through the door and slammed it, I sometimes lost control and wet myself. Disgusted with me, he would force me down the basement stairs into the darkness while he took out his rages on my mother. I spent too many nights in that darkness, listening to my father's wrath and my mother's pleas when he taunted and beat her. When he finished with her, he always came for me as I huddled again in the darkness of that cold, dark basement.

Four weeks ago, my quarters became a basement room again, with the same small locked windows near the ceiling, like the ones through which I peered as a boy, praying that someone would hear my cries and rescue me.

In these new quarters, I could no longer bear my imprisonment. The damp concrete walls and floors in that basement cell, the locked door, the smells rising from the floor drains - all these waited for me at the end of each day. They brought back the terrors that ruled my dreams as a boy. I had to get away.

I can't be a prisoner like that again, Mr. Moreland, but I blame no one. I know now that my father was an injured man. He could not give me something that he had not received. I can only pray - something else that you taught me - that the memories that continue to wake me will fade over time.

I have unfinished business in Canada, but, again, you and yours will neither see me nor face any danger from me. When my business is complete, you will hear from me only once more. I hope my final message will bring a measure of relief to you.

I remain ever indebted to the only man who listened, did not judge, and gave of himself for my sake.

Ernest

Michael read the letter a second and a third time before starting his truck and driving home. Of course, he had to share the letter with Sir Richard, whom he was sure would be concerned about an escaped German prisoner. However, Michael also felt somehow protective of Ernest Duncan. He sensed a genuine change in the man and didn't feel that anyone at Highfield was at risk. He also felt that, out in the open, Ernest Duncan would be hard to find if he didn't want to be found. Duncan had posted the letter days ago. He could be anywhere now. He said he had unfinished business in Canada, but that didn't necessarily mean Prince Edward Island. Michael didn't know what to think, but he was about to find out.

Chapter 10

An older woman, a regular patron among the neighbors who frequented the farm stand, spoke to Ingrid one day.

"He was a strange one, he was. Not one of us, you know," she said. "He was on a bicycle with a basket on the front and one on the back, too. He was wearing a fedora for a hat, not like anything our men wear. He looked hungry and proved it as he ate several tomatoes and most of a loaf of your mother's bread, he did. He looked up the driveway toward the big house several times. The way he looked made the hair on the back of my neck stand up," she said. "I know when something's not right, and this man was not right."

Ingrid asked a few questions and learned that the man was perhaps thirty and had blond hair and blue eyes. There was some straw stuck to his clothes, suggesting he might have spent time in a barn somewhere close by. Everything the woman said was genuinely mysterious.

Ingrid was good with a secret and kept everything to herself until she could talk with Michael. Then, she told him everything.

"Did she say when she saw him?" Michael asked.

"Yesterday at dusk," Ingrid answered. "One other time, it was very early, at first light. She's seen him several times, but always at dusk or dawn, as if he doesn't want to be seen. And he always rode north, toward the schoolhouse, which is strange because there's nothing that way to speak of," she said.

"Thank you, Ingrid," Michael said. "You've been very helpful. I think I may know this man. Yes, he seems a bit odd, but I think I can help him if he comes again. If you can, let me know, OK?"

"I will, Mr. Moreland. I will," Ingrid said.

A week later, when Michael arrived at the farm stand with a bushel of new potatoes, Ingrid ran up the driveway to meet him.

"I heard your truck coming, and I need to tell you," she said, breathing hard. "That man was here, but he just left, riding north. I think you could catch up with him if you hurry."

Michael started north immediately, but after driving two miles, he had seen nothing. On his way back, he stopped at the Henault's home, but neither Alida nor Phillipe had seen anything, either. Michael was perplexed until the next morning.

He remembered what their neighbor had said about some straw stuck to the man's clothes, and he had a new thought. Just north of Highfield on the east side of Suffolk Road, there was an abandoned driveway overgrown with brush. It led to what had been the Kendall Farm. A fire had destroyed the farmhouse sometime in the 1920s, but a substantial part of the barn still stood, though in a sad state of disrepair. Michael was intent on taking a closer look at the barn this morning.

As he suspected, there was evidence in the brush at the driveway of some recent foot and bicycle traffic. Just past the remains of the farmhouse foundation, Michael found a newly trampled path through the undergrowth to what remained of the barn. He found signs inside that someone had recently made the barn an overnight home. Now abandoned, the barn held nothing for anyone to come back and claim except for a short-handled spade, an empty canning jar, and a worn grey fedora, like the one that Highfield's neighbor had described. The hat's label bore the name of a merchant in Halifax.

Michael needed to see no more. Yes, Ernest Duncan had been here, but why? He might have left his hat to pique Michael, but why did he leave a canning jar and a spade? Michael brought both home to share with Sir Richard, but neither man could offer a logical guess regarding them until almost two weeks had passed.

That morning, Michael made his regular stop at the post office, but this time, he discovered a small parcel posted in Burlington, Vermont. Michael recognized the hand at once and opened the parcel to find a letter and several small, hand-drawn maps. The letter told him everything he needed to know.

Dear Mr. Moreland,

By now, I'm sure you have learned that I spent a few days near Highfield some weeks ago. I kept my promise to remain undetected and left only a few indicators to help you confirm that I had been about. Here is the reason for my visit to PEI.

I spent many hours mapping the island's shores for my former employer. My work required locating secluded sites where invaders from U-boats could land small inflatable watercraft with a minimum risk of detection. My assignment also required burying a small cache of goods that invasion forces would require once they landed.

I am including maps and coordinates for the three locations where I buried these goods. A short-handled spade will suffice to discover a single, common waterproof container at each location. With your permission, Mr. Moreland, I would like you to deliver particular items of value in each container to the young man injured at Highfield's sawmill last year. Please extend my sincere apologies to him for his pain and suffering.

Also, please accept my heartfelt thanks for extending yourself and coming to my aid when I was imprisoned. The kindness you offered me provided the possibility of a new beginning. Fr. Hunt, whom you sent to me, provided counsel that proved particularly healing. Please extend my thanks to him.

Someday, perhaps a long time from now, our paths may cross again. For now, though, my best gift to you is that I remain only a memory. Although memories will fade in time, for my part, they will remain fond.

E.D.

The day after Michael shared the letter with Sir Richard, the two men traveled with Armand to locate the three sites Ernest Duncan indicated on his maps. After some exploration, they discovered the three caches he described. Buried about eighteen inches underground at each site, they found a single well-sealed canning jar. When they opened the three jars back at Sir Richard's study, they found that each contained hand-drawn local maps and the names and addresses of local officials such as police chiefs, fire chiefs, and others in charge of civil defense. Each jar also held a sum of cash in Canadian currency. The total value of the currency among the three jars amounted to nearly $4,000, a small fortune for any farmer or fisherman on PEI.

Sir Richard and Armand marveled while Michael merely pondered. When he first came to know Ernest Duncan, he witnessed a man with a hard, calculating, and unforgiving heart. Now, that same man was willing to forfeit thousands of dollars for the peace of mind he needed to confirm his heart had changed.

All three men concurred that they could report to SIS only that after landing at the port of Providence, Ernest Duncan was known to have traveled in Rhode Island and Vermont before his trail went cold.

"As a naturalized US citizen and a civilian, he won't be pursued as a war criminal," Sir Richard said. "Furthermore, he paid for the crimes he perpetrated against shipping in Halifax several times over during his service to the RCN as a double agent. I believe he offers no further threat to Canadian or British interests. When his German counterparts fail to hear from him regularly, they'll send someone to look for him. He'll need to go to ground and disappear. Until he reappears, I have to consider this case closed. Our energies are needed on other battlefields."

Neither Armand nor Michael could disagree. Ernest Duncan's whereabouts would remain a mystery. Perhaps there were some secrets worth keeping. Michael, however, felt a twinge of sadness. He had watched Duncan change from a hard, ruthless man to one whose injured heart, mind, and spirit had found an amazing measure of healing. His new journey had just begun. Michael regretted that he would be unable to follow it further.

Chapter 11

"Michael," Susan called on her way upstairs. "You have to see this! It's a parcel that just arrived by courier. It's from Grayson and Michelle."

Michael had been dozing in the nursery while Case and Reed enjoyed their afternoon naps. Although he hadn't planned on joining their naptime, the hour or two he and Susan lost each night changing diapers, feeding, and burping their boys had caught up with him after lunch. Half-awake, he remembered leaning forward to marvel at their two little faces, so alike, but each day offering just a tiny hint of individuality. Naptime was a particularly singular event. Before he yielded to sleep, Case preferred to kick his way out of the blanket Susan wrapped around him. Reed, however, was happy to snuggle down right away and usually fell asleep first. Watching his sons nod off was the last thing Michael remembered before Susan woke him with her news.

He stood quietly, easing out of the nursing rocker and taking a last peek at the boys before closing the door and joining Susan in their bedroom. In one hand, she was holding a parcel addressed to them from New Mills, Derbyshire, England. Her other hand held a large photo album, the kind with three or four photos on each page.

"I couldn't wait, Michael," she said as she sat on the bed. "I had to look. You've got to see this," she giggled.

Michael joined her, and they laughed together. Photo after photo captured an ecstatic father and mother with their newborn son, Logan.

"He's got Michelle's hair, don't you think?" Susan asked.

"Her eyes, too, but he's got Grayson's forehead and chin. He looks a little serious already, doesn't he?" Michael laughed.

"I won't disagree," she said, "especially in this photo with Grayson's mother."

"Ah, yes," Michael said. "And here's Grayson's sister. I haven't seen Nancy in years, but she looks like a very content and adoring aunt."

"There's a letter here, too. I haven't read it all, only the first sentence mentioning a miracle that brought Grayson home when Logan was born. Here," she said, "we can read it together."

Michael leaned in as they learned about Grayson's flight to Manchester and the overnight he enjoyed in New Mills when Logan was born.

"Things like that don't just happen," Michael said. "I know divine intervention when I see it."

"No disagreement here," Susan added. "Nothing else could have brought them together at just the right time during a war."

"This parcel was posted weeks and weeks ago. By now, Logan is already becoming a little man. Someday, when he gets together with our boys, we'll have our hands full," Michael laughed.

Just then, there was a knock on the door, and Patrice called quietly, "Mr. Moreland?"

"Yes, Patrice. I'll be right there," Michael answered as he kissed Susan's temple and walked out to the hall. "What is it, Patrice?" he asked.

"My father is downstairs in the kitchen. He'd like a word with you if you can," she said.

It wasn't like Jacques to appear at the house this way, so Michael went downstairs right away. Jacques was waiting at the kitchen table, hat in hand.

"Could I bother you for a minute?" he asked. "Sir Richard called me in this morning to give me this," he said as he held up a thick envelope, "but he had to take a telephone call and never told me what it was about. He said that you could explain, Michael."

Michael recognized the envelope immediately. It was the same one Ernest Duncan posted to him a week ago. The envelope was void of Duncan's letter but was now full of money. Michael motioned to Jacques to follow him out the rear kitchen door.

Once they were away from the house, Michael said, "That's a lot of money, isn't it."

"It certainly is, Michael. And Sir Richard said it's for Joseph from the man who set the trap at the sawmill last winter. That man wanted to kill us then, but now he wants to give us a fortune like this?" Jacques marveled. "What happened to him?"

"He had a remarkable change of heart, Jacques," Michael began. "He was an injured man who got some help, found a way to forgive those who hurt him, and is now seeking forgiveness himself. The money is for Joseph—to cover his injuries, hospital expenses, and anything else he needs."

"Well," Jacques began, I must say I'm amazed, and it couldn't have come at a better time. Joseph opened a letter yesterday from his RCA recruiter. Joseph failed his physical examination. He doesn't have full movement in his legs yet, and his back isn't fully healed, either. They suggested he re-apply for enlistment a year from now. He won't be going to basic training when Luc goes, after all."

"Wow," Michael said, "he must be shattered. I know how much he was looking forward to serving."

"But that's where all this money comes in, Michael," Jacques explained. "Dr. MacMillan is arranging for Joseph to train at a hospital in Montreal. He'll have regular classroom studies and be learning on the hospital floor. If he does well, he could go on to medical school and be a doctor someday."

"And how does Joseph feel about all this?" Michael asked.

"He was slow to come around at first," Jacques explained, "but he began to get excited when Dr. MacMillan described the path of study he'd be following. After a year's training in Montreal, he'll be free to re-apply with the RCA or return to Montreal for a second year at the hospital. Of course, he's still upset about missing basic training with Luc, but he's also excited about the opportunities in Montreal. And this," Jacques said as he held the envelope over his head, "will pay for everything he needs for the next three or four years."

"You and Doris must be relieved to have one son out of harm's way and staying on this side of the ocean rather than serving on a battlefield," Michael said.

"True enough," Jacques agreed, "and the girls are relieved, too. Luc will get used to the idea. If all goes as expected, he'll be headed for basic training in New Brunswick the week after next. Doris and I were thinking about a going-away party for him this weekend. You'll all be coming once we make the plans, right?" Jacques asked.

"We wouldn't miss it," Michael promised, shaking Jacques' hand. "All of Highfield will be there to celebrate one of our own."

Chapter 12

Although letters from Nigel and Boyd were few, and those that arrived were usually six to eight weeks old, Sir Richard and Lady Moncrieff looked forward to every one. Sir Richard's SIS sources were able to inform him of the general locations of both the HMS *Ark Royal* and the HMS *Revenge* but could reveal little more. The Moncrieffs and the Morelands wrote regularly, regardless of the long delay their letters would endure before delivery. What mattered was that the Moncrieff men at sea could rest assured that they were remembered and mentioned in prayer every day.

The *Ark Royal* had been deployed in the Mediterranean since late June, where she was instrumental in neutralizing the remainder of the French fleet before they could be seized by the Nazis and deployed against the Allies. Nigel had enjoyed his share of flight time, providing reconnaissance, bombing, and torpedo launches from the air. The *Ark Royal* went on to defend the island of Malta from Italian attacks while delivering fighter planes to British airfields and launching a successful air attack against Italy's air base at Cagliari. After sailing to Alexandria, she was deployed to West Africa before returning to England for refitting. From the first week in October, she was docked in Plymouth, and work continued until the third of November.

During the same time, Boyd was serving aboard the *Revenge* when it left its North Atlantic convoy escort duty to attack German transport ships along the English Channel, where they lay waiting for orders to invade Great Britain. When Germany relented and canceled her invasion plans, the *Revenge* returned to duty in the North Atlantic.

On the continent, the news remained grim, especially for the Jewish populations in every country Germany had invaded. As early as October, the rump state of Vichy France, under Marshall Phillipe Pétain, called on its police to begin a census of the country's Jews. Within days, they passed legislation banning Jews from holding jobs in many occupations, both public and private. In Poland, the Nazis forced all of Warsaw's Jewish population to move into a ghetto established to separate them from the general population. Immediately after invading Belgium, the German occupation force announced anti-Jewish laws and began confiscating Jewish property and businesses while banning Jews from many professions. Similarly, the Nazi occupation force in the Netherlands immediately began separating Jews from the general population, forcing Dutch officials to participate in the process.

Unfortunately, much of this news never reached the press in Canada or the United States. Thankfully for Highfield, Sir Richard was willing to share the news he could, exclusive of any intended for SIS eyes only. An end to the evil that the Nazi victims in Europe endured every day remained the subject of Highfield's prayers each morning.

When Japan joined Germany and Italy in the Tripartite Pact in September of 1940, it became clear to many that the war in Europe had become a world war, now called by many "World War II." The Tripartite Pact provided that any country not currently at war with Germany, Italy, or Japan would become the enemy of all if any of the three was attacked.

The pact was aimed squarely at the United States, which had officially maintained neutrality thus far. While Germany and Italy extended their aggression in Europe to North Africa and beyond, Japan had already invaded China and French Indo-China. To the US, the Tripartite Pact provided a threat of war it could no longer ignore. Axis threats surrounded the nation as the war expanded from Europe to China and beyond.

In conversation with Lady Moncrieff, Susan, and Michael after dinner on a cold November night, Sir Richard offered some hope for the war that the UK was shouldering alone.

"Since Japan joined Germany and Italy in September, the United States appears to be preparing to enter the war," he said with his sherry glass in his hand.

"What makes you think so, Richard?" Lady Moncrieff asked.

"Several things have come to light," he began. "Until now, US aid to Britain has been limited to supplying military goods, arms, and munitions, first on a cash basis, but later under more liberal payment options. We understand that there is support in their Congress for legislation permitting even more freedom for them to supply armaments while maintaining their neutrality. But," he added, "that's not all."

"Please, say on," Michael said.

"Two months ago, the US instituted peacetime conscription for the first time in history. All men between the ages of 21 and 45 are required to register," he said. "They've already got thousands of men in basic training, readying them to serve."

"That sounds serious," Lady Moncrieff said. "Conscription has never been popular anywhere, especially when one's country is not at war. They must believe war is imminent."

"Exactly," Sir Richard said, "but there's more. Their legislature has approved a defense budget that has been increased five-fold since the previous year. They are also expanding their navy, adding more than 250 vessels, including carriers, destroyers, cruisers, and submarines."

"That's quite a fleet, Father," Susan said as she handed Case to Michael for his burping. In exchange, Michael handed Reed to her for his feeding. "How long will it take for them to have them battle-ready?" she asked.

"It will take some time, of course, but the Americans have a manufacturing history second to none. Shipyards are plentiful on their east, west, and southern coasts, materials are available, and the American workforce has always been up to a challenge," he said. "While others spend years retooling, the Americans will need only months. By the way," he added, "the legislation their Congress approved was called the 'Two Ocean Navy Act.' Clearly, the US is already preparing for a war not limited to the Atlantic theatre."

"I must say, Richard," Lady Moncrieff began, "that although the Americans appear to be preparing for war, it is hard for me to believe they will enter the war unless attacked. They are peaceful people and not given to aggression. Thus, even from their birth in 1776, they have always been more reactors than actors. Nonetheless, history has shown us that once Americans go to war, they go to win. It may sound rather radical, but I look forward to the day when the Axis powers attack them. I believe their response will be immediate and their counter-attack relentless. Their attackers will rue the day they dared to pique this giant. Once they are in the fight, I am confident they will fight shoulder-to-shoulder with us until we attain victory together."

"Well spoke, Angela, well spoke," Sir Richard said, applauding, "and with your usual gifts of discernment and wisdom. Perhaps you would have some spare hours to advise my compatriots at SIS? They could do with your gifts, some of those men," he laughed.

"Let's just say, 'Not today, thank you,'" she laughed as she rose and turned toward the center stair. " I have an appointment with my pillow just now."

As she stood, all rose to bid her goodnight. Those remaining lasted only a few minutes longer before succumbing to her wisdom and seeking their pillows, too.

Chapter 13

It had been more than five months since Nurse Emily Langdon's marriage to Dr. Andrew MacMillan when she telephoned Highfield one afternoon and asked for Susan. Fortunately, Case and Reed were settled and asleep after their afternoon feeding, and Susan could take the call.

"Hello, Emily. It's been some time since we last spoke. I hope you and Andrew are well," she said.

"Oh, yes, very well," Emily answered, but followed with, "Actually, I'm not doing as well as I'd like. Would you have a few moments when I could drop by to talk?"

"Of course," Susan answered. "The boys are sleeping right now, but you're probably at the hospital."

"Yes, but I'm just about to leave. I could be at Highfield shortly if that would be all right," Emily said. "Andrew is meeting with the hospital's finance committee, and I have the car for the afternoon."

"Of course, Emily," Susan answered. "I'll brew some tea."

Until a month ago, Emily had been a regular visitor at Highfield, attending Lady Moncrieff for brief routine checkups and always eager to see Case and Reed. The boys were the first twins whose birth she had attended since her training in London years and years ago. She was a natural with babies, and Susan and Michael had already begun to call her Aunt Emily whenever she visited. Susan tried to recall the last time Emily saw the boys and realized it had been over two weeks. She wondered if something was awry.

Susan smiled when she thought back to the hour she and Michelle had spent with Emily in July, a week after she and Andrew returned from their honeymoon. Emily had an irresistible way of recounting events that kept her two friends on the edge of their seats.

"About our honeymoon, ladies, you must remember," Emily began, "that I have seen a few more years than either of you but never with any thought of a husband. I planned on dying a spinster, as most nurses in London do. Remember, too, that Andrew has five years more than I have, and he also hadn't given marriage a serious thought for some years. So, we were both somewhat surprised by our relationship's whirlwind acceleration, which eventually included our wedding plans. And," she went on, leaning forward to say quietly, "personally, my expectations for our honeymoon were limited to my vague recollections of love stories I had seen in films at the theatre, which were precious few."

"But, Emily," Michelle said, looking at Susan, "we both know that you and Andrew are very much in love, and we haven't forgotten how specific and detailed you were when telling us about the first kisses you shared. You told us that Andrew was very much a gentleman then, although you did say he was eager, and, as I remember," Michelle said, "you described him as 'hungry.' Isn't that correct?"

"Yes, I did," Emily admitted, blushing. "However, once we left the wedding reception for our hotel, I was somewhat surprised at the extent of our mutual, how shall I say," she hesitated, "*energy* once we were finally alone with one another."

"Emily," Susan had said, looking at Michelle and smiling knowingly, "we are not so far from our honeymoons that we have forgotten how new and exciting those first nights and days were for us."

"Yes, of course," Emily said as she put her teacup on the table, took a deep breath, and smoothed her hair. "But, because I never expected to marry, neither had I allowed myself the luxury of looking forward to a wedding night. Looking back at that night now, I find it somewhat of a blur. I remember the bellman leading us to our suite," she said, "and Andrew carrying me across the threshold. It was a lovely suite with several rooms. Each had high ceilings and was furnished with every comfort—lovely linens, plush carpets, and even his-and-her robes, hanging on brass stands beside the bed."

"It sounds lovely," Michelle said.

"Yes," Emily said as she reached back in her memory. "I remember Andrew tipping the porter and closing the door. But when he turned from the door to look at me across the room, our eyes locked, and in an instant, we found ourselves rushing toward each other and meeting in the center of the room. We seemed to agree, and it was as if our minds were one and we hardly needed any words. Perhaps an hour passed—again, it's all a bit of a blur for me now—until I rose, reached for my robe, and tried to find my way to the bathroom. But, as I raised my eyes, I was suddenly ashamed and so, so embarrassed."

"Ashamed and embarrassed?" Susan asked. "But why, Emily?"

"Because while donning the lovely robe the hotel provided, I looked across the room to discover that we had left a veritable trail of clothing behind us. Some things were on the carpet, some on the furniture, but none had been properly folded or hung," she said, looking down at her teacup. "And you two, my best friends, had given me some lovely intimate things to wear for that night, and I hadn't even considered opening my suitcase. As I was retrieving our clothes from the carpet, Andrew rose to help me. He could see my embarrassment but smiled and helped me gather our things together."

"I see," Susan said, glancing at Michelle, who was working hard to contain her smile.

"It was not yet seven o'clock that evening when we showered, made ourselves presentable, and walked to the hotel dining room. I don't know why I was so hungry, but the menu boasted a wonderful coq au vin, and I ate all of it, every bite, and followed that with dessert, a lemon tart. Andrew ordered calves liver and onions. You know," she said, "I had no idea he fancied calves liver. That was a surprise to me."

"Calves liver," Susan echoed. "Interesting."

"We shared a bottle of wine at dinner, a cabernet sauvignon if I remember correctly. I had never enjoyed more than a single glass of wine in one sitting, but before I knew it, I had consumed two. Perhaps that is why my memory is so hazy," she said, knitting her brow. "But then Andrew asked the waiter to deliver a bottle of champagne to our room. When we returned to our suite, it was waiting for us, and Andrew opened the bottle and poured two glasses. It might sound extravagant, but we sat together on a small red velvet sofa and never took more than a sip before our eyes locked again, and we were suddenly, well, how shall I say? Perhaps a good word would be 'occupied.' Yes, we were *occupied* again," she said as she looked into her teacup.

"Occupied?" Michelle asked with raised eyebrows, looking at Susan.

"Yes," Emily said, looking up. "Occupied. *Completely* occupied. So occupied were we with each other that were a locomotive to have passed through our room, I'm not sure we would have noticed."

"Oh," Susan said as she grasped Emily's meaning.

"Again, we had some picking up to do, but soon it was time for bed," Emily said. "However, we were already there, you see, only now we had to get used to sleeping in bed with another. But it wasn't 'another,' now was it? Now, it was 'each other,' which was such a comfort because our marriage was finally real somehow."

Michelle and Susan looked at each other and nodded before looking back as Emily began again.

"And then, sometime shortly before dawn, I rolled over in bed to look at Andrew. You see, I could hardly believe we were truly a married couple." Then, glancing left and right, she said in a whisper, "Truth to tell, I had already visited the bathroom, freshened my breath, combed my hair, and given my cheeks some color. That's when I found out that Andrew had been there before me. You see, I discovered his toothbrush was wet, and his razor was, too."

"Of course," Susan said, smiling.

"We both lay there for a moment as if we had just awakened. But when I looked at him, I discovered his eyes were open, too, and he was looking right back at me. All it took was that one look and a single morning kiss, and we found ourselves, well, occupied again."

As Susan recalled Emily's six-month-old honeymoon conversation, she couldn't think of a single reason why Emily should sound as concerned as she did on the telephone. Perhaps she was worried about something besides her marriage, and Andrew wasn't involved at all. Whatever the reason, Susan knew Emily would explain everything before long.

Susan was waiting at the front door when Emily arrived. They walked to the west sunroom, where Susan knew they could enjoy the sun's warmth on a cold afternoon. While seated on opposite sides of the tea table, Susan poured their tea, and they enjoyed a first bite of Alida's cinnamon sugar cookies.

"So what is it that has you so concerned, Emily?" Susan asked. "I trust everything is all right between you and Andrew."

"Well, yes and no," Emily answered. "There's nothing wrong between us, no dispute, no misunderstanding. We're just not happy right now."

"How so?" Susan asked.

Emily paused a moment before answering. "I suppose we're both afraid that we waited too long," she said as she looked wistfully out the window toward the setting sun.

"Waited too long? For what?" Susan asked.

"To have what you and Michael have and what Michelle and Grayson have, Susan," she answered.

"Oh-h," Susan said. "I think I understand."

"We have done nothing to prevent conception," Emily began, "and we know of nothing in our medical histories that would prove a problem. We've been following a German doctor's discovery that a slight rise in basal body temperature can indicate ovulation, helping us to tell when I am most fertile. However, now our most intimate moments have begun to feel like work. One day, when my temperature was right, Andrew and I left the hospital to go home and returned an hour later so that I could finish my shift. Andrew's mother has been hinting regularly, worrying that she'll be too old to enjoy grandchildren. We certainly don't want to disappoint her. Perhaps our medical training is not a boon to either of us. Perhaps we know too much. Nonetheless, we have made an appointment at Royal Victoria Hospital in Montreal, where we scheduled some tests. We only hope we're not too late," she said, lowering her eyes and looking at the floor.

"Emily," Susan said, "when you become pregnant is not up to you or Andrew and certainly not to your mother-in-law. And, at thirty-two and thirty-seven, neither you nor Andrew is too old to start a family. My mother was older than you when I was born. Furthermore, you've been married less than six months. Michael and I waited longer than that before our boys were conceived."

With a surprised look, Emily said, "Pardon me for being so forward, Susan, but I must ask. You hadn't used any means of prevention?"

"No," Susan answered, shaking her head.

"But that means you tried for almost a year," Emily said.

"Yes, it was almost a year, Emily, but we weren't trying. We're not in charge of these things, you know. Michelle and Grayson hoped to start their family right away, and it must have been the right thing for them. And, although Michael and I were married months before them, Michelle and I found ourselves delivering only a few weeks apart. The timing is not in our hands, Emily. I think you're worrying too much about something over which you have very little control," Susan said, "and turning something precious into a chore. If you and Andrew relax and become more of a mutual comfort to each other, then I believe your intimate moments will not feel like work."

Emily stopped for a moment to breathe before relaxing her shoulders and sitting back in her chair to say, "Thank you, Susan. I was sure you and Michael had been waiting purposefully, perhaps concerned for your brothers who were away at war, Sir Richard's commitment in London, or perhaps your mother's health, or for some other reason."

"No, Emily. We knew someone other than us was in charge of a schedule that important. Of course, we also never suspected He would send twins," she laughed.

"No," Emily agreed with a laugh, "but they are the most handsome young lads on this island, wouldn't you agree?" she asked, smiling broadly. "No nurse on the maternity ward has forgotten them yet. And they are all jealous that I am 'Aunt Emily' to your sons."

"I wouldn't disagree, Emily," Susan laughed. "They are fine-looking boys, but I will look forward to your children whenever God chooses to send them. His timing will be perfect."

"I've experienced that timing in the past, but I too often forget it, Susan," Emily said. "All my hospital training in London led me to my work with Dr. Merrill in Suffolk, and he brought me to your mother at Clifton Manor, which, in turn, brought me here to Highfield. And here I met my future husband at the hospital. I've had a charmed life, I have. How could I doubt that the best is yet to be? Thank you, Susan."

When the ladies had finished their tea, their next stop was the nursery, where Emily could hold the Moreland boys again. Susan felt assured that it would not be long before Emily and Andrew held their own.

Chapter 14

Michael didn't see the pile of icy bricks in the road ahead until he was nearly upon them. The tailgate on a truck in front of them had fallen open, spilling the bricks onto the pavement on Suffolk Road. Michael had only seconds to avoid hitting the bricks, but his mind turned to Susan and the boys in the back seat and Lady Moncrieff sitting beside him in the 1939 Ford sedan. His first instinct was to pull the steering wheel left to avoid the bricks, but he discovered an oncoming car approaching in the opposite lane. He realized he had no choice. He risked a head-on collision if he swerved left. Neither could he brake too hard without risking injury to everyone in the car. So, he gripped the wheel until his knuckles were white, stayed in his lane, and applied the brakes, unable to do anything more than say, "Hang on!" As they hit the pile, the car lurched upward and back down, making a noisy impact while the bricks clashed with the car's undercarriage near the right front wheel. The truck, now stopped half off the road on the shoulder ahead, grew larger while Michael stepped on the brake pedal again, but something was wrong. The pedal went to the floor in one swift motion, but without slowing the car. With the truck ahead looming larger every second and seeing no way to avoid a collision, Michael reached for the emergency brake and pulled with all his strength. The car slowed gradually and finally rolled to a stop, a single car length from the truck.

Everything happened so fast that neither Susan nor Lady Moncrieff had been able to utter a word.

"Is everyone all right?" Michael asked.

"I think so," Susan answered. "The boys slept through it all."

"And you, Mother," Michael asked, "I hope you weren't too frightened. Are you well?"

"Yes, Michael," she answered a bit haltingly. "Thank you for keeping us on the road."

"Well, that is a relief," Michael said. "Please stay right here in the car. I'm going to check a few things outside. The Boucher house is only a short walk from here. I'll see if Jacques can give us a hand."

Assured that no one was injured, Michael left the car to assess the damage. The truck driver was unharmed and full of apologies. The driver of the oncoming car had stopped to help and volunteered to direct traffic safely around Highfield's sedan, the truck, and the hundred-foot-long load of bricks strewn across Suffolk Road.

What Michael discovered under the right front wheel didn't surprise him. Several of the front-end components had felt the impact of the bricks and bore red dust, while small pieces of brick were lodged in every crevice. But then he saw something else.

Near the right front wheel, there was a small puddle of fluid on the road. Michael discovered a fluid trail on the road leading back to the pile of bricks the car had hit.

"Brake fluid," he said to himself. "One of those bricks must have severed a brake line. No wonder I couldn't stop. The more I pushed on the pedal, the faster the fluid found its way to the road. Thank God for the emergency brake."

The Ford Motor Company had introduced hydraulic brakes on their passenger cars in 1939, the same year Michael bought the new sedan for Lady Moncrieff. Until then, Ford cars and trucks had used a mechanical braking system. Pressing on the brake pedal in earlier cars extended solid steel rods to engage the brakes on each wheel. However, with the new hydraulic brake systems, depressing the pedal sent brake fluid under high pressure through metal tubes called brake lines to each wheel to engage the brakes. Today, a brick bouncing off the road severed one of the sedan's brake lines. When Michael stepped on the brake pedal, all the brake fluid spurted onto the road, causing the brakes on all four wheels to fail.

Michael returned to the car and limped it to the side of the road, able to stop it by using the emergency brake once again. When Michael appeared at the Bouchers' door, Jacques' was surprised to see him but was more than happy to drive Michael to Highfield. Once Michael returned with the older Ford sedan, the Moreland family and Lady Moncrieff were safe at home within a few minutes. A half-hour later, a tow truck arrived from Freeman Ford to take the damaged sedan to their service department for repairs.

Thankfully, Lady Moncrieff and Susan treated the incident as an adventure. To Michael, however, it presented a serious problem to solve.

Before bed that night, Michael spent some time at his desk, making notes about the incident.

"If one brake line fails," he thought aloud, "the whole system fails. That is too dangerous for my liking. The front brakes always take the biggest load every time a vehicle stops. The car's forward momentum sends much more weight to the front of the car. That's why front brake shoes always need replacing before rear brake shoes. But," he thought again, "that's not the problem. Our issue is that one severed brake line caused the car to lose all its brake fluid, so neither front nor rear brakes functioned. That's a dangerous situation, and there must be a solution."

By morning, a solution was brewing in Michael's mind.

"If there were two hydraulic systems, one for the front brakes and one for the rear brakes, then if one failed, the other would still be available to stop the car. It's not an ideal plan, but it's better than what we endured today. The front and rear systems would have to be calibrated to work together smoothly, and there would be other details to work out, but I'm going to spend a little more time finding a way to provide my family with a more reliable way to stop our cars."

Two days later, Jacques dropped Michael off at Freeman Ford to pick up the 1939 sedan. Before he stopped to see Steve Freeman to pay his bill and collect his keys, he wanted to see his friend, Bill Stewart, at the Parts Department.

"Michael," Bill called as he left his place at the counter to greet an old friend, "it's good to see you. I'm guessing you're here to pick up your sedan."

Michael shook Bill's hand and said, "That's right, Bill, but I have a question for you first."

"What's that?" Bill asked. "I hope I've got an answer for you."

"I was wondering if you have a master cylinder and all the other components needed to install it," Michael said.

Bill answered, "I'm sure I have everything you need on the shelf in the back, but from what I understand, your sedan only needed a piece of brake line and a new supply of brake fluid. The rest of the undercarriage cleaned up just fine. A little paint down there finished the job like new."

"I've got another idea I need to explore, Bill," Michael said. "I'll go settle up with Steve and be back to get those parts in a few minutes if that works for you."

"It works for me just fine, Michael, but now you've got my curiosity up. I smell another surprise like that radiator cooling shroud, don't I?" Bill asked.

"Shh," Michael said with a smile. "I'll let you know as soon as I know."

Twenty minutes later, Michael was driving home with a box of brake parts and a quart container of brake fluid on the seat beside him.

"Now," he said, "if I can get Charlie Hawkins to listen to my idea and help me out, we'll have a much safer car to drive."

Chapter 15

Lois Wilshire, the oldest among the evacuees to come to Highfield at almost eighteen, had made a fast friend in Ingrid Boucher, who was a match for her age. A tall young woman from London with long dark hair and blue eyes, Lois hadn't failed to capture the young men's attention, especially Luc's. Like most guest children, Lois arrived unprepared for life on an active country estate with fields, woods, gardens, and livestock. With so much to learn, the Boucher teens became teachers for all the guest children. Under their care, Lois learned about planting, harvesting, and animal husbandry, but she also had other skills she was happy to share with the Boucher girls.

When she arrived at Highfield, Lois brought a small wooden case filled with art supplies, everything she needed to create simple pencil drawings, watercolors, and oil paintings. She also brought an easel that folded into a canvas case and a supply of brushes and palette knives. From time to time, when she traveled with the Bouchers to Charlottetown, she stopped at the art supply store *For Art's Sake.* On one occasion, she shared her portfolio with the owner—pen and ink drawings, finely detailed sketches, oil paintings of the flower gardens, and even the henyard, full of chicks. After one look, the owner invited her to do a small showing and perhaps offer lessons to anyone interested. Ingrid and Patrice were already eager students who spent early evenings with Lois at the guest cottage twice a week learning to sketch and hoping to add color to their work.

Always quiet and unassuming, Lois made a rare request to speak with Susan on a mid-December afternoon. Susan was glad to meet her in the library.

"Mrs. Moreland," Lois began, "thank you for taking the time to speak with me. I'm sure your twins can be very demanding, and I promise not to keep you more than a few minutes."

"Thank you, Lois," Susan said, smiling. "Yes, Case and Reed seem to be either hungry or wet, or wet and hungry, most of the time. At present, however, they are sleeping soundly. I'm sure we will have all the time we need."

"I wanted to tell you about Biddy and Wilfred, my younger sister and brother who couldn't come here with me," Lois said.

"Tell me, if you will, Lois, why were they unable to come with you?" Susan asked. "If it was a matter of cost, we will be happy to help . . . " Susan began, but Lois interrupted her.

"It's not money, ma'am," Lois said. "That's not the problem. You see, they both suffer from tuberculosis, and in my last letter, I learned that they're both doing very poorly and may not . . . "

Lois couldn't finish as the tears came. While handing Lois her pocket handkerchief, Susan rushed to embrace her on the settee.

"I'm so sorry, Lois. I had no idea that your sister and brother were ill. I simply expected them to arrive here someday as you did," Susan said. "We're expecting seven more children soon, and I so wish Biddy and Wilfred could be among them."

"As do I," Mrs. Moreland, "but I can't believe that is to be. We've seen tuberculosis attack children their age before. Few recover, and those who do suffer weakness as long as they live. It took my father, too. It's seven years ago now that we buried him. My mother still grieves."

"I am so sorry, Lois. That's more grief than any young woman should have to bear. Is there any way I can help?" Susan asked.

"I hope so, Mrs. Moreland. I've come to ask a boon of you, and I hope it won't sound ungrateful," she said, looking down at the floor.

"I'm pleased to favor you however I can, Lois. Please tell me how," Susan asked.

"It's just this, Mrs. Moreland," she began. "You know that Ingrid and I have become very close, and Patrice is like another sister to me. I'm alone in the cottage now, and it's all very comfortable there, but Luc will be leaving next week for the army, and Joseph is away training at the hospital in Montreal. I'm doing more and more painting these days, and Ingrid and Patrice are almost ready to start painting, too. Teaching them helps me to forget about . . . "

She stopped to dry her eyes and wipe her nose before continuing. "Ingrid and Patrice asked their mother if I could move from the cottage to be with them. Luc and Joseph's room will soon be empty, and it has wonderful light and space for an easel. I'm sure I could paint there. I have two pieces I need to finish to send home to Biddy and Wilfred. They'll arrive too late for Christmas, but I want to send them as soon as possible. It's a bit lonely where I am in the cottage, and I don't want to sound ungrateful, but . . . "

Susan interrupted, saying, "Lois, I think you have a capital idea. I've heard about the lessons you've given Patrice and seen some of her work, and I know you will be such a help in the Boucher home. I have only one boon to ask of you first, though."

"What would that be?" Lois asked through her tears that had become tears of relief accompanied by the hint of a smile.

"I should like to see the contents of the portfolio I've seen you take into Charlottetown on occasion, and I would like your opinion on several small pieces in my own collection, pieces I never quite finished when I studied in England at about your age," Susan said.

"Oh, my, Mrs. Moreland. I will be happy to run for my portfolio even now," Lois said, "and to see your work would be my delight."

She was on her feet and turning toward the door when Susan said, "Not so fast, my dear Lois." Then Susan stood and offered her open arms.

Lois melted into Susan's embrace and let her tears fall once again. Susan gathered her in and held her tight until her sobs and quivering breaths relaxed into a sigh full of relief. Only then did Lois leave Susan, offering a smile over her shoulder as she ran for the portfolio on her bed at the cottage. When she returned, Susan was waiting, and for some reason, Case and Reed took their longest afternoon nap on record. Two artists' hearts enjoyed their first hour together that week, with the promise of many more.

Chapter 16

On a particularly cold Saturday afternoon near the end of December 1940, Sir Richard found London's most recent war reports unusually distressing. They were summary reports that he had decoded as part of the overnight radio transmissions sent from SIS in London, some recounting events now weeks old.

He learned details of continued Luftwaffe localized blitzes in the UK throughout December. Sheffield was especially hard hit, enduring four nights of heavy bomb attacks. Liverpool also faced three nights of relentless bombing, while the bombs that exploded for two nights in Manchester left over 650 people dead and more than 2,000 injured. To their credit, the RAF answered the German blitzes in kind when 134 RAF bombers attacked the industrial city of Mannheim, dropping over 100 tons of explosives during a nighttime raid. The attack began at eight o'clock in the evening and continued until the following morning. When the RAF returned home after dropping another 14,000 incendiaries, the fires in Mannheim on both sides of the Rhine remained out of control for several days.

Sir Richard read better news originating on the Canadian side of the Atlantic. Most encouraging was intelligence from London indicating that the anti-war sentiment that had long ruled politics in the United States had begun to wane. President Roosevelt's influence fueled the momentum behind a change of heart among American politicians and their constituents. Roosevelt's remarks made at a press conference earlier in the week indicated his concern for Britain's industrial centers, which suffered from fierce and frequent Nazi bombing attacks. Furthermore, he recognized that sea routes for ships carrying the raw materials needed to manufacture the weapons Britain required remained under constant attack. Convoy after convoy succumbed to attacks by relentless U-boat wolfpacks. Roosevelt, a man able to see the future better than many politicians in the US, had openly suggested that the US might be able to sell or perhaps lease Britain the weapons they sorely needed. He said, "The best defense of Great Britain is the best defense of the United States," and "these materials would be more useful to the defense of the United States if they were used in Great Britain." Two days after making this statement, Roosevelt also approved an aid package for the Republic of China totaling $25 million. The package aimed to bolster the Chinese air defense against Japan's continued attacks. By the end of the month, Roosevelt had been bold enough to coin a phrase while addressing his constituents on the radio, referring to the US as an "arsenal of democracy."

Churchill considered Roosevelt's words a promise of support from America and her people who manned the factories in industrial centers across the US, the strength of which was unmatched in the world. He was also reassured that the US would soon supply raw materials and the weapons, armaments, and ammunition essential to Britain's defense.

Meanwhile, other reports in Sir Richard's hands indicated that a substantial number of pilots who had joined the RAF during the Battle of Britain had arrived not only from countries in the Commonwealth like Canada and New Zealand but also from Poland, Belgium, France, and the US. Hundreds of airmen from the US had found their way into Canada to join the RCAF. Some had already been deployed to the UK as part of three Eagle Squadrons established in the fall of 1940. Although the US had remained officially neutral thus far in the war, hundreds of her men had found their own reasons to come to Great Britain's aid and were already serving the RAF in the air.

Sir Richard's thoughts went to his sons, both aboard ships that were choice targets for German U-boats. Boyd was once again in the North Atlantic, while Nigel was not out of danger in the North Sea. Both faced the heavy presence of the Kriegsmarine battleships as well as their U-boats. Suddenly recognizing his distraction, Sir Richard asked himself, "Why am I thinking of my sons in the midst of reviewing reports meant for my eyes, on this day, at this hour? Why am I so easily distracted today?" He knew it wasn't worry for his sons that had taken his mind from the reports he was reviewing. No, his distraction lay elsewhere, and he suspected there was no singular cause for the discord in his mindset.

A man of self-discipline, habitual in maintaining a single focus, he tried to take stock of the events and circumstances he had allowed to dissuade him from the needful things to which he owed his attention.

Immediately, he thought back to his arrival at his study that morning. He was then aware that he missed his office in London, his proximity to key personnel, and access to the Prime Minister. Of course, he was grateful for the Prime Minister's confidence in him and for the value Churchill placed in his work on Prince Edward Island. He was still overwhelmed by the foresight in Churchill's orders that kept him an ocean away from the bombs dropping in London. Nevertheless, he was distracted by his misdirected craving for the usual, the customary, and the comfortable.

He recognized a second dissatisfaction that had stolen his peace this morning. He found himself courting memories of his service with the Royal Navy during the Great War. Now, more than twenty years after retirement from the Royal Navy and serving SIS ever since, he felt passed over, like a soldier made for war who had been banned from the battlefield. Although he knew his work at SIS was vital to the war effort, he felt himself withering as the war persisted. Still, he had to ask himself why he had fallen to chewing on himself, prizing only his past, and feeling worthless and unnecessary in the present.

He rallied briefly to remind himself that he was doing his part. His operatives behind enemy lines were working with the resistance in every country under Nazi control. Their regular reports of troop movements, traffic at airfields, and fleet movements in harbors were invaluable. No, his work, which determined his worth to a man like him, was intact. "So, what is my problem?" he asked himself.

He knew the Prime Minister had called on him to make a sacrifice. Now, however, he was living it out, putting flesh on the bones, and finding out what that sacrifice meant.

"Time to get over it, Moncrieff," he said aloud. "This is your hour of watch on the bridge, and this is no time for distractions. Snap yourself to attention and salute, sailor. The Captain is aboard, and this ship is underway."

In the next moment, however, his thoughts went to his trips during the past two years as Rear-Admiral Moncrieff, sailing again with the Royal Navy from England to Halifax and back. On both occasions, he was charged with the responsibility for much of the planning and execution of *Operation Fish.* With his assistance and leadership, the wealth of the United Kingdom's gold bullion had arrived safely in Canada, preserving it against capture by Nazi Germany.

Those had been his first opportunities to serve his King and Commonwealth at sea during wartime since the Great War, now called World

War I. He had fought at sea during that war in several crucial battles, including the battle of Jutland. Nonetheless, a generation away from World War I, away from the bridge of a battleship, away from the immediate danger, and away from the challenges that faced him so many years ago, something in Sir Richard felt impotent.

"I miss it . . . I don't like being old . . . I can't be old," he shouted inside.

Thankfully, at that moment, his reason returned to acknowledge the authority to whom he had bent his neck a generation ago. Reminding himself, he said, "Today it is my honor to serve the Commonwealth at the pleasure of King George VI, his Prime Minister, Winston Churchill, and the Admiralty of the Royal Navy, who no longer require my services at sea. They need me at the helm of a ship no longer, for I am of greater service to them here, and I shall make my peace with that, God being my helper," he pledged. Then, reaching into his bottom drawer, he retrieved a bottle of Dewars, one of the last remnants of his office in London. He poured two fingers and raised his glass to say, "To all of you men, my brothers, my sons, my fellow officers, and every fellow sailor who knows the burden and joy that lives within each of us whose blood is mixed with salt water, know this: I long to be with you, to fight beside you, to bear the burdens of King and Country with you. But, I shall serve you better here, remaining faithful in my work and prayers. So be it, gentlemen," he said, raising his glass, "as I pray with you, pray with me, and together, let us carry on until our foes lie vanquished at our feet!"

Just then, he heard a knock at the study door and Angela's voice. "Richard?" she said, "We need to talk."

Chapter 17

Sir Richard had learned long ago that when Angela came to talk, it was rarely because she had something he wanted to hear. Nonetheless, on too many occasions when she confronted him in the past, he had learned to respect her wisdom and thank her for the insight and peace that she often brought him.

"Yes, Angela," he said as his bottle and glass found their place back in his lower drawer. "Please come . . . "

But before he could add "in," she was already in, and as he stood, she was taking a seat at the leather armchair she had re-arranged to face his desk. She didn't look unhappy, but after more than four decades of marriage, he knew the look she called "concerned." Today, he could tell that she was *very* concerned.

"Richard," she began, "I have been observing your decline for some time, but I have kept my concerns to myself, hoping you would return to the man I have known and loved for over four decades. Tell me, Richard, where has he gone?'

"Gone, Angela? Nowhere, I assure you, though I have spent an hour this afternoon sorting through several distractions as I read through my reports," he answered.

"Can you share them, Richard? I'd be interested to see if they are related to some of the distractions I have observed," she said.

"Of course," he said, wondering what sort of distractions she had on her list. He went on to explain that he simply missed his office, the faces he took for granted there, and the proximity of everything that was part of his daily routine.

"Routine," he said. "I just don't know if anything will ever be routine again. I arranged this office to resemble my London office. Nonetheless, nothing about it is as I hoped it would be, Angela. I know the Prime

Minister called on me to make a sacrifice, which I was happy to do. Now, however, in living it out or putting flesh on its bones, if you will, I am finding out what sacrifice requires."

"Go on," she said, somehow knowing there was more.

"I was thinking about Nigel and Boyd, both of them serving at sea and the perils they face. I know they are in God's hands. I know I can do nothing to protect them during this war, but my thoughts went back to my time sailing in those same waters during the Great War, or World War I, or whatever name is appropriate now. I could do something then: lead my men, strategize, maneuver, and attack the foe. And I was good at it. Now, I can do nothing to protect our sons, and the impotence I feel is profound."

"Please go on," she said.

"I thought back to the two voyages I made with the Royal Navy recently, the one that brought me here for Susan's wedding last year and the one that brought me back this year. Angela, it was so good to be at sea again, and it was even better to know that the missions entrusted to me were vitally important to our King and Country. My father served in the Royal Navy, as did my grandfather. There must be salt water in our veins. Masefield's words came to mind, '*I must go down to the seas again, to the lonely sea and the sky*.' I still miss my place on the bridge, Angela."

"I know you do, Richard," she said, "I know. Those seasons, the one at sea and the one in London, were seasons where you devoted all your wit, energy, and enthusiasm, and they brought you a grand satisfaction, did they not?" she asked.

"Oh, yes, they did, Angela," he answered, reaching for the handkerchief in the breast pocket of his tweed jacket, "yes, they did."

"Then please note that you are speaking in the past tense, Richard," she said.

"Past tense?" he questioned.

"They *did*, Richard. In the past, Richard, in seasons of your life that have passed," she added.

Sir Richard stood and walked around his desk to sit in the chair beside her.

"Those seasons were grand," she said, "God given and God blessed, but they have passed. While you lived them, you gave your all and were rewarded appropriately with the satisfaction of jobs well done and the respect of many. But, Richard, those seasons are over. What you owe King and Country now will be accomplished on this side of the ocean - in a new season," she added.

"A new season? What do you see in this new season?" he asked.

"First," she began, "you must finish what you have begun with SIS, Richard. That is a given, and it will require the continued hard work and devotion for which you are known and respected. However, you entered a new season when Winston Churchill sent you to this side of the Atlantic, and this new season has some very different requirements for you to satisfy, but all with the same energy and devotion as the last two seasons," she said.

His face told her she must exercise the patience and grace she had learned to use with her husband whenever they reached a crossroads like this. She reached over to his chair to take his hand.

"Richard," she said, "you are a man of inspiration. Your inspiration brought us to Highfield. You saw things across the ocean that no one else saw. You had a vision that you felt compelled to complete. Today, we are safe and not surviving but *thriving* because you were obedient to pursue your inspiration. But now, you are in a new season of your life and of our life together. Your malaise today is because you demand to stay in the past."

"I must ask you to say on, Angela, because I don't see all that you see," he said.

"I will," she said. "You thought of Nigel and Boyd this morning, concerned for them at sea while at war with a deadly enemy."

"Yes," he answered.

"And your concern for them is . . . ?" she asked.

"Well, ultimately, that they won't return home, of course." He stood and reached for the family portrait that sat on his desk. Returning and handing it to her, he said, "What will become of us then, without our boys, Angela? I can't see a future without them, without someone to carry on the Moncrieff name when I am gone," he said.

"And that is part of the problem, Richard. We can do nothing to ensure that our sons return to us well and whole and able to give us grandsons. That is to be decided in a season yet to come. We can only live today, in *this* season," she said. "This season, Richard, today."

As he sat again, looking at her for an explanation, she began to speak softly as he drew closer to her across the arm of her chair.

"Richard," she said, "you are missing so much. It's right here in front of you. You have a daughter who has birthed two sons, our grandsons."

"Yes," he answered, "Case and Reed."

"Correct, and both with the middle name Moncrieff. That name was given them at their christening at Michael's insistence and Susan's acquiescence."

"I don't remember hearing that in the church," he said.

"I'm not surprised, Richard, but it is very telling. You have already made them distant, and you are at risk of losing the only grandsons we may ever have," she said.

"I don't understand," he said.

"Children relate and form a bond with their parents almost immediately, but only over time to those a generation removed. Those boys know *me*, Richard, but they don't know *you*. That fault is yours," she said.

"But, what have I done wrong?" he asked.

"You haven't sought, held, or loved them, Richard. They already know that. What's worse, there's another generation you are at risk of losing," she said.

"Another generation?" he asked. "I'm lost, Angela. What do you mean?"

"Their father," she said. Seeing the puzzled look on his face, she continued. "Richard, Michael is still a hireling to you. You haven't accepted him as family. You've allowed his marriage to Susan, and you endure it now, but he still works tirelessly every day and every night to earn your respect, something he should never have to earn."

Sir Richard sat silently, puzzled by her words but willing to listen as she explained.

"In the past, you saw him as the sole son of his father, the superintendent at Clifton Manor. Today, you see him as the superintendent here at Highfield, but Richard, he is so much more. Every part of the dream you had for Highfield, every detail, he made his singular goal, all because of his grateful servant's heart. You cared for his father until his death when you gave Michael his father's position, which he fulfilled with the heart of a devoted son. At Highfield, he installed every hinge on every door, every carpet in every room, every drapery at every window, every baluster at every staircase, and every lockset at every door. He refurbished a decades-old fire tower so you could send a radio signal to London from your desk. And how many buildings has he built from lumber milled here on the estate you wished to be self-sustaining? Richard, we have barns, stables, a smokehouse, an ice house, two cottages, a schoolhouse, a boat shed, and so much more, all because Michael gave himself to fulfilling your dream. Consider also the acres and acres under cultivation that were once overgrown fields. He made them into crop-bearing gardens that feed all of us and many of our neighbors. But he is so much more than the superintendent of this estate. When you needed a code for SIS communications with Highfield, you mentioned that need to Michael. How long did it take him to respond and offer a code? And how many of your agents use that code daily?" she asked.

"He responded within days, and hundreds use his code daily," he answered quietly.

"And yesterday, Richard, you went pheasant hunting and took Simon, Highfield's dog. You came back with four pheasants, bragging about Simon, who led you to each bird, flushed it into the air for your shot, retrieved it from where it fell, and, with the softest of mouths, delivered each to your hand unbruised. Correct?" she asked.

"Yes, Angela, that is correct."

"And who do you suppose was the man who sought that dog, chose that dog, and trained that dog?" she asked.

Sir Richard didn't have to answer.

"I will pain you, Richard, with one more bit of information concerning your son-in-law, Michael Moreland, another gift of which I believe you are ignorant," she said.

Quietly, he answered, "Please, Angela, say on."

"When you acquired Highfield, how many vehicles were included in the sale?" she asked.

After thinking for a moment, he answered, "Three. One sedan, one flatbed truck, and one tractor."

"And how many are on the premises now?" she asked.

Again, after a moment, he said, "Why, seven, I believe. Your new sedan, Susan's cabriolet, a second truck, and a second tractor."

"And who purchased the last four vehicles, Richard?" she asked.

"I must assume that the monies came from the Highfield account," he answered, "but why does that matter, Angela?"

"Because, Richard, Highfield had nothing to do with the purchase of those vehicles. Michael Moreland bought and paid for each of them, gifting both Susan and me with our own automobiles, paying for all of them out of his own means," she said.

"But how can that be, Angela?" he asked. "His salary at Highfield would never support such purchases."

"That's just one more thing you don't know about your son-in-law," she said. "You see, he is also a talented inventor, having patented an invention used internationally by several major automobile manufacturers who pay to license his product on thousands of vehicles yearly. That young man can buy virtually anything he wants, Richard, but when he does, he usually spends his money to help others."

"I am so embarrassed, Angela," Sir Richard said as he sat and melted into his chair. "I had no idea. I feel so ashamed. I am so sorry for demeaning Michael, Susan, and our grandsons out of my pride and ignorance." Hesitating for a moment, he asked, "But what can I do now?"

"What are you willing to do, Richard?" she asked.

"I have no wisdom to offer, Angela, but I am willing to do whatever you suggest," he answered.

"Then let us start at the beginning," she said. "To this day, Michael still addresses you as 'Sir Richard,' as a hireling would. Tomorrow, when he does so, you will insist he calls you 'Richard' from now on, reserving 'Sir Richard' solely for appropriate social situations where propriety is required."

"And so I will, Angela," he said, adding, "and, with your help, I will also embrace my daughter and our Moncrieff grandsons."

"Splendid," she said, "but there is one further practical suggestion I will make concerning Michael. You mentioned the salt water in your veins a few moments ago, correct? she asked.

"Yes," he answered, "I did."

"Well, after you left the breakfast table this morning, Michael mentioned that he planned to spend evenings in the boat shed over the next two weeks painting the bottom of the *Lady M*, stripping the mahogany in the cabin, and adding several coats of fresh varnish. I suggest that you join him there for those evenings. After all, the *Lady M* will be back in the water in a few short months with a captain at the helm who has salt water in his veins."

"It will be my honor," he said quietly. "I will look forward to those hours every day."

"That is a beginning, Richard, and if you are willing, I will offer further suggestions as they seem appropriate."

"Yes," he said, "I hope you will."

As she stood, he needed his handkerchief again to dry the tears that were not yet ready to abate. His wife added her handkerchief to his remaining hand, and as his tears subsided, she whispered in his ear amidst their embrace, "Now that's the way to begin a new season. I can't wait to see it in full bloom!"

Chapter 18

"You're the fourth recruit from the States today," Corporal Williams said as he reviewed the application in his hand.

The RCAF recruiting office in Montreal had processed several hundred applications from Americans over the last several months. With the advent of the British Commonwealth Air Training Plan came a virtual open door to qualified men and women who wanted to join the RCAF, regardless of nationality. Not every young man or woman in the US agreed with the neutrality policy that Congress had dictated since the war began in Europe. Many of them sought opportunities to serve in Canada. By the winter of 1940, several thousand Americans had flooded across the Canadian border to enlist. Some were experienced pilots who spent only a short time training in Canada before shipping out to airfields in the UK. Those who didn't qualify as pilots often trained for positions as flight engineers, bomb aimers, navigators, air gunners, or wireless operators. Others served on the ground, maintaining and refueling aircraft or loading bombs and ammunition. Still, other experienced American combat pilots enlisted and went immediately into service as flight instructors.

"You're a little older than some of the recruits we're seeing lately," the Corporal said, but men in their late twenties are always welcome. You meet the physical requirements for height and weight, but your application indicates you have no prior flight training. Is that correct?"

"Yes, sir," the recruit answered, "that is correct."

"Have you had any mechanical experience with engines, machinery, or maintaining industrial equipment, including farm equipment?" the corporal asked while looking down at the application.

"No, I haven't," the recruit answered.

"What kind of work have you done in the past?" the recruiter asked.

"I've done shipping and receiving at a large company on the East Coast, and before that, I clerked in a retail store," the recruit answered.

"What level of education did you finish in the States?" the corporal asked.

"I finished high school in New Jersey before my father's job took us to Europe. I went to university there."

Surprised, the recruiter asked, "University? We don't get many college men in this office. What did you study?"

"Cartography," the recruit answered.

"Cartography?" the corporal asked. "What is cartography?"

"It's the science of drawing maps. It involves quite a bit of engineering and a similar investment in mathematics," the recruit answered. "It's not all done on the ground, either. Our professors and my fellow students were airborne for a large part of our study. Some of our work was accomplished from dirigibles, and at other times, we flew in military aircraft, mostly bombers. Their bomb bay doors helped with the photography. I loved flying. That's why I want to enlist."

"Photography? So you know photography, too?" the recruiter asked.

"Yes, but not the kind of photography most people might understand. Ours was accomplished using sophisticated cameras equipped with lenses that could capture ground-level images at altitudes where ordinary cameras were useless," the young man answered.

"And did you also develop and print the photos you took?" the corporal asked.

"Yes," the recruit answered, "but only because our professors left all that to us. The chemicals and their odors were too much for them, so I learned all the darkroom procedures and produced my share of finished photos."

Corporal Williams made some more notes on the application before continuing.

"And where was the university you attended?" he asked.

"Munich, in Germany," the recruit answered, "although my father's business travel took us to several other countries."

When he heard "Germany," the corporal raised his head.

"You lived and studied in Germany? For how long?" he asked.

"Almost five years," the recruit answered, "but we left when I was twenty-one. My mother died there, and my father and I came home. I haven't been back."

"I see," the corporal said, "I'm sorry about your mother."

"Thank you," the recruit said. "It was sudden and unexpected, and my father was shattered. He's at peace with it now."

"Do you speak any foreign languages?" the corporal asked.

"Well, I had to learn German, but I can get along with Dutch, and I have some French," he said.

"So, you've lived in Germany, you speak German, and you've flown over Germany drawing maps from the sky?" the corporal asked.

"Yes," the recruit said, "Most of our flight time was spent over major cities. Several of my professors were involved with a government initiative to improve highways, bridges, and railroad lines, so my experience is limited in mapping open, unpopulated spaces."

"I don't think you will have to worry about that," Corporal Williams said. "Wait here for just a moment. There is someone I need to consult. I'll be right back."

The recruit's eyes followed Corporal Williams as he walked to a glass-partitioned area at the rear of the recruiting office, where an older man was sitting at a desk and talking on the telephone. The recruit watched the two men begin their conversation but quickly looked away. Although he listened carefully, they were too far away for him to hear anything.

"Wait a minute." the older man said. "Are you telling me that you've got an American recruit at your desk who is fluent in German?"

"Yes," Sergeant Miller, but that's not all. He studied cartography at a university in Germany. Cartography is mapmaking, you know," the corporal added.

"I know what cartography is, Williams," the sergeant said, disgusted. "Just finish what you started to say."

"My apologies, sir, but you should know that he took pictures from dirigibles and through the bomb bay doors of airplanes in Germany to make the maps. He also developed and printed the pictures. This man is not our usual recruit."

"No, he isn't, Williams," the sergeant said as he stood and glanced in the recruit's direction. "I'll finish this interview myself," Sergeant Miller said as he stepped away from his desk and put out his hand to receive Corporal Williams' clipboard.

When Corporal Williams returned to his desk, he wasn't alone. Sergeant Miller was standing beside him.

"Sergeant Miller would like to complete the interview with you," the corporal said.

The recruit looked up at the sergeant, who said, "Follow me to my office to complete your application, Mr . . . ," the sergeant hesitated as he looked back at the application for the recruit's name.

"Duncan, Sergeant," the recruit said as he stood and offered his hand. "Ernest Duncan."

Chapter 19

"Susan, I can't stand idly by any longer," her mother said, holding a letter in her hand. "If we have room for British children at Highfield, we also have room for Jewish children who have fled from persecution. Millie writes from home that there are hundreds of Jewish refugee children in Lowestoft and more in Reydon and Pakefield, not far from Clifton Manor. The Suffolk coastline could be invaded at any time, and those poor children, already displaced from their parents and families, need our help. They should not have to endure any further horrors."

Susan was not used to seeing her mother in such agitation. Clearly, whatever their cook in England had written to Lady Moncrieff had been upsetting.

"I would not disagree, Mother," Susan said. "No one deserves a safe home more than those children, but you know how horribly restrictive the immigration policy here in Canada has been, even concerning children. Remember, in May of 1939, Canada turned a ship away with more than 900 Jewish refugees and forbade them to land at any Canadian port. Eventually, that ship faced the danger of German U-boats in the North Atlantic for the second time when it sailed back and landed in Belgium. It was a miracle that the ship and her passengers could complete that voyage and land safely."

"I remember it well, Susan, but I would feel terribly irresponsible if we didn't make some sincere effort to help these children. I have an idea and, I believe, a relatively simple solution."

"Well, tell me, Mother. I'm not big on suspense, as you well know. What is your plan?" Susan said as she motioned toward the divan, where the pair sat down.

Lady Moncrieff began, "Our friends in Suffolk have sent dozens of children to us thus far, correct? I'd wager and win if I were to say that they know all about the Jewish children in Lowestoft. I'm sure they could find a way to send some Jewish children with the next British group they send here. What do you think?" she asked.

"Of course, they could," Susan agreed, "although there could be some administrative obstacles—paperwork, you know. Who do you think we could contact to make the arrangements?"

"Leave that to me, Susan. I'll have your father's ear after lunch. He has access to SIS personnel up and down the coast with their eyes always watching for the enemy. With their help, he'll know who to call among the local officials who can make things happen. I'm sure he'll be able to find us a sympathetic soul among the fine people caring for the children in Lowestoft. Under his auspices, I suspect those children, when mixed among the British children, will have no trouble entering the country," she said.

"Then let's see what he can do. We'll have room for ten or more at midmonth. Perhaps some of them will find their safe haven here, " Susan said.

"I do hope so. On second thought, though, I'll not wait until lunch. I'm going to visit your father in his study now," Lady Moncrieff said.

Susan had to smile. When her mother was this eager to help a worthy cause, she knew her father would be powerless to refuse her. Mother's latest cause was always at the top of his priority list.

As Susan started up the stairs to check on her napping boys, she heard the door close in the kitchen. She suspected Michael had returned from his morning errands and would be looking for his lunch. Only minutes ago, she had left a crock of lamb stew on the stove, several raised biscuits, and a piece of Alida's peach pie. She turned toward the kitchen just as he sat at the table.

"I thought it was you," she said from behind his chair as she wrapped her arms around his neck and kissed his cheek.

"How could I stay away with a lunch like this waiting for me?" he asked. "I'll confess, though, it also makes me wonder if dessert will be its equal," he said with a wink as he turned to return her kiss.

Shaking her head, she said, "Do you ever think of anything else, Michael Moreland?"

"Not when you're around, Susan Moreland, mother of my sons and love of my life. But right now, I've got something to tell you. Can you sit for a minute or two?" he said.

"I need to check on the boys, and if all is well, I'll be back soon," she said.

Michael was already reaching for his pie when she returned.

"So what do you have to tell me?" she asked as she sat across from him.

"It's about my meeting with Charlie Hawkins this morning," he said. "He's the man who owns the machine shop in Charlottetown."

"What's a machine shop?" she asked.

"It's a shop where a man like Charlie can create almost anything out of metal. He has machines that can take a piece of solid steel and shape it into almost anything you can imagine. The machines can work magic, but it takes a genius like Charlie Hawkins to get it done."

"So why were you there?" Susan asked.

"It all began when we hit the bricks on Suffolk Road in your mother's sedan. That collision broke one of the brake lines and caused the entire brake system to fail. It gave me an idea that could keep half the brakes working even if a brake line was compromised," Michael said.

"How does it work?" Susan asked.

"Well, when a new car comes from the factory, pressing the brake pedal forces brake fluid in what is called a master cylinder to flow under pressure to engage the brakes on all four wheels. I had the idea to install a second master cylinder so that the front and rear brakes could be isolated from each other. That way, if a front brake line is broken, the rear brakes will still be available to stop the car."

"And likewise, if a rear brake line is broken?" Susan asked.

"Exactly," Michael agreed between bites of pie.

"So, where does Charlie Hawkins come in?" she asked.

"I needed him to machine a manifold and a rod to engage the second master cylinder when the brake pedal is pressed. Susan, the man, is a real artist with steel. His work makes it look like everything came as original equipment on the car," Michael said, smiling.

"You mean it's already installed?" she asked. "I thought it was still an idea."

"No, once Charlie had all the parts machined, we worked together for the morning and got it installed. I think he has almost every tool in the world in his shop. Once the cylinders were proportioned correctly, a thorough test drive told us the system worked like a charm. I was elated, but then I had another thought," Michael said.

"Which was?" Susan prompted.

"Well, fitting two master cylinders in a space made for only one was challenging. So, I asked Charlie to look at another idea that came to me overnight. Why not make a master cylinder with two chambers and a proportioning valve between them? He said he could have it done in a week or so."

"Michael, is this another invention you can patent like the last?" she asked.

"That's one of the best parts, Susan," he said. "Charlie has a man in his shop who has already produced all the mechanical drawings. I'm ready to send them to Atty Leighton. I'll get them to the post office in Charlottetown later today. Then, he'll have everything he needs to apply for a patent."

Susan followed as Michael stood to clear his dishes to the kitchen sink. She reached up to hug him around the neck and said, "You've done it again, Michael Moreland. Just when I thought you had no more surprises in you, you've done it again. What will you think of next?"

"Well, actually," he said, "I was thinking about dessert."

"But, you just had dessert," she said as she leaned to look past him at the empty dish in the sink.

"Oh, that," he said, following her eyes. "Sure, that was dessert, all right, but I was thinking of another sort of dessert that's a lot better than that."

"You'll have to settle for this," she said, adding a quick kiss. "It sounds like the boys just woke up. Duty calls!" she laughed as she turned and hurried toward the stairs.

Michael smiled as he took inventory: Susan, their boys, and another new invention. Life could hardly be better.

Chapter 20

The last time twelve-year-old Jacob saw his parents, Daniel and Deborah Abrams, was at the train station in Leiden. He and his sister, Naomi, eleven, had been waiting on a bench inside the station near the exit to the street. They had rehearsed this location with their parents several times the previous week. Only their father and mother ventured further toward the platform whenever they arrived at the station. Their plan relied on their parents to assess potential dangers on the platform before allowing their children to join them.

Since the Nazi invasion last May and the subsequent Dutch surrender five days later, a substantial number of Dutch police and Leiden administration officials had capitulated with the Gestapo, especially in identifying and isolating Jews. As in other German-occupied countries, the Jewish population was subject to harassment and persecution, which often ended only when whole families were arrested, spirited away after dark, and never seen again. Any form of resistance often meant death. As more and more Jews tried to flee the city, the train depot became a prime Jewish hunting ground for SS and Leiden officials.

Daniel Abrams had been born in Rotterdam, but he moved to London with his British father and mother when he was very young. Daniel's gifts in art eventually led to a teaching position at the Royal College of Art. There, he met Deborah Weil, a student who had emigrated from Leiden to study painting. After a whirlwind romance, they married, and now thirteen years later, their family found themselves in Leiden, Nazi prey on a railway platform.

They had returned to Leiden nine months ago before the imminent Nazi invasion of the Netherlands in a desperate attempt to convince Deborah's mother to return to England with them. They brought their children on this second visit more than six months later, but even her grandchildren could not convince Ruth Weil to leave Leiden. Frustrated and saddened, the Abrams family began their trek home to London.

Daniel wished the platform was busier. He had heard that during the last forty-eight hours, the Gestapo and local officials had begun stopping passengers randomly to verify their papers. Fewer people on the platform meant a greater chance of being stopped and questioned. Although Daniel knew his family's papers were in order, he also knew those papers meant nothing to the Gestapo if one was suspected of being Jewish. With their British passports buried deep in their luggage, they carried their Dutch documents in their hands, papers that identified them as Dutch citizens, both by birth and family heritage in the Netherlands.

If the Nazis detained their parents in Leiden, Jacob and Naomi were ready to rely on a well-practiced set of instructions. They knew exactly what to do in the event their parents were stopped and arrested. So, when Jacob and Naomi heard their father's raised voice coming from the platform, the shouts that followed, a dog barking, and a single gunshot, Jacob took Naomi's hand as they quietly rose, calmly left the train station, and didn't look back. Entering the busy afternoon sidewalk traffic, they walked with purpose, bags in hand, toward the setting sun.

Only when they were alone on the road did they dare to speak. Jacob played the elder brother and comforted Naomi when her tears came, tears that came again and again. All the while, Jacob was on the verge of his own. Alone now, the two shared the same fear—they feared they would never see their parents again.

After walking for several hours while the shadows behind them grew longer, the worst day of their lives met some relief. A middle-aged woman, a widow with a well-tanned and wrinkled brow, calloused hands, and a sensitive eye, watched the pair on the road from the covered porch of her aging farmhouse, following their every move. These weren't the first well-dressed children carrying traveling bags she'd seen fleeing Leiden. They weren't the first she had befriended, either. When she managed to stop them, they remained wary until she showed them the pendant she wore around her neck. It was engraved with a six-pointed star. That evening, she shared a warm meal with them and provided a safe place where they could spend the night.

Before they left the next morning, their host schooled Jacob and Naomi in ways to help them fit in away from the city. She helped them soil their clothes at the knees and elbows and rub some wear into them with a coarse stone. She helped Jacob tear a pocket here or there and fray the exposed stitches to give them some age. After telling them what not to say or do to draw attention to themselves, she helped them act out an interview where she played a stranger who asked too many questions. Before leaving her home, they had memorized their new traveling names, the name of their home village near Leiden, and the name of the fictitious aunt they were to meet when they reached their destination. The widow, whose name was Ruth, also had them memorize an address in the next town near the coast. She instructed them to go nowhere else to find shelter.

And so their trek continued for over a hundred miles, traveling from safe house to safe house as they walked west and south along the coast to find a safe port. With help from some former members of a group called *Kindertransport*, Daniel and Naomi secured a place on a ferry with other children evacuating to England.

It had been two months since Jacob and Naomi landed in Harwich and traveled north to Lowestoft on England's east coast. A matronly older woman, Mrs. Goodwin, had become their fast friend from the day they moved to the shelter at St. Felix School in Reydon. There, they joined several hundred Jewish children who had been separated from their parents and somehow found their way to England. Mrs. Goodwin spent several hours daily among the children and was the first to speak with Jacob and Naomi about an opportunity to evacuate to Canada.

"But, where did you learn to speak such fine English in Holland?" Mrs. Goodwin asked when they first arrived.

"Oh, Jacob and I were born in London," Naomi explained. "Father came to London when he was very young. His father and mother had always lived there. He was born in Rotterdam, but only because grandfather was helping to build a factory there."

"Yes," Jacob said. "Mother was born in Leiden but left to study art in London when she was twenty. That's where she met my father, an art professor, and they got married. Mother taught him Dutch, and he helped her improve her English. Jacob and I learned some Dutch at home, too," she said.

Mrs. Goodwin saw the tear start in Naomi's eye when Jacob mentioned "home."

"Your parents sound like very bright and astute people," Mrs. Goodwin said, "parents who have raised some very bright young folks like you."

"Naomi's the bright one," Jacob said. "I'd rather play football with these other blokes, but they're hard to get to know. They say I don't look Jewish. How am I supposed to look?" he asked.

"I think it's your fair hair, Jacob. Your sister has it, too," Mrs. Goodwin said.

"Yes," Naomi agreed. "Mother told us our grandmother was an orphan who was fortunate to be taken in by our Jewish great-grandmother in Leiden. So, our grandmother wasn't born Jewish, and she had the lighter hair that Mother has and has given to us."

"Well, that solves the mystery, Jacob," Mrs. Goodwin said. "It hardly matters what color your hair is; it's the color of your heart that matters. You two have good hearts that cared for one another on your impossible trip to safety here in Lowestoft. And now you have a marvelous opportunity to sail to an even safer destination in Canada. Someone," she said as she pointed toward the ceiling, "is looking out for you. Princess Juliana and her children fled Holland to go to Canada for their safety, you know. You fled Holland, too. Soon, you may find yourselves among Dutch royalty in Canada," she smiled.

"That's lovely, Mrs. Goodwin, it really is," Jacob said, "but I'd sooner be here waiting for my father and mother to arrive. What if they come here to find us? Will you be able to tell them where we are? They may be able to follow us here to Lowestoft, but I'm sure they'd never think to look for us as far away as Canada."

Mrs. Goodwin's face grew very serious as she said, "I promise you, Jacob, and you, too, Naomi, that when your parents come to get you here, I will tell them where you are and help them find you. That is my solemn promise. Thanks to the papers you hid in your bags, we've already posted news of your arrival here in Lowestoft to your home in London, your neighbors there, and the Royal College of Art. Among all those good people, someone will inform your parents when they arrive home."

"If they ever get home," Naomi said, looking at the floor, "if they're still alive," she cried as she ran to her cot in the girls' dormitory.

As Jacob rose to follow her, Mrs. Goodwin said, "Let me take care of her this time, Jacob. You have your own tears to shed," she added as she handed him her handkerchief.

Jacob nodded as he turned and walked away, drying his eyes. He felt helpless, no doubt, because he *was* helpless. In their two months here, neither he nor Naomi had seen a mother or father arrive to rescue their children and take them home. None of the other children had received a letter from their parents. Why should he and Naomi have any reason to hope that their parents would be the first to write?

Thankfully, his dormitory was empty when he arrived, for when Jacob lay down on his bunk, his pillow knew nothing but his desolate tears and desperate sobs.

Chapter 21

Michael awoke feeling no respite from the awkwardness he felt with his father-in-law. No promise the early morning sun could offer in the spring of 1941 would help. When first asked to call him "Richard" instead of "Sir Richard," Michael's spirit rebelled. There was an order and a tradition, something akin to the sacred, that had to be maintained. He had always been "Sir Richard" to Michael, to Michael's father, and to everyone who wasn't immediate family. All of Michael's world knew him as "Sir Richard." How could that change now?

But, beyond tradition, Michael's family history, or the simple respect due to a man knighted by the King, there was another debt that Michael felt he owed. Sir Richard had given Michael the gift of a secure childhood following his mother's early death and during his father's recovery after the war. Even more, though, was the trust Sir Richard had placed in him, initiating his training as a SIS field operative, helping him to secure that position, and trusting him with the fit and finish of Highfield, an ocean away from his office in London and his home overlooking the English Channel.

Beyond all those gifts, honors, and trust, Sir Richard had received Michael as a son and given him his daughter, entrusting her to Michael's care forever. No man could earn that kind of trust, Michael knew. It was a gift, plain and simple. "And, so," Michael asked himself, "how can I address this man as anything but 'Sir Richard,' a title earned and well-deserved by one more generous to me than I could ever hope to be to another?"

Michael thought for a long moment before a smile awoke on his face. It wasn't a smile wrought by humor but a smile wrought by the satisfaction of a simple discovery. Ever the problem solver, Michael had come to a conclusion that he knew hadn't come from within.

"I *can* call him 'Richard,'" he affirmed aloud. "And why? *Because he asked me to*. I need no other reason. Out of respect for his request, I will address this honorable man by his first name."

After the inevitable awkwardness of their first few evenings preparing the *Lady M* for launching in the spring, the two men discovered a remarkable commonality in their thought processes. Sir Richard learned logic at a chessboard with his father as his teacher. Michael, too, had learned from his father, but his logic came through a keen mind expressed through simple but systematic engineering solutions. Both Michael and Sir Richard enjoyed a systems approach to getting a job done, shunning disorder and wasted time. Once they discovered that they thought alike in many ways, they could anticipate each other's next step in their work process. Often, they would arrive at like solutions for a problem left over from a previous night's work. Together, they made a good team.

On Sunday, both their families were at the early mass at St. Peter's, but Sir Richard and Lady Moncrieff were seated near the front of the nave while Susan, Michael, and the boys sat near the back. The Morelands found it much easier to care for their boys from the back of the church where they weren't as likely to distract the entire congregation. Interestingly, Fr. Hunt referred to Psalm 133 in his homily. The psalm's first verse read, "Behold, how good and how pleasant it is for brethren to dwell together in unity!" Hearing Fr. Hunt expound on that verse brought a smile to Michael's face, one that Susan acknowledged just before she glanced toward her father and mother, ten rows in front of them. Not surprisingly, she saw her parents nodding together at the same moment.

For Susan, the changes she had seen in the relationship between Michael and her father brought mixed feelings. Of course, she was happy to see these two men more relaxed and closer to one another than they had ever been. However, she found herself yearning to return to the status quo, where her father's role in the family kept him in authority and comfortably untouchable. She had found an odd security in the familiar distance he maintained.

She recalled the conversation they shared during one of his rare visits while she was studying in Oxford. He had asked her if she had met any interesting men there. She had to smile as she remembered how frank she had been when she described the few men she had met. She recalled saying, "Father, most men I have met here in Oxford are consumed with themselves; they constantly compete with other men who threaten to become their equals. These same men fear women, regularly reminding us of the limitations they have put on us and the role they expect us to play. I suppose that having a woman in his life is convenient for a man's career, but because men take themselves so seriously with other men, they can't relax with women, either. It seems all they want from us are bed partners and cheerleaders."

As she thought back to that moment, she was surprised at how open she had dared to be with her father. Then again, she knew that women often had an easier time being honest with a man than men had being honest with each other. With a woman, there wasn't the same fear of vulnerability that kept men from sharing with other men. She had learned that from her mother before Michael finally dared to propose.

At the same time, Susan was jealous for her brothers, whose relationships with their father were not nearly as open as Michael's had become. Perhaps when they returned from war, Nigel and Boyd would also build a new relationship with their father. Funnily enough, though, she felt her own twinge of jealousy about Michael's new relationship with him. It was hard to admit, even to herself. Her father had always maintained a curious distance from her. "Perhaps he could do no other," she wondered as she recalled her grandfather, another man she found just slightly larger than life. Her father spoke of him regularly, even to this day, and always in terms that left her slightly in awe of a man from her childhood whom she hardly remembered. Then, it came to her.

"He can't give away something he never had," she said aloud. Her father's relationship with Michael was something entirely new, and though still a bit uncomfortable, it offered her father a freedom he was beginning to enjoy. Her grandfather was another man who lived at a distance from others, no doubt because he had learned that from *his* father a generation earlier. Susan marveled for a moment. "Perhaps generations have reached a moment of healing," she thought. And then she could add, "and Michael was here for its beginning." Suddenly, she felt ashamed of her jealousy. "I know it wasn't easy for him. He told me so. But he was willing to do as Father asked, despite his reluctance," she thought. Looking over at Case and Reed napping in their cribs, she said, "Perhaps I should support these men by sacrificing my jealousy and joining them. Then, perhaps our boys will never feel the need to keep an overly respectful distance from their grandfather as I did. I was afraid then. Now, perhaps, Case and Reed will never need to know that kind of fear."

Just as her mother had been instrumental in freeing Michael to propose to Susan more than two years ago, her mother had prompted the change in Sir Richard's and Michael's relationship, the two most important men in Susan's life.

"Mother," Susan thought with a smile, "I believe you've done it again!"

Chapter 22

Three days after Germany invaded the Netherlands on May 10, 1940, Queen Wilhelmina gratefully found refuge awaiting her and the Dutch government in London. Thankfully, most of the Dutch Royal Navy's fleet was in the East Indies, but the remainder fled to England. Many Dutch airmen found their way to the UK and joined the RAF, fighting in the Battle of Britain. At home, however, the Dutch resistance faced overwhelming odds against the terror tactics of their Nazi invaders.

As with the other countries the Nazis invaded, their plan included transforming the Netherlands into a socialist state that would be absorbed into the Nazi German state. The Nazis were also eager to exploit the Dutch manufacturing economy and its workforce. A third goal required first subjugating and then eradicating the Dutch Jewish population.

When Daniel and Deborah Abrams were taken into custody in Leiden in December, Jews had already been banned from civil service occupations and forced to register the assets of their businesses. Although both the Abrams were born in the Netherlands, their British passports made them Nazi enemies. To be both Jewish and British subjects detained by the Nazis in the Netherlands in the winter of 1940 left the Abrams little reason to hope that they would ever be free again.

It was not a German but a Dutch official appointed by the Reich Commissar who arrested the Abrams on the train platform in Leiden. The pistol shot their children heard was a warning shot that brought many on the platform to their knees in a frightened halt. Something about the Abrams looked suspicious to their appointed captor, and they were quickly ushered to separate cells in a basement jail beneath City Hall for interrogation. It was two weeks later that a German officer interrogated Daniel.

Standing inside his cell while the officer remained seated outside, Daniel said, "We registered with the British embassy in London before we traveled here. They know we are here. I am a professor at the Royal College of Art in London. When we do not return on schedule, you will be held responsible," Daniel warned his interrogator, an SS officer named Rauter.

"And who will the British Embassy contact here?" Rauter asked calmly. "As I understand the situation, the government of the Netherlands, her ambassadors, and all other Dutch government representatives have fled to London. Perhaps the British and the Dutch can discuss your situation there," he smiled. "I'm sure it is only a short walk between their offices."

"I demand to speak with the local authorities," Daniel said. "They arrested me without cause. I demand that my wife and I be released to return to London. Since they arrested me, they can release me."

"I'm afraid you don't understand, Mr. Abrams," Rauter said. "When you came here from London to spy on the Third Reich, you forfeited any possibility of appeal to the local authorities. No, I am afraid you have become my prisoner now. The local authorities take their orders from me, you know. However, if you choose to cooperate and confess your crimes, I would be more inclined to help you and your wife . . . "

Rauter hesitated while trying to remember her name.

"Deborah," Abrams said quietly.

"Ah, yes, Deborah," Rauter agreed. "Of course, she will also be interrogated, but not today. I will have to travel to meet her. You see, moving her to another facility has become necessary for her safety."

"Her safety?" Daniel demanded. "What do you mean, 'for her safety'?"

"Mr. Abrams, you must understand that the people of Leiden are a peaceable lot. However, they don't take well to British Jews who come to their city to disturb their peace. I am responsible for defending that peace, but I cannot guarantee that other prisoners or even those who guard the prisoners here will always remain civil. Some have been known to express their outrage physically. It is unfortunate, but it happens, Mr. Abrams. Fortunately for you, I am a reasonable and generous man. Your cooperation could convince me to intervene to provide the safest accommodations within my power for your wife and for you before..."

Daniel looked into the eyes of evil and the smirk on a face that knew no shame. He was helpless, and Rauter knew it and was thoroughly enjoying the fear and torture he was inflicting.

"Perhaps you will have something more to tell me tomorrow, Mr. Abrams. Perhaps my schedule will allow me to make another visit, although I may have to send one of my staff in my place. Unfortunately, they are often not as, how shall I say it?" he asked as he lifted his eyes to ponder, "I believe the word would be, 'patient,'" he said. "That will be up to you, Mr. Abrams."

With that, Rauter stood, put on his SS officer's visor cap, and, after adjusting it carefully, followed the jailer to the door at the end of the dimly lit corridor.

Despite every threat that Rauter had made, one thing he didn't say gave Daniel hope. Rauter never mentioned Jacob and Naomi. Daniel rejoiced that his children might yet be safe. He knew that God was good and that God heard his prayers. Tonight, he would center his prayers on Deborah and her welfare, wherever they had taken her. She needed his prayers, and he needed to offer them.

It was only a few hours later that his prayers were answered. In the silence of his basement cell, he heard a woman's voice. He sat erect on his cot and listened more closely. Yes, he wasn't dreaming. It was Deborah's voice. She was singing a lullaby, the one she sang for Jacob and Naomi. "Slaap Kindje, Slaap," he heard, "Sleep Baby, Sleep." It was the lullaby Deborah's mother sang to her as a baby and the one she sang to their children. Rauter had lied. Deborah was still here, perhaps several cells away, but still here. She, too, was praying for their children. The one who answered prayers would hear both of them tonight. Daniel was sure of it.

As Deborah sang, Daniel dared to echo each line. He heard her voice hesitate as he finished, but she began again, this time louder. They sang together for perhaps an hour. Daniel refused to close his eyes until he could no longer hear her voice. Only then did he offer his "Amen."

"Tomorrow night, we'll sing to our children again," he promised. Within a few moments, he found he could close his eyes and give himself to his dreams.

Chapter 23

It was early in the evening after supper when Michael finally got to look at the mail he picked up this morning at the post office in Charlottetown. The stack of letters included a thick envelope addressed to Michael from Atty Leighton in Quebec. Michael opened the envelope, perused the cover page quickly, and opened the second envelope. The second envelope always held the bank draft from the proceeds of Michael's invention, the Moreland Radiator Cooling Shroud. This quarter's bank draft was similar to many others except in its amount. This draft was written for $18,348.72.

Michael could not restrain the tears that came to him at that moment. Deep inside, his heart cried out in joy, but at the same time, he felt like an interloper, one who had claimed something that was not his own.

Walking up behind him, Susan couldn't help but recognize his emotion as he held the letter in his hands.

"Michael," she asked, "is something wrong?"

As she looked over his shoulder, he answered with a handkerchief in hand, "No, Susan, everything is fine. I'm simply feeling a bit out of place."

"What do you mean?' she asked.

"It's this," he said as he showed her the letter and the bank draft from Atty Leighton's office.

Susan skimmed the letter and turned to the draft in Michael's hands. "Eighteen thousand three hundred forty-eight dollars and seventy-two cents?" she asked. "Isn't that a small fortune, Michael?"

"Yes, " he replied, "to many, it would be. It's enough to feed and house a family like the Bouchers," he hesitated, computing figures in his head, "for over ten years."

"Then why the tears, Michael? Please tell me. I need to know," she asked.

Michael thought for a moment before answering. "I think it has something to do with your father," he said. "Ever since I've begun to call him 'Richard,' I've been forced to confront the differences in our stations. It's hard to reach out and pretend equality with a man I've always revered. Suddenly, he asked me to forget the past and address him, my benefactor, Sir Richard Moncrieff, as simply, 'Richard.'"

Susan listened and nodded as Michael continued.

"I've never considered what it would be like to be wealthy, Susan. It was never possible for a simple man from my family, a proud family of loyal caretakers of a master's estate. But now, I feel a great responsibility for all the money that has come to us from a simple solution to an overheating problem on a 1936 Ford truck." Shaking his head, he added as he turned toward her, "A check like this means that I can care for you and our boys properly, in the manner that you've always known, the same way your parents cared for you—and also for me," he remembered with a smile. "It's humbling," he said, "and I am very grateful. I deserve none of this," he said as he pointed to the bank draft on his desk.

"I wouldn't dare claim to understand your feelings, Michael," Susan began. "I've never known anything but the privilege that comes from social rank and wealth. However, you have a heritage that none of us can claim. You also have riches that none of us could earn."

"What do you mean?" he asked.

"Your wealth comes from a heart that claims no deserving and requires nothing from any man but this," she said as she walked around the desk to face him, "Respect," she said, "respect for your ingenuity and your hard work. You, Michael Moreland, are a self-made man but not one who set out to be anything extraordinary. No, Michael, you are talented and genuine, your reward is due, and the return on your genius arrives every few months in an envelope like this," she said, as she lifted the envelope to his eyes, "to prove to you once again that you are worthy."

Michael stood to face his wife, still shaking his head in disbelief. Taking her in his arms, he said, "I have no deserving, Susan, but the blessings keep coming—you, our boys, our home. I'll get used to it," he said, as he held her tighter, "but I will always need your help. Only when I first felt that you could love me as desperately as I loved you could I finally raise my head from the earth to look up and believe in our future. And now, our future has come upon us, and we are blessed beyond my wildest expectations. And, you, Susan, were the beginning."

"Well, Michael, you should know that four years at Oxford, surrounded by everything the socialites and wealthy young men in England could offer, never held a candle to the man I first came to love when he taught me how to drive a little car called 'Bessie' in Suffolk. I waited patiently to set my trap for him on this side of the ocean because I knew I would never be happy with any man but him. Now, if wealth comes, too, that's just icing on the cake, as they say," she laughed.

"Then," Michael said when their kiss ended, "do you think Ingrid and Patrice could babysit Case and Reed for an hour? Then, you and I could drive into Charlottetown tonight to find a place that serves some of that cake and icing."

"Oh, Michael," she said, "I haven't been outside the house in what feels like forever. That sounds wonderful."

"Then, what's to stop us?" Michael asked.

"Nothing," she answered. "If you will call the Boucher house to see if the ladies are available, I'll attend to the boys' last feeding now. If Ingrid and Patrice are willing, and if you could help with the burping, we could be ready to leave in about half an hour."

"Consider it done," Michael laughed. "I'll have your cabriolet warming out front when we're ready to go."

As Michael walked to the garage to get Susan's car, a thought passed through his mind. It was a novel thought for him, something he'd never considered. At first, he drew back from the idea as if it was somehow suspect and out of place. To clear his mind, he found himself speaking aloud as if to another who could be his sounding board.

"So, you, your wife, and your children live together in her parents' home, correct? So, what would be wrong with building your own home?"

Michael didn't know where the idea came from, but he didn't reject it immediately. Instead, he asked aloud, "So, what *would* be wrong with having our own home?"

He laughed as the answer came out of his mouth a second or two later. "The problem, Moreland," he said laughing, "is spring. We've got gardens to plow and plant, fields that will soon be full of hay to cut and bale, and everything else summer brings. When things quiet down in the fall, perhaps we'll dream of a new home and make a few sketches. Besides, Susan needs to be part of everything. Perhaps I could tell her about it tonight," he said. "I'd love to hear what she might think."

Chapter 24

"World War II," Lady Moncrieff said, shaking her head. "It's hard to believe how many countries and peoples are involved in this conflict, Richard. I marvel that you can keep so much information at your fingertips."

Sir Richard nodded as he poured his second cup of breakfast tea. "I was late coming to bed last night amid the latest reports, some of which worry me."

"The Germans?" she asked.

"Always," he said while spreading marmalade on his scone, "but there are so many other fronts to consider. When the Soviets joined the Nazis, one battle on the continent ended with the Soviet occupation of three Baltic nations. Now, I'm afraid that Estonia, Latvia, and Lithuania will never escape Soviet domination. Since Poland, Norway, and Denmark fell to the Wehrmacht, along with the Low Countries and France, one might think that battles on the continent could be contained after Hitler added Yugoslavia and Greece. But then Mussolini raised his head from Italy to attack southeast France and begin further havoc in the Mediterranean," he said.

"Are our men still fighting in North Africa?" she asked.

"The Italians have attacked us in Palestine, Egypt, and Somaliland, and battles have continued there since German forces joined them," he said. "Further, shortly after Germany invaded Yugoslavia last spring, the Italians attacked Greece. In my mind, though, Italy will prove a distraction soon. They lack the capital, industry, and military manpower to sustain a war that Mussolini can never win."

"And the Japanese?" Angela asked.

"The Japanese have been at war with China since 1937," he said. "Since Britain and the United States have historically supported China, the Japanese consider us their enemies. Furthermore, while the French have been in no position to oppose them, the Japanese also invaded and occupied northern Indochina."

"Do you believe the Japanese could prove a threat to the Commonwealth in Australia and New Zealand?" she asked.

"Absolutely," he answered, "anywhere in the Pacific could be their target, but besides their British, French, and Dutch targets, I believe the United States has a target most likely to draw their fire."

"And what is that, Richard?" Angela asked.

"It's called Pearl Harbor on the Hawaiian Islands," he answered. "President Roosevelt moved the US Pacific Fleet from San Diego, California, to Pearl Harbor six or seven months ago. Although three thousand miles from Japan, it is well within range of Japan's aircraft carriers," he said.

"You said some of your overnight reports had you worried, Richard. Among all these you've mentioned this morning, which has you most concerned," she asked.

Richard paused before responding. "None of these, Angela," he answered. "My concern is more personal, but I don't want to alarm you."

"So, it concerns our sons, then?" she asked.

"It could, but I have no immediate intelligence suggesting that either of our boys is in particular danger. The reports I have received are quite general but serious, nonetheless," he said.

"What can you tell me, then, Richard? There must be something," Angela asked.

"In a way, it's very old news concerning two German battleships that have been under construction for years. SIS has monitored their progress since their keels were laid in 1936. However, these aren't ordinary battleships, Angela. They're monsters," he said, shaking his head.

"Why do you say that?" she asked.

"Because these ships are larger and better equipped than any ship Germany has ever built. Hitler and his Kriegsmarine have tried to keep them a secret, but to no avail. The first is called the *Bismarck*, and the second is the *Tirpitz*. The *Bismarck* was launched last year but was commissioned only a few months ago. Since then, it has remained hidden. We expect the Kriegsmarine to launch the *Tirpitz* very soon as well."

"I see," Angela nodded.

"So far, the *Bismarck* hasn't been sent on a mission, but we know it is located somewhere in the North Sea," he said. "When it is launched," he added, "the *Tirpitz* will probably follow soon after."

"Nigel is with the *Ark Royal* in the North Sea, if I'm not mistaken," Angela said.

"That is correct," he said, "and Boyd, aboard the *Revenge*, may also be there."

"No further encouragement has come from the United States recently?" she asked.

"There is some news on that front. Denmark has signed an agreement allowing the US to take over the defense of Greenland. In return, the US will enjoy the right to build air and naval bases there. Roosevelt was once again able to overcome those who remained adamant about maintaining US neutrality. Furthermore, Churchill, before the House of Commons, had this to say," Sir Richard said as he raised a paper from among those lying on his desk. "Churchill said, 'Once we have gained the Battle of the Atlantic and are sure of the constant flow of American supplies which are being prepared for us, then, however far Hitler may go, or whatever new millions and scores of millions he may lap in misery, we who are armed with the sword of retributive justice shall be on his track.'"

"Churchill sounds confident that the US will continue to support our cause," Angela said.

"Yes," Sir Richard answered, "and I have more good news to add. Several months ago, we captured the *München*, a German weather ship. Discovered onboard by Royal Navy Captain John Haines were secret papers related to the German Enigma machines. With the help of this intelligence, we have been hoping to find a way to break German codes. Even better, however, was news that came in overnight. Three of our convoy escorts in the Atlantic captured a German U-boat, *U-110*. Onboard they found an intact Enigma machine along with an entire set of Nazi code books. With the *Bismarck* and the *Tirpitz* scheduled to be at sea soon, I can think of no better time for us to be able to intercept and decipher their communications."

"I so hope they are successful," she said.

"And I am thankful for this," he said, "that our sons are aboard the best-equipped ships in the Royal Navy, manned and commanded by the best officers in the free world. Because they are at sea, they can maneuver and fight or, if necessary, flee to come back to fight another day. The defense of the common folk, be they British or otherwise, is our one noble goal. I believe with all my heart that God is on our side and that we will prevail."

Angela was quiet for a moment before asking, "How do you do it, Richard?"

"Do what?" he asked.

"How do you carry all of those terrible things you know—the evil, the horrible, the frightening, the things that threaten all that is good and noble in our world when it seems we are helpless to effect any change for the good? I know I could not bear it all as you do, but I also know one thing more. We are fortunate that there are men like you, Richard, who bear impossible burdens and do it willingly. These men are noble, self-sacrificing, and admirable, but still men. I'm sure the burden impacts you in a thousand ways, but you bear it willingly, and I, for one, am grateful," she said.

"You honor me with your kind thoughts, Angela, but I only do what I have been called to do, and I do it thankfully. Yes, my work is tedious, and sometimes its weight feels overwhelming, but I comfort myself with the call I answered even as a young man. God being my helper, I will continue to listen for that voice that reminds me of all the good gifts given to me, your love chief among them."

"And so may our prayers be answered," she said, "Amen, and amen."

Chapter 25

Daniel Abrams marked one more day of captivity, using the buckle on this belt to carve a hashmark on the wall of his cell, adding it to all the others. He dared not count the marks again. The number didn't matter anymore. No one was coming to their aid. He and Deborah had no one to defend them, no one to question the charges against them, no one who cared.

When he buckled his belt again, he could not tighten it securely. He had lost so much weight that his clothes hung on him as if on a hanger in a closet. He shuddered to think how Deborah must feel about herself. She had always been a striking woman who carried herself proudly and attended to her good looks. Perhaps it was a mercy that he had seen no mirrors in the jail. The short walk down the windowless corridor to the small paved courtyard where he could occasionally see the sun offered nothing to grant a reflection. Once, though, after a rain, a puddle in the courtyard offered a face to him that was bearded, gaunt, aged, and ill. Daniel remembered turning away in disgust.

Their jailers were neither uniformed nor professional in their manner. There were but few, all short-spoken. Before they spoke, they often looked over their shoulders down the corridor to see if their superiors could overhear them. Daniel gathered that they were among those who needed jobs during wartime and had chosen this, the lowest civil service post available, despite its evils. All seemed to live in fear of a man named Faber, a local politician in charge of the prisoners and who reported to Rauter, the SS officer Daniel would never forget. The mention of Faber or Rauter was enough to stiffen the guards' gait and remind them of their status in the new order that the Nazis were imposing on the people of Leiden.

A new guard, a young man in his twenties, stopped at Daniel's cell door late one night while Daniel lay sleepless on his cot.

"Mr. Abrams," he said in a hoarse whisper. "I have something for you."

Daniel raised his head, surprised to hear his name but more surprised that the guard offered something other than the cold rations that came twice a day. Though he said nothing, Daniel raised a shoulder from the cot and leaned on one elbow as he faced the young man.

"Please," the young man said softly, "do not be afraid. Here," he said, offering something in his outstretched hand that the darkness hid from Daniel's eyes.

Slowly, Daniel swung his feet to the dampness of the stone floor, stood, and took the three short steps to his cell door. He saw what looked like a piece of fabric in the young man's hand. Daniel reached out to take it. However, when he drew it closer to his eyes, he found it wasn't just a piece of fabric. It was the edge of a handkerchief embroidered with blue flowers, a woman's handkerchief, Deborah's handkerchief.

Daniel fell to his knees, sobbing while at the same time conscious to stifle his sobs, all the while clutching the handkerchief to his breast, covering his heart.

"How," he whispered through his tears, "how did you get this?" he begged as he glanced toward the corridor outside.

"Please, Mr. Abrams, do not be afraid," the young man said. "My name is Jan. Please ask me nothing more about my identity for now. I am new here, and I hope you will let me help you."

"No," Daniel said, "no. First, tell me how you got this."

"Of course," the young man said. "I'm sorry. Your wife is in a cell two corridors away. I spoke with her today. She asked me to give it to you."

"Is she well?" Daniel asked. "Please tell me she is well."

"She is well, Mr. Abrams, as well as she might be, given the circumstances. But I can stay no longer," he whispered, looking down the corridor. "Is there anything you would like me to give to her, say to her?" Jan asked.

Daniel looked down at his soiled shirt, once white but now soiled, stained, and gray. On the pocket was his monogram, the one Deborah had embroidered. He tore the pocket from his shirt and handed it to Jan in one motion.

"I must go," Jan whispered, but she will have this within minutes," he promised.

Thus began a series of night visits, all whispered and short. In less than two weeks, Daniel learned a great deal.

Rauter, the SS officer assigned to monitor the Jewish cleansing in Leiden, had been transferred to Rotterdam, where the Nazis required his expertise in questioning captured members of the Dutch resistance. Faber, the man in charge of the jail in Leiden, was a civilian citizen of Leiden and a member of the NSB, the fascist National Socialist movement in the Netherlands. Anxious to climb the ranks of the NSB and earn the respect of the SS, Faber kept a close watch on his prisoners and regularly provided detailed reports to Rauter.

In the late evenings, when other guards were sleeping through their shifts, Jan spent a few moments with either Daniel or Deborah whenever he felt they could talk safely.

"I was an art student here at Leiden University," Jan whispered to Daniel. "The Nazis closed the university because many professors and administrators protested the Nazi racial policies against Jews. Some of the more outspoken professors and students have disappeared. We know the Nazis have kidnapped them, killed some, and deported others."

Jan took a brief moment to compose himself.

"I am one of the few they call 'dissidents' who have remained undetected. My employment under Faber in the jail, where many protesters have been questioned, has kept me safe thus far. However, I need to escape the city, and I can help you escape as well," he said.

Daniel could hardly believe what he was hearing. "But how could you do that?" he asked.

"Faber is traveling to Rotterdam in two weeks. He will be there for four days, meeting with other NSB members and Nazi organizers. That will be our opportunity," Jan said, "but I must have your promise of help."

"But, what can I do for you?" Daniel asked.

"Everything," Jan answered. "I was hoping to become an architect someday, but that can never happen now that the Nazis have closed the university. You are a London art professor, yes?" he asked. He continued in his hoarse whisper, not waiting for an answer, "While Faber is in Rotterdam, I can help you escape from this jail. I have contacts in the resistance who are ready to help us get to the coast."

"But, again, what kind of help do you think I can promise?" Daniel asked.

"I have no English, Mr. Abrams. I will need your help to learn enough English to apply to study at the Royal College in London. I will guide you safely to the coast where we can find passage to England, but you must help me when we arrive in London."

"But, our children, Jan," Daniel said. "I've never mentioned our children, but they must be somewhere here in the Netherlands. They escaped from the train station when we were arrested. My greatest joy has been that neither Rauter nor Faber has mentioned our children. I trust that they do not know our children exist. We must find them before we can return to London. I have to believe they are somewhere not far from Leiden. I only pray that they are safe."

"No, they are not," Jan said.

"They're not safe? How do you know? Tell me, Jan," Daniel demanded.

"Shh!" Jan ordered as he looked over his shoulder again. He whispered, "They are safe, but they are very far from Leiden, and quite luckily so."

"But, how do you know? You must tell me everything you know, Jan," Daniel begged.

"Late on the day you were arrested, a member of the resistance, a trusted woman outside of Leiden, observed them on the road," Jan began. "That woman, a widow who lives alone, invited them into her home, fed them, and prepared them for their journey to another safe house a day's travel away. They traveled from safe house to safe house until they reached the coast. Our last information was that they joined a group of several hundred other refugee children, some of whom were evacuated from the country. Your children sailed with them to England more than a month ago," Jan answered.

"But, how do you know it was them?" Daniel asked. "There are thousands of Jewish refugees hoping to find passage to England. How can I be sure the two you describe are my children?"

Jan took a small notepad from his pocket and flipped through several pages, scanning each until he found what he needed. "Would it suffice for me to say that your son's name is 'Jacob' and your daughter's name is 'Naomi'?" Jan asked. "And following your practiced instructions, when they left the train station in Leiden, they walked toward the setting sun?"

With tears running down his face, Daniel nodded, "Yes, those are their names, and those are the instructions we rehearsed."

"Quickly now," Jan said. "We have two weeks to prepare, and there is much for me to do. Every day the Nazi presence in Leiden grows. Every day a Nazi convinces another desperate citizen to join them and betray their neighbors. All have eyes eager to discover the overland and water routes we use. The Nazis thrive on making examples of the resistance and of others who have escaped their capture. If we fall into their hands, our death is certain, Mr. Abrams," Jan said. "For the moment, however, we remain in God's hands."

"May it ever be so," Daniel said, "may it ever be so."

Chapter 26

Two weeks passed too slowly for Daniel, who had missed the sight of Deborah's face and heard her voice only in the lullabies she dared to sing from time to time. Feigning sleep until the regular guards had made their last check on the prisoners, Daniel waited for Jan to keep his promise. His reward came at last.

Among the shadows of the darkened corridor, Daniel sensed movement that sounded labored. Every breath and step that approached brought Daniel closer to his cell door, peering into the darkness until he could see two human forms turn the last corner and creep toward him. Finally, he could make out Jan and someone behind him, who had to be Deborah. Leaving her at the corner, Jan arrived with a key to the cell door, and he unlocked it as silently as possible. The squeak the door issued as he opened it forced Jan to open it only inches at a time. When the gap was large enough, he guided Deborah inside and followed behind.

One look into her eyes drew Daniel forward with tears that rolled down his cheeks into the beard on his face that aged him by twenty years. Cupping his face in her hands as if holding a delicate flower, Deborah kissed his cheeks and forehead as he wrapped his arms around her shoulders. Careful to maintain their silence, neither could say what each had seen. Their partners were thin, emaciated, and severely weakened by their incarceration. Still, the spark in their eyes at seeing their beloveds brought smiles to faces that had not known them for months.

Jan drew a finger to his lips as Daniel and Deborah leaned forward to hear his whisper.

"See, here, I have two haversacks. Both have men's clothing. You, Deborah, must travel as a man for your safety," he said.

Deborah nodded, her eyes signaling her understanding.

Jan continued, "Faber kept a meticulous history of your arrest and incarceration. He also maintained an untouched cache of all the personal items taken from you at your arrest. Your valuables are all here," he said, pointing to Daniel's haversack, "passports, jewelry, even your cash. Now, you must dress in silence. Deborah, you will find a pair of scissors. You must wear a man's hair now. Daniel," Jan said, "you must help her to cut it close. I will return after I am sure the others are where I left them, sleeping and well overcome by the two bottles of schnaps I brought them tonight."

Daniel and Deborah began to change their clothes even as Jan passed through the open door and started up the corridor, "I will return within five minutes. If, for some reason, I am delayed, take this key to the courtyard door," Jan said, handing a large skeleton key to Daniel, "and leave without me. The courtyard gate leads to a path that runs parallel to this building. Turn right onto the path and follow the canal toward the sounds of the train yard. I will meet you there." With that, Jan was gone.

Daniel and Deborah were dressed within minutes. The last of Deborah's long hair was lying on the floor when Jan returned. Smiling, he whispered, "They are sleeping the sleep of the just, but they will awake with headaches. Fortunately, they will see us no more."

With only a sliver of the moon glowing in the starry sky, the trio made their way through the darkness of the courtyard onto the footpath beside the canal and to the train yard, where a westbound train with several empty boxcars stood waiting. Within a few hours after climbing into an empty boxcar, they were several miles southwest of Leiden and had several more hours left before their absence at the jail would be discovered. Daniel and Deborah spent the time huddled in a corner against the boxcar walls, content to rest in each other's arms. They talked of everything good, old, and familiar, but they always returned to their children, thanking God that Jacob and Naomi had found a safe route to England. They prayed together for a reunion, and that right soon.

Jan sat at the boxcar door, taking in what landscape he could see in the darkness. It would be hours before dawn, but he knew they would have to leave the train behind in Voorschoten while darkness prevailed. His contact with the resistance awaited them, ready to guide them further south before they could turn west toward the coast. Jan had planned their route carefully, avoiding populated areas and using backroads where they were unlikely to be discovered. But all that was a few hours away, and Jan succumbed to the rhythm of the boxcar wheels on the rails and took his rest. There would be much to do when he awoke.

All were asleep when there was a sudden jolt as the train braked and began to slow. Jan looked out the door toward the front of the train, but he couldn't see the station lights. There were no lights at all. He realized the train hadn't yet reached the city but was making an unscheduled stop. All Jan heard was some confused shouting in Dutch, but then he heard some unmistakable orders barked in German. Daniel and Deborah were already at his elbow when headlights appeared in the distance, and Jan turned to them to say, "Now. We must go *now*. Follow me."

With that, he leapt to the railway path below, waiting to help Deborah down as Daniel followed. In seconds, they found the dark of the woods to the southwest and moved as fast as they could away from the railway. Behind them, they heard voices shouting in Dutch and German, and behind the voices, they heard barking dogs. Jan knew their pursuers were intent on finding their prey in one of the boxcars, and he feared their scent would be strong enough for the dogs to follow them. The trio ran and ran, stumbling in the darkness, with the crescent moon their only source of light. It was almost an hour before they stopped to rest and take shelter in a long-abandoned farmer's shed where they could hear the sounds of a swift-flowing stream. They waited, listening intently, saying nothing. Finally, Jan spoke.

"We've missed my contact in Voorschoten," he said. "We'll not encounter another for many miles. In the meantime, we must rest and eat. While you rest here, I will find food somewhere nearby at a farm or in a village. Do not venture away. Do not be seen. I will return as soon as I can."

The sun was up before Jan returned. With Daniel's money, he bought enough food to keep them for several days - bread, cheese, sausages, and two bottles of red wine.

As they ate and drank, Jan said, "My next contact awaits us in Leidschendam, a small village to the southwest. He will have a place for us to stay. Until then, we must fend for ourselves in places like this, places of interest to no one but us. We can light no fires or lanterns. The darkness will be our friend."

And so they traveled by night and slept by day, resting a full day in Leidschendam before reaching Rotterdam. They traveled west to the shore, where the money Jan recovered for the Abrams proved enough to secure passage south to Dunkirk and pay for a room in an inn. Far from those pursuing them, Deborah could finally leave her men's clothing and boots behind. Able to embrace civilization once again, the trio enjoyed hot baths, clean clothing, and adequate grooming to make them comfortable. None but Jan, however, was able to abandon the terror of their journey and the fearsome memories of Leiden. He was looking forward to arriving at the Royal College in London, his determined destination. At every opportunity, he prevailed on Daniel and Deborah for another lesson in English. Another day passed before they continued across the Channel to England, landing in Harwich.

On their second day in Harwich, Daniel learned of an organization called *Kindertransport*, an agency that had helped thousands of Jewish children escape to Great Britain several years earlier. Jan believed some of her former members may have helped Jacob and Naomi reach England. Within a few short hours, Daniel and Deborah were overjoyed to meet a man who identified himself only as "Dexter," a former *Kindertransport* agent. He assured them that upon their arrival in Harwich, Jacob and Naomi had been bussed north to Lowestoft with other Jewish children. Because Lowestoft was less than a day's journey north by bus, the trio from Leiden purchased tickets and boarded a coach. Daniel and Deborah were sure it would carry them to a reunion with their children.

"Jan," Daniel said, "when you first came to me in the jail, you told me it was best for us that you keep your identity a secret. You have done so much for us, but we've realized we don't know your last name. Is it safe to tell us now?"

"Of course," Jan answered, blushing. "I am Jan, Jan Molenaar."

"We owe you so much, Jan Molenaar," Deborah said, "and when we arrive in Lowestoft to collect our Jacob and Naomi, I'm sure they will agree."

What Daniel and Deborah didn't know was that Jacob and Naomi had left Lowestoft by bus for Liverpool two days earlier. The British merchant ship they boarded this morning in Liverpool, *Mulbera*, was sailing in convoy to Halifax, Nova Scotia. Their children's final destination was Highfield, an estate in the village of Suffolk on Prince Edward Island.

Chapter 27

"So, what's the news from our friends in England?" Michael asked while Susan read the letter he had handed her minutes ago.

"Michael Moreland," she began, "just because you retrieved the mail from the post office and handed it to me a moment ago doesn't mean I've already been able to read it. If you can't wait until I finish, come here and read over my shoulder."

"That sounds like a dangerous invitation," he smiled, "especially if you're still wearing that perfume I like so much."

"Then stay where you are," she laughed, "but please, let me finish this while the boys are still asleep. I'll tell all, or you can read all then, all right?"

"So, I can check on your perfume when you finish reading?" he asked. "Fair enough," he said, feigning innocence, while her best school teacher look kept him at bay. When she finished, though, she began summarizing everything Michelle had written.

"OK, Michael, here are the high points," she began. "Michelle is well, and Logan is healthy, happy, and growing as fast as our boys."

"And they've remained safe there? Safe from the bombings?" he asked. "From your father's latest reports, Liverpool endured a week of bombing, and Belfast has suffered three raids. Greenock, in Scotland, was also hit over two nights. Then, there were raids on Kingston, Hull, and Nottingham. The Luftwaffe targets are all over the map of the UK, now."

"Nothing in her letter indicates any attacks in her region," Susan said, "but my prayers haven't ceased for their safety."

"And they are doing well in their household despite the rationing?" he asked.

"She doesn't mention anything in particular except that it takes Nancy a good deal more time to shop. Every trip involves queuing up at the greengrocer, the baker, and the butcher. Every member of the family, even Logan, is registered and has a ration book with coupons. Since spring arrived, they have also settled a vegetable garden, sacrificing some of their flower beds. A new government program called 'Dig for Victory' has some of the parks in the village allocating space for vegetable gardens, too," Susan added.

"Thankfully, we won't suffer here at Highfield if rationing is promulgated in Canada," Michael said. "There's no reason to believe that we won't still have more than we need and plenty to help our neighbors, too. But what about Grayson? What does she have to say about him?"

"Let me see," Susan said as she looked through the pages in her hand. "Ah, here it is. She says Grayson got a three-day family leave over Easter, but she doesn't expect to see him again soon. He isn't flying missions just now because the RAF needs him to train a recent infusion of Polish, Czech, and American pilots to fly RAF fighters."

"Well, that's good news. I'd rather see him at the base training others than meeting the Luftwaffe in the air," Michael said.

"And it seems that some of our bombers returning from the continent have had to land at Kirton in Lindsey for repairs from time to time. Michelle mentioned that Grayson heard some news of an American who joined the RCAF a couple of months ago here in Montreal. After training as a navigator in Canada, he arrived in England and has already become quite a celebrity. It seems he spent considerable time in Germany as a student in years past and is proving himself a remarkable asset to the RAF as a navigator. His knowledge of German industrial targets, shipping routes, and bridges has led our bomber squadrons to success again and again."

Michael sat up straight in his seat. Susan had his full attention. He stood and reached out his hand for Michelle's letter.

"I haven't finished yet, Michael. There's more you haven't heard," she said.

"You don't need to summarize anything further for me," he said quietly. "I can read it for myself. Take a well-deserved break while the boys are still quiet. You deserve a rest."

"You don't need to convince me," she said. "I'm going to sit right back in this chair and close my eyes."

Michael retrieved the letter from her hand and took it downstairs to Sir Richard's study. When he arrived, he knocked at the door and called, "Richard? I have some news you'll want to hear."

"Come in, Michael," Sir Richard said. "I could use some good news."

As Michael sat down, he said, "I'm not sure it's good news, but it is intriguing. Grayson mentioned news of an RCAF airman that Michelle included in this letter. I'll be interested to see if your suspicions match mine."

Michael indicated the paragraph in question and watched his father-in-law suddenly raise his eyebrows and read further before handing the letter back to Michael.

"Could be our man, Ernst Hoffman, but he's probably using his alias as Ernest Duncan, I would guess," Sir Richard said.

"Yes," Michael said. "I believe so. Ernest Duncan. He continues to amaze me."

"As I remember," Sir Richard began, "he indicated in his last communique that we'd not see him in these regions again. He appears to be a man of his word. Furthermore, though a one-time double agent, he appears to have chosen one side, *our side,* over the other."

"Yes," Michael said, "and his cartography training could continue to be a uniquely potent weapon in the RAF's arsenal."

"Strange how these things turn out, isn't it?" Sir Richard said. "A young man with a tortured past finds a way to escape those chains and to champion a righteous cause, however dangerous that cause may be. It will be a shame, though," he added.

"A shame? What will be a shame?" Michael asked.

"It will be a shame if he survives the war and keeps his promise not to return here," Sir Richard said. "I, for one, would like to meet this young man and shake his hand. Then, I'd like to hear the *whole* story."

"You know," Michael agreed, "so would I."

Chapter 28

Michael returned from his daily errands in Charlottetown on a Monday morning in late May to find Emily MacMillan's car parked in Highfield's driveway near the front door. Michael still found thinking of her as Emily *MacMillan* strange. For years, she had been "Emily Langdon," "Nurse Emily," or simply "Emily." Now that she was married to Dr. Andrew MacMillan, Michael was still getting used to calling her by her new name.

Though not a frequent visitor of late, Emily was always welcome as part of the Highfield family. As he entered the house, Michael was not surprised to hear women's voices and laughter from the parlor. Since it was mid-morning, he guessed the pastries he carried in the box under his arm might find welcome appetites in the parlor. He knocked at the open door.

"Pardon me, ladies," he began, "but *Tea for Two* sent me home with this box for you. I'll return in a moment with plates, napkins, and a pair of scissors to cut the string, if that will fit your schedule," he said, smiling. "I'll also prepare a fresh pot of tea and deliver it momentarily," he added.

The ladies were glad to oblige, and Lady Moncrieff reached out to Susan to receive Reed while Emily sat on the sofa holding Case. The boys gurgled contentedly, enjoying the full attention of the women in the room. Susan followed Michael to the kitchen.

"I can take care of this, Susan." Michael said, "You don't get to see Emily these days, and it sounded like you three were thoroughly enjoying your conversation before I interrupted."

"Yes, we were," Susan said, "and that's why I need to run upstairs to get something I've been saving for Emily, a gift for this very day."

"Is it her birthday?" Michael asked.

"No," Susan answered. "It's much more exciting than a birthday. It's a day for which several of us have been waiting, but mostly Emily and Andrew."

Susan watched the light go on in Michael's head as he turned and began, "Then she's . . . "

"Yes," Susan said with a broad smile. "They are expecting a baby in late November. I've had a gift awaiting her announcement for some time."

"A gift?" Michael asked. "When have you had time to shop?"

"I haven't," she answered. "It's a pair of warm booties and a matching hat that I've been knitting from lambswool. A November baby will need warm booties and a warm hat. I'm running upstairs to get them now."

While Michael boiled the water for the ladies' tea, Susan wrapped her gift and penned a short note. When she came downstairs, Michael had prepared the tea tray and was ready to deliver it to the parlor. When he arrived, the ladies were kind enough to invite him to stay to enjoy some of the pastry he had provided.

"So, Emily," Lady Moncrieff said, "how soon will you find respite from your hospital duties? Surely, your administration and teaching responsibilities will be burdensome as your pregnancy continues."

"Andrew expressed the same concern, Lady Moncrieff," Emily said, "but I have some very good news to assuage his concern and yours."

"I love good news, Emily. Please say on," Lady Moncrieff smiled.

"A fine, well-trained, and well-experienced nurse is ready to join us at the hospital. Her name is Mary Clark. Her past is really rather sad. After finishing her nursing studies in Montreal and serving at the hospital there, she fell in love and married a bush pilot whose work took them to Cuba. Sadly, he contracted malaria there and died. She only recently returned to Nova Scotia and has now come to Charlottetown."

"How terribly difficult it must be for her," Lady Moncrieff said, "heart-rending, I would imagine."

"Yes," Emily said. "Tragic, so very tragic, but Mary seems ready to move forward with her life and is eager to begin work as soon as possible. I must say, her credentials are stellar. She will benefit from several weeks of orientation at the hospital, of course, but she appears ready to take on my responsibilities as soon as I am ready to leave my work behind."

"Emily," Susan began, "you couldn't have planned anything so fitting. You will be available to acquaint Mary with Charlottetown, the hospital, and the nursing staff, and I'm sure she will be available when you are ready to deliver your baby. Andrew must be thrilled."

"Oh, he is," Emily said, nodding. "I must say he is already doting on me much of the time, treating me as if I was breakable, you know."

Susan looked at Michael and said, "Yes, we know what that is like, don't we, Michael?"

Of course, Susan caught Michael with his mouth full of peach pastry. Still, he was able to nod and, after swallowing, say, "Guilty as charged, I confess, but as penance, I'll be happy to call on Andrew to give him the benefit of my experience, if you'd like, Emily."

"Thank you, Michael," Emily said. "He's quite alone in this right now. I'm sure you'll be a great help to him."

"It will be my pleasure," Michael said with a nod.

"I have a little something for your baby, Emily," Susan said as she produced a wrapped package and card.

"Oh, my," Emily said, surprised. "It's his . . . or her," she caught herself, "first gift. Of course, we're enjoying a lot of 'firsts' these days."

"And I hope you enjoy every one. Go ahead, please. Open it," Susan said.

Parting the ribbon and the folds in the wrapping carefully, Emily found the white box within and the oh-so-soft cream-colored hat and booties. Tears came to her eyes when she realized Susan had knit them herself.

"But how did you find time with your two boys needing you every moment?" she asked. "These will be our treasure when our baby arrives."

"Fear not," Susan said, "even twins have to sleep sometime. You, too, will find time to enjoy friends and family, even after your little one arrives."

At that moment, Reed awoke and began to cry. Susan checked her watch and said, "Right on time. Their appetite never fails."

True to form, Case found his voice, and the duet called Susan and Michael to duty upstairs for feeding time. Lady Moncrieff and Emily were left together.

"Emily," Lady Moncrieff said, "when it seems appropriate, I hope you will bring Nurse Clark to Highfield so that I might meet her. She seems like a fascinating woman, a courageous survivor. I should like to get to know her."

"Of course, Lady Moncrieff," Emily said. "She will need wise friends to help her through some times of adjustment. She has already met Fr. Hunt at St. Peter's. I'm sure she will also be happy to visit with you."

Chapter 29

Lady Moncrieff was used to waking most mornings to find her husband's side of the bed empty. Sir Richard often woke before dawn to monitor overnight communications with London or to send reports. Today was different, however. On her way to the dining room, she stopped at his office in the study but didn't find him. He wasn't in the kitchen either. As Michael returned from the stable, she stepped outdoors to ask if he had seen her husband.

"Good morning, Michael," she began. "Tell me, have you seen Richard this morning? I checked, but he's not in his office."

"Yes, I have," Michael answered. Looking at his wristwatch, he said, "A little over a half hour ago, he appeared at the garage to take your car to Charlottetown. He said something about getting to the newsstand early and told me he'd spare me having to stop there on my regular errands today. I expect he will return soon."

"What kind of news could he be expecting to find, I wonder?" she asked.

"I'm sure I don't know," Michael said, "but he seemed excited and happy. Whatever it is, it must be good news."

"Well, I'll look forward to that," she said.

Looking down the driveway, Michael said, "It seems you won't have to wait too long." Pointing to her sedan and the red dust that followed it, he said, "He'll be parking the car right here in another minute."

Lady Moncrieff turned to look down the driveway as her car came into sight. Sir Richard was driving faster than usual, bringing even more red dust. As he drew to a halt at the kitchen door, he stepped out of the car but reached back inside to blow the horn again and again. Lady Moncrieff noticed several newspapers tucked under his arm. Then he opened the rear door and handed Michael the first of four large bakery boxes. While the sweet scent of pastry began to fill the air, all within earshot left their work and started toward the kitchen door.

As the Highfield family was still gathering, Sir Richard turned to Lady Moncrieff. "Angela," he said, "we have reason to celebrate this morning. Come along to the kitchen now."

While Lady Moncrieff stood with him at the door, Sir Richard turned to the group to say, "We have good news to share with you this morning. Please come closer to hear it."

Just then, Susan appeared in the kitchen, only steps behind her mother, with her arms full of Moreland boys. Lady Moncrieff stepped through the kitchen door to take one of the boys from her as Michael handed the pastry boxes to Doris inside the kitchen. A moment later, Sir Richard raised his voice to address the Highfield family.

"Friends and family, all," he began. "The last few days have been especially perilous for the Royal Navy in waters north and west of the UK. Recently, the Germans sent their newest, largest, and most powerful battleship, the *Bismarck*, out of the North Sea into the Denmark Strait on a mission to raid the commerce lanes of the North Atlantic, hoping to sink ships bound for Halifax. It was the first mission for the *Bismarck*, and the Royal Navy immediately responded when two of His Majesty's battleships confronted her. Sadly, I must report that the guns of the *Bismarck* prevailed against the HMS *Hood*, sinking her and taking the lives of nearly all aboard."

Sadness filled every face as Sir Richard continued.

"But the story does not end there," he said. "Damaged in the battle and blocked from reaching the Atlantic, the *Bismarck* turned back and sailed east. Poor weather prevented the Royal Navy from pursuing her initially, but, in the end, just eight days into her first offensive mission, I can tell you she now lies at the bottom of the sea!" he said as he opened one of the newspapers to reveal the headline, "*Bismarck Sunk with Admiral and 2,000 Men*".

A cheer erupted among all present as Sir Richard handed newspapers to eager hands.

"Please join us in celebrating this victory with pastry and tea in the kitchen," he said. As the rest of the Highfield family found their way to the kitchen, Lady Moncrieff, Susan, and Michael joined Sir Richard in his study.

Always a step ahead of them, Doris had already sent Patrice to the study with a fresh pot of tea. The family sat to hear all that Sir Richard could divulge.

"As I said," he began, "the battleship *Bismarck* and *Prinz Eugen*, a heavy cruiser, were attempting to break out of the Denmark Straits between Iceland and Greenland to reach the North Atlantic shipping routes. The *Hood* and the *Prince of Wales* engaged them there on May 24. A shell fired from the *Bismarck* hit the *Hood* near her aft ammunition magazines, and the *Hood* exploded and sank within minutes. Only three of her crew survived. After firing on the *Bismarck* successfully, the *Prince of Wales* was also hit and broke off the engagement. Subsequently, the *Bismarck*, which suffered substantial damage to her fuel tanks, turned back toward the North Sea."

"How many souls were lost on the *Hood*?" Lady Moncrieff asked.

"I'm sorry to say more than fourteen hundred, Angela," he answered.

"God be with their families, every one of them," she said.

"Amen," Michael added.

"What happened next, Father?" Susan asked.

"The *Bismarck* set sail for the French coast to find repairs for her wounds. The Germans sent *Prinz Eugen* to other waters. Amidst a gale, the Royal Navy lost contact with the *Bismarck* for a day before sending nearly every available ship in the flotilla to find and destroy her. Among them was the carrier, *Ark Royal*," he said.

"Nigel's carrier?" Lady Moncrieff asked.

"Yes, Nigel's carrier," Sir Richard answered, "and Nigel and his fellow airmen may well be called heroes after this battle."

"What do you mean, Father?" Susan asked.

"When the *Bismarck* was finally located, the Fleet Air Arm sent fifteen Fairey Swordfish into the air, all armed with torpedoes. Those boys had to dive from a mile in the sky and level out twenty feet above the waves to fly directly toward the hull of that monster before releasing their ordinance. Because the Swordfish could fly beneath the huge ship's guns, all the *Bismarck* could do was send rounds into the waves in a vain attempt to splash the planes out of the sky," he said.

"But what did you mean when you mentioned the airmen might be called heroes, Richard?" Lady Moncrieff asked.

"Of the fifteen Swordfish, only two were able to launch torpedoes that hit and damaged the *Bismarck*. The first fired a torpedo that hit the *Bismarck* amidships but with little consequence. However, the torpedo fired by the last Swordfish hit the *Bismarck*'s rudder, leaving the ship unable to steer. As a result, the *Bismarck* could do little more than sail in long, lazy circles. Disabled as she was, our flotilla fired round after round from shorter and shorter distances until *Bismarck*'s captain gave his remaining crew the order to scuttle the ship. She went to the bottom, taking more than 2,000 men with her. Our ships rescued a few more than a hundred others," he said.

"Richard, it's possible, then, that the Swordfish pilot who disabled the *Bismarck* was our Nigel, correct?" Lady Moncrieff asked.

"Yes, Angela," he answered, "it is possible, but we shan't know that for some time. For now, I recommend celebrating only the best news, the answer to our prayers."

"And that best news is?" Susan asked.

"That no pilots were lost or wounded and that Nigel is well and whole. I will thank God for those gifts again and again."

"As will we all," Michael added, "as will we all."

An instant later, as he lifted his teacup, Sir Richard's eyes rose in a smile, piquing his wife's attention.

"What is it, Richard? I know that look. What do you find amusing?" she asked.

Regaining his serious tone, Sir Richard said, "I was just thinking about those fifteen small bi-planes buzzing around that huge battleship."

"I see," she replied with a nod. "They must have seemed a harmless hive of hornets to a ship that size."

"Yes, Angela," he answered, "until one of them stung it in the aft," he said, winking at Michael.

"Richard!" Lady Moncrieff said, feigning shock before succumbing to her smile.

As Sir Richard's laugh subsided, Michael couldn't resist adding, "A very cheeky fellow, that pilot."

"Oh, Michael!" Susan said as she rolled her eyes and giggled. "Let's serve these men some pastry, Mother, to fill their mouths so this will stop."

However, Sir Richard couldn't resist one more salvo as his wife reached toward the plates.

"Actually," he said, "my latest reports from our most clandestine operatives in Berlin report that the Füehrer was so fu-r-r-ious last evening that he banned a former favorite entrée from future dinner menus."

"Really?" Lady Moncrieff said, and waiting for what would come next, she asked, "And what would that be, Richard?"

"Swordfish, of course," he said with a grin.

Chapter 30

"You're the first," Mrs. Goodwin said incredulously, her voice shaking. "I'm sorry; we simply didn't expect you. We never expected to see Jacob and Naomi's parents. We never expected anyone to come for them."

"It's never happened before?" Daniel Abrams asked. "Parents have never come to find their children?

"No," Mrs. Goodwin said, shaking her head. "No parent, aunt, uncle, or family member has ever come for one of the children here. I was so happy your Jacob and Naomi could be evacuated to safety, but now I am so, so very sorry that you are here and they have gone."

"And where have they gone?" Deborah Abrams asked. "Where have you sent them?"

"Their bus left Lowestoft two days ago. They were bound for Liverpool, where a ship traveling in convoy awaited them. They departed for Halifax yesterday," Mrs. Goodwin said.

"Halifax?" Daniel asked, shaking his head. "I don't understand. No one needs to board a ship to reach Halifax in Yorkshire."

"I'm sorry," Mrs. Goodwin said, "I meant Halifax, Nova Scotia, in Canada."

Shaking her head as if she didn't understand, Deborah looked at Daniel before turning back to Mrs. Goodwin. "They are sailing across the ocean to Canada," she cried, "in waters where ships are sunk by German torpedoes every day?"

"Yes," Mrs. Goodwin said. "I'm so sorry. The bombing here in Britain has been unceasing. City after city faces bombing attacks every day. We believed your children would be safer away from here, especially away from the coast where we fear the Germans may invade at any moment."

While Deborah translated for Jan, who could only see how upset she and Daniel were, her husband paced silently, trying to discover a way to retrieve their son and daughter. Finally, he interrupted Deborah and said, "We must travel back to Harwich today and find our way to London. We'll sell everything we have there to buy passage to Canada. We can't lose our children like this. I won't let it happen." Desperate, he turned to Mrs. Goodwin and asked, "Can you hold the bus for us, please? We need to purchase tickets and travel back to Harwich immediately."

"I believe I can," Mrs. Goodwin said. "The driver has a one-hour layover here before returning." Looking over her shoulder at the office clock, she said, "That's thirty minutes from now. He should be in the pub around the corner having his midday meal."

"Then please certify our children's documents and ours during that time, and provide us with their photos and anything else we might need so that we are not prevented from retrieving them once we find them. Can you do that?" he asked. "Will you do that?" he pleaded.

"I'll do everything I can," she said. Squaring her shoulders, she turned to a young woman sitting at a desk behind her and called, "Blanche? I need full files of all records for Jacob and Naomi Abrams as soon as you can prepare them. I'm going to keep the bus from leaving without these folks. Everything else can wait. Is that clear?"

"Yes, Mrs. Goodwin," she said, but I have lunch in fifteen minutes."

"Not today, you don't, Blanche," she said. "I'll see you get your lunch break as soon as you finish. I hope that is clear?" she asked, looking over her eyeglasses.

"Yes, Mrs. Goodwin," Blanche replied as she stood and walked to her filing cabinet.

Turning to the Abrams and Jan, Mrs. Goodwin said, "Blanche is a good sort, and she'll have things together in a few minutes. Once you have everything you need, you will find me outside, standing at the bus. It will not leave without you."

Mrs. Goodwin was true to her word. Fifteen minutes later, Blanche, carrying a thick brown envelope, led Daniel, Deborah, and Jan to the waiting bus. Mrs. Goodwin stood beside the uniformed driver, who didn't appear concerned about keeping a schedule. Instead, he doffed his cap and smiled at the approaching party.

Still in a hurry, Daniel reached into his pocket and apologized.

"I'm sorry for any delay," he said, "we need to pay our fare to Harwich."

"No, Mr. Abrams," Mrs. Goodwin said, "you don't. Your fare is paid, and not just to Harwich, but all the way to London."

“But, how can that be?” Daniel asked as he stopped fumbling for his wallet.

“Because we are a God-fearing people, Mr. Abrams,” Mrs. Goodwin said as she moved closer, holding a small stack of tickets. “We know you are, too. We are a praying people also, and we know that we all pray to the same God. So every one of us,” she said, as she pointed to the office steps behind her where every staff member had gathered, “has donated all we can to help you find your way to Jacob and Naomi.” She handed Deborah a small, heavy leather purse, so full that it barely clipped together at the top.

Tears welled up in Deborah’s eyes as she received the purse from Mrs. Goodwin and managed to whisper, “Thank you.”

The office staff drew in closer as Mrs. Goodwin pointed to the football field where nearly two hundred refugee children had stopped their matches to gather at the edge of the field. There they stood waiting, looking up at the small group of people standing at the bus.

“You’ve given all of these children hope today. What has never happened here before is happening today, and every one of those children sorely needs a reason to hope. We make only one request of you,” she said as she handed Daniel the brown envelope that held his children’s records. “Inside, there is a postpaid envelope addressed to this office. When you are reunited with Jacob and Naomi, please send us a photo of your family so we can share it with all our children.”

On that day, there were no Christians, and there were no Jews in Lowestoft. There were only grateful people who would never doubt that they all prayed to the same God.

Chapter 31

After learning from Sqn Ldr Grayson Royce about the remarkable success of an American named Duncan, a navigator on a Vickers Wellington twin-engine, long-range medium bomber, Sir Richard made some further inquiries. It turned out that the intuition he and Michael shared was correct. A US citizen, Ernest Duncan, currently served at Newmarket Heath in Suffolk. Sir Richard's intelligence operatives had confirmed the impressive success Airman Duncan enjoyed as a navigator, especially when bombing targets in Germany.

When he arrived at Newmarket Heath, Duncan's former flight experience was years old and limited to a period during his university studies in cartography. Several of his courses required flight time over principal cities and manufacturing centers in Germany. His early experience as a navigator on a Vickers Wellington bomber following RAF protocol had been disappointing. Because many RAF maps were outdated, they often failed to indicate important prime and secondary targets such as major bridges, railways, railway depots, and manufacturing centers.

RAF bombers proved far less successful in hitting their targets than expected. Furthermore, after losing too many aircraft in daylight bombing raids, the RAF began limiting their raids to nighttime hours, even though visibility was severely restricted. However, Duncan believed he had discovered a reason for the disappointing results the RAF had experienced in both daytime and nighttime raids.

Following a navigators' review briefing, which included recent bombing results and RAF reconnaissance photos, Duncan sought an opportunity to offer his thoughts. He waited until the Senior Air Staff Officer was available when the other navigators had been dismissed from the briefing.

Upon approaching the officer, Duncan saluted and said, "Permission to speak freely, sir?"

Officer Kirkpatrick returned his salute and said, "Granted, if it's short. What's on your mind, Duncan?"

"Sir," Duncan began, "I believe I can offer a potential solution to the accuracy problem our bombers have been experiencing. Since my solution falls outside our customary protocol, I request permission to exercise that solution on our next mission."

Duncan had Kirkpatrick's attention immediately.

"If you can be succinct," Kirkpatrick said as he finished filling his briefcase with documents from the briefing, "I'll be happy to listen."

"Thank you, sir," Duncan said as he produced several maps and other documents from the case hanging on his shoulder.

"You came prepared, Duncan," Kirkpatrick said, surprised as he looked at the maps and charts on the table before him, "But, again, give me the short version."

"Sir," Duncan began, "I spent considerable time in Germany as a cartography student some years ago. We often did our mapping from the air. I am familiar with several potential target cities within our range from Newmarket."

"Interesting and potentially helpful, Duncan," Kirkpatrick said, "but what does that have to do with our accuracy?"

"Nothing, sir, except for the experience I gained in dropping markers from the air for mapping purposes. In many ways, that experience is relevant for our bombers," Duncan said.

"Go on," Kirkpatrick said.

"Yes, sir," Duncan replied. "It all concerns some elementary physics we learned at university. All the markers we attempted to drop from our aircraft traveled at the same speed we were flying. We learned that nothing drops straight down from an airplane. It follows the same trajectory, even when gravity draws it closer to the Earth. In time, we learned how far ahead of our targets we had to drop our markers so they would land where we needed them."

"Continue, Duncan," Kirkpatrick said as he turned to take a closer look at the maps and charts that Duncan had provided.

"I believe that the Vickers Wellington's customary altitude and airspeed when delivering its payload requires that we release our bombs approximately 4.9 to 5.1 miles before we have eyes on our target. If we wait for a visual, it will be too late to release our ordnance. Our bombs will land well beyond the target," he said.

"Interesting," Kirkpatrick said as he momentarily held one finger in the air and retrieved some documents from his briefcase. After finding the papers he sought, he looked back at some of the equations on Duncan's papers and said, "Your data agrees with the results our reconnaissance team has recently documented. However, there's a fundamental problem yet to be solved. You see, Duncan, we don't have the level of mapping and up-to-date surveillance that would allow us to send our payloads to targets we can't see until we fly over them."

"I understand, Sir," Duncan said. "It sounds risky because it's never been tried. However, if you allow just one experiment at my hands, I believe you will be satisfied."

"What kind of experiment?" Kirkpatrick asked.

"The mission you announced a half hour ago is aimed here," Duncan said, indicating a city on a topographic map he had provided. Pointing to a ridge a short distance outside the city, he said, "I climbed that ridge every day for two weeks while I was a student here. I hiked from the city limits and back every day. I know its distance from the city and the ball-bearing factory on its outskirts," he said, pointing at the map. "If we release our bombs as we fly directly over this ridge," he said, pointing again, "they will fly with us for the next 4.9 miles to the factory that is our principal target. Shortly after we drop our bombs, we will see the results as we fly over the factory precisely as our bombs land."

"And if we wait until we see the city?" Kirkpatrick asked.

"Then the factory will remain untouched, and the population center beyond it will be destroyed," Duncan said.

"So, Duncan," Kirkpatrick asked, "you're saying the success of this mission depends on you?"

"Only as far as identifying the position of the ridge, sir," Duncan said. "We need to fly when there is just enough light to verify our position—dawn or dusk. Unless other men are as familiar with the landscape as I am, I am your man, willing and able. But you might also be interested in knowing that there is an appropriate secondary target, a railway bridge to the north. It is essential to the city, servicing travelers, commerce, and industry. I believe I could also help to target that bridge," he said.

As Duncan handed him another page and indicated the bridge, Kirkpatrick said, "And you believe you can guide our bombers to these targets as early as tomorrow?"

"Yes, sir, I do," Duncan said. With your permission, sir, let that be a test because," he said as he handed the Senior Officer another page, "here is a list of cities where my past training carried me. I would also be pleased to help when we have targets in those cities."

"One target at a time, Duncan," Kirkpatrick said. Pensively, he examined Duncan's list and waited another moment before adding, "Prepare to execute your plan tomorrow, Duncan. Depending on the results, we may consider other targets. In the meantime, get some rest, and we will see what tomorrow brings."

Not surprisingly, Duncan's first mission verified his predictions. The industrial complex at the outer boundaries of the city lay in ruins, while the populated regions were essentially unharmed. A day later, the railway bridge was a smoking ruin where no trains would travel for a long time to come. Within weeks, Duncan had become an RAF secret weapon, eliminating the need for the carpet bombings of cities that destroyed not only principal targets but population centers alike. How many lives Duncan's skills saved would probably never be known.

Chapter 32

Nurse-in-Training Joseph Boucher was shadowing Nurse Witter, following her on rounds on the third floor at Royal Victoria Hospital in Montreal. His practicum would be finished by fall when he would become one of the youngest male nurses the hospital had ever known. A year and a half of study and work under Nurse Emily MacMillan at Charlottetown Hospital had accelerated his schedule by almost a full year. When morning rounds were over in a few minutes, he had an afternoon planned in the library.

"I don't know why you need me any longer, Joseph. You know what to do and how to do it," Nurse Witter said.

"Maybe on this floor," he answered, "but I'd be lost caring for babies or little kids."

"Understood," she answered, "but your schedule on those wards doesn't begin until the end of the month. Don't let it worry you yet. You'll have weeks and weeks to get familiar with the little ones. For now," she continued, "just remember how I take my tea, which," she said, looking at her wristwatch, "I'll be expecting in about five minutes."

"I'm on my way," Joseph smiled, "Cream, one sugar. I'll have it prepared and at your station on the spot."

Joseph had the tea ready at Nurse Witter's desk before she arrived. As he set it down on the counter, he heard a voice behind him that he recognized immediately.

"Nurse-in-Training, Joseph Boucher, you have visitors."

It was Nurse Emily MacMillan's voice, which took Joseph entirely by surprise. When he turned around, he was overwhelmed to find Nurse Emily, Dr. MacMillan, and Ingrid Boucher standing on the other side of the nurses' station.

"Surprise!" Dr. MacMillan said. "We have an afternoon of routine appointments downstairs for this expectant lady, and Nurse Witter informed us that your rounds are finished for today. Is that correct?"

Smiling broadly, Joseph raced around the counter to Nurse Emily, who met him with open arms. His smile grew as he shook Dr. MacMillan's hand. To his surprise, Ingrid rushed to him with a hug of her own, which he returned in kind. He noticed she was wearing perfume, a scent that was sweet and warm. Her strawberry blonde hair was in shoulder-length curls instead of the braids she usually wore at home. There was more of a woman in his arms than the girl he left at Highfield six months ago. Their embrace was more familiar, too, and lasted longer than it might have then. When they parted, he was still looking into her brown eyes. She was blushing, but their smiles continued.

"While we're with the doctors," Nurse Emily began, "we were hoping you could show Ingrid some of the city. It's such a lovely day, absolutely made for a nice walk. We've just come from lunch, but we won't be finished here for almost three hours. Would that fit your schedule, Joseph?"

Joseph looked at Ingrid, who looked right back. "Of course," he said, never letting his eyes drop. There's a lot to see, but I'll be sure to have her back at about 3:30?" he asked.

"That would be just right," Dr. MacMillan said. "We'll meet you right here at 3:30."

Joseph and Ingrid waited as Nurse Emily and Dr. MacMillan returned to the elevator.

Ingrid was the first to speak.

"You look so official in your uniform and wearing your name tag, but I'm glad you don't have to wear a nurse's hat," she laughed.

"No," he grinned, "just this operating theatre cap, but give me a moment, and I'll get rid of it, OK?"

"OK," she said. "Do you have to go far? I'm feeling a bit small in the city and even in this hospital. It's so big, so come right back, please."

"I will," Joseph said. "I'll be right around the corner, one door past the Nurses' Station, so if you sit here by the window, I promise you won't get lost. Give me two minutes."

True to his word, he was back and wearing street clothes in no time at all.

"There," he said, "that wasn't so bad, was it?"

"No, it wasn't," she said as she rose and reached to hold his hand.

Her hand was soft and feminine, but her grip was intentionally warm, and he couldn't help but return it. One smile later, they were on the elevator, through the lobby, and out onto Pine Avenue, hand in hand, in front of the hospital. Over the next several hours, Joseph showed Ingrid some of the best parts of the city, including McGill University, the superb shopping district on St. Catherine Street, and several churches that made St. Peter's look very small.

They started back toward the hospital at three o'clock, stopping for an ice cream sundae at a little shop where they could sit beneath an umbrella in the shade. Ingrid filled Joseph in on everything he had missed at Highfield.

"Things have slowed down a little bit since you and Luc have been gone. It's just Patrice and Lois and me at home. I'm sure Lois has a crush on Luc. She writes him a letter, and sometimes two or three every week," she said.

"The baby boys must be growing up, aren't they?" Joseph asked.

"Yes, they are cute, but they keep both the Moreland's busy. Either Case or Reed always needs a bottle, burping, or a diaper change. It would wear anyone out, but Miss Susan is as beautiful as ever," she said.

"Like you?" Joseph asked before he realized what he had said.

"Me?" Ingrid asked. "Oh, don't be a tease. I know what beautiful looks like, and I've also got a mirror, so I won't be fooled about that."

"Well, they say that beauty . . . " he began.

"Is in the eye of the beholder? I know," she said. "That's just something people say to keep us plain girls hoping."

"What do you mean, 'plain,'" Joseph said. "No one could call you plain and mean it, Ingrid. I'm not a world traveler, but I've seen a lot of young women in Montreal over the last several months, and I know what I like when I see it."

Ingrid couldn't contain her smile. Blushing, she said, "So, are you saying you think I'm . . . "

"Pretty?" he interrupted. "Yes, that's what I'm saying. I've always thought so, but I feared you'd laugh at me if I told you."

"Why would I laugh?" she asked.

"Because fellows aren't supposed to say what they feel. It makes them look weak. I've always looked weak next to Luc, anyway, so I decided to keep quiet," he said.

"I don't think that's weak," she said. "I think a man who knows what he feels and isn't afraid to say it is strong. He doesn't have to apologize for anything."

"So, you wouldn't think less of me if I told you everything I feel?" he asked.

"No, Joseph, I wouldn't. I'd like to hear everything, but . . . "

"But, what?" he asked.

"But especially if there was something about me," she said, looking down.

"You want to know how I feel about you? You don't already know?" he asked.

"Not really," she said, looking into her ice cream dish.

Joseph stopped and reached toward his back pocket to find his wallet. When he retrieved it, he took out a folded sheet of paper that looked like it had been wedged there for some time. He carefully unfolded it but didn't show Ingrid its contents. It took him a moment to read it before he folded it again.

"You know Mr. Moreland writes poetry, don't you?" he asked.

"Yes," Ingrid said. "He writes sonnets. Miss Susan has several framed in her dressing room," Ingrid said.

"Well," Joseph began, "he taught Luc and me about sonnets and told us what they meant to him. So, I wrote one and kept it with me in case I needed to share it one day."

"But his are all love sonnets written about Miss Susan," Ingrid said.

"Yes," he said, "and mine is a love sonnet, too. Only mine is about you," he said quietly, looking down.

"Joseph Boucher," Ingrid began firmly, "don't you dare be ashamed to say how you feel. I want to know. No, it's stronger than that," she said, correcting herself. "Joseph, I *need* to know."

Slowly, he began to read aloud.

Again, I wake, too early, for the night
Holds dawn at arm's length, and, once more I sigh,
For though my limbs seek sleep, my eyes crave light
The moon holds pris'ner till the morn be nigh.
And though the night bore sleep, dreams it withheld,
And thus for hours I've not seen your face;
And this cruel fast I've borne with spirits felled

For want of art none other can replace.
And hours yet 'twill be before it's day,
Before one glimpse of you I'll realize.
Till then all thought of sleep I'll cast away,
While with my mem'ries I will feed my eyes.
Poor food, this fare on which I'm forced to feed;
Grant audience, I pray; supply my need.

His British accent made his words all the more sincere. "How long," she wondered, "have I not seen what now seems so obvious?"

Ingrid reached out her hand and took his as he looked up.

"Those are not the words of a weak man," she said. "Those are powerful words, Joseph, strong enough to win a young woman's heart."

"But, a man with this impossible dark hair and this nose?" he asked.

"Your hair isn't impossible, Joseph," she said. "It just has natural waves. And you have a Roman nose, the kind Miss Susan showed us on all the statues of Caesar in her art books. It's noble."

He nodded as the hint of a smile grew across his face. Then, as he folded the paper and reached again for his wallet, Ingrid said, "Not so fast, Joseph Boucher. You said it was for me, didn't you?"

"Yes," he said, just louder than a whisper.

"Then, I will have it, sir," she said as she reached out her hand.

Finally, his smile grew to fill his face. He put the copy in her hand, and they laughed together.

Then, as their laughter dissipated, something inside Ingrid brought a second laugh. She said, "Do you remember the day you left for Montreal when we were surrounding the car and saying our goodbyes?"

"Yes, I do," Joseph smiled. "There were hugs and kisses all around, and when you and I hugged, I tried to kiss your cheek, but I was so awkward that we both turned our faces at the wrong moment and almost shared a proper kiss. At the last instant, we managed to find each other's cheek. I was so embarrassed."

"Yes," Ingrid said, "but when we part today, let's be sure we don't miss our targets. Let's make our kiss today a *proper* one."

And so, a half hour later, after practicing in the shade of a maple tree beside the ice cream shop, Joseph said his goodbyes to Dr. MacMillan and Nurse Emily in front of Royal Victoria Hospital. Then, he turned to Ingrid as they joined hands and shared an entirely proper kiss.

Chapter 33

Luc Boucher had never heard of most of the places where Canadian units shipped when he left Canada. He'd seen maps of England and France and Spain, of course, and others that included countries like Norway, Finland, and Sweden. However, in the last two weeks, he had landed in Greece and learned of battles in Yugoslavia, Bulgaria, and Croatia, places he couldn't remember on the maps at home. Then, without seeing combat in Greece, he was suddenly shipped out to an island called Crete, where troops from Australia, New Zealand, and Scotland had already landed. At that time, no one in Luc's unit knew what awaited them. One thing was sure, though. The Expeditionary Force was in a hurry to get all the Commonwealth forces out of Greece and over the sea to Crete.

Aboard the light cruiser, HMS *Coventry*, that night, Luc found a corner below decks where he could clean his Lee-Enfield No. 4 rifle and his No. 32 scope. He hadn't yet been called to the front to fire his rifle. Nonetheless, it seemed like a friend, a reliable model used successfully by many snipers before him. At that time, he didn't know how it would feel to aim his rifle at another man during battle. He only knew he was tired of shipping from port to port and doing nothing but waiting in between.

The seas were calm for the 200-mile overnight cruise, but tensions remained high on board. Everyone knew that U-boats could be awaiting them at sea, and dawn could bring fire from the Luftwaffe. Every soldier onboard felt helpless against such attacks, and the fear and frustration were palpable. Luc tried to sleep, but he could only doze for minutes at a time. Just before dawn, however, he fell hard asleep.

That's when he woke to hear aircraft overhead, felt the shudder of bombs exploding on the beach, and heard officers shouting as soldiers followed each other out to the decks and down to the landing craft. From the deck, Luc could see parachutes in the sky, all of them German. The battle was behind them from the sea, waiting for them on the ground and falling on them from the sky.

Once organized, Luc's unit left the waterfront behind, finding its way inland and stopping to await orders. They didn't have to wait long but were immediately called to higher ground, where Luc was deployed just behind the advance unit.

Luc could hear the groundfire ahead. He knew that neither German artillery nor tanks had been deployed because he heard only small arms fire. From what he could tell, his unit had stopped outside the fighting, not far from a small village. That was when he got the call.

"Yes, Lieutenant," Sgt McAllister said into his radio microphone. "I see it on the map. Galatas, a half mile south of Brest. The church? Yes, sir, on our way."

"Boucher," Sgt McAllister called at half voice. "Follow me."

The two men left at a dead run for about a quarter mile over rocky terrain before some stray enemy fire forced them to the ground.

Able to move forward only at a crouch, Luc followed his sergeant, who was moving slowly a few yards ahead. In another fifty yards, though, both were forced to their stomachs as bullets flew just feet over them. They found cover behind an ancient stone wall a short distance away, its mortar joints loosened by mortar explosions and ground fire. When Sgt McAllister stopped, an officer, Lt Lang, met them.

"There's a church ahead with twin towers," Lt Lang said. "There's a sniper in at least one, but possibly another in the second tower. We haven't yet verified the second sniper, but the amount of fire they're sending us tells me there are at least two. We have four dead and two wounded already. The rest of our men are pinned down by enemy fire advancing on our left and right flanks, so we've got to move straight ahead through that churchyard before we're overwhelmed. Boucher," Lt Lang said, looking into Luc's eyes, "I need you to take those snipers out."

Luc nodded and said, "Yes, sir."

"We can give you plenty of cover to reach a position where you can target both towers. We'll decoy them by raising helmets on my signal to keep them aiming away from your position. That's your chance to see exactly where they are and take your shot. Will that work for you?" the lieutenant asked.

"Sir, yes, sir," Luc answered.

The lieutenant heard something in Luc's response or saw something in Luc's eyes that made him pause.

"Pvt Boucher," he said, "you've trained for months to meet this moment. Your qualifications are without question. Make this only one more training exercise with a single objective—you are here to save lives. Can you do that?" he asked.

"Yes, sir," Luc answered. "Yes, sir, I can."

"All right then, on your belly and follow me," Lt Lang said.

About fifty yards ahead, the two joined a half dozen other riflemen positioned behind the low stucco-covered stone walls surrounding the church on top of the hill. The other riflemen kept up their cover fire toward the towers while Luc found a loose stone in the wall. In another minute, he had the stone on the ground before he removed two others, which gave him a clear view of the south tower. He estimated the distance at about one hundred fifty yards. He cleaned the lens on his scope and looked as long as he dared at the round-topped stucco openings at the tops of the towers.

Lt Lang motioned for the firing line to cease fire and gave Luc a thumbs-up signal. The sun was still low, and the interior of the open towers was in shadow, making it hard to see anything inside. Luc trained his eyes through his scope, first on the north and then the south tower. He sensed movement among the men in his firing line to his right and saw one man raising a helmet on his rifle. Luke returned to his scope as the infantryman's helmet drew fire from the towers.

Luc saw a muzzle flash at the lower corner of the far right opening at the top of the north tower. Silently re-positioning his weapon and himself, he focused all his attention on the source of that muzzle flash.

The infantry line set up its decoy to Luc's left this time. Luc thought, "He'll have to sweep to his right to get a shot on this side. That will open him up for me. Get ready, Boucher."

Luc didn't have to wait long. With the sun behind him, Luc's scope revealed a glint of light coming from the movement of the sniper's scope in the tower. Aiming just behind that flash, Luc waited to hear the report of the sniper's rifle.

As the sound reached Luc's ears, he squeezed his trigger.

After his shot, all Luc saw was a rifle barrel leaning out through the tower window and pointing upward. It wasn't moving. The man holding that rifle a moment ago was now on the floor on top of his rifle butt. One threat had been removed.

With his position compromised, Luc quickly backed away from the wall and crawled to the opposite end of the firing line. Meanwhile, the other riflemen kept bullets flying toward the tower to cover him until he found a second position with an unobstructed view through a chink in the stucco wall.

The sun was higher now, high enough to push his adversary to the west window of the south tower, the place with the best shadow cover. Concentrating on that window, Luc made his nest on the ground and waited. He didn't have to wait long.

The firing line quieted on Lt Lang's signal. He gave Luc a second thumbs-up. Luc's eye was in his scope, and he was trained on his target. This time, however, the sniper didn't fall for the decoys as readily as the first had. The morning turned into a waiting game.

Luc was grateful for his sleep below deck on the HMS *Coventry* the night before. He needed to keep his eyes trained on the darkest shadow in the tower window until he saw movement again. When he did, he drew his scope in tight and blinked once to clear his vision. When he focused on his target again, he found himself looking directly into another scope, this one more than one hundred fifty yards away. He didn't have time to think. He squeezed the trigger, and, in the same instant, the stucco wall before him exploded.

More than an hour passed before Luc awoke on a stretcher at a hastily assembled field hospital on the same waterfront where his unit had landed only hours earlier. He couldn't see anything past the bandages that wrapped his face. His right shoulder screamed with pain. He wanted to speak but couldn't find his voice. Then he heard someone calling from a distance, "Boucher? Pvt Boucher? Can you hear me, Private?"

Luc couldn't see where the voice came from but answered, "I hear you. Where am I? What happened? I can't see anything."

"Not to worry, Private," the voice said. "I'm Corpsman Bill Enright, a medic at the field hospital. Just call me 'Bill'. Let me remove some of this bandage so you can see."

Somewhere a distance away, Luc could hear some guttural cries of pain in what sounded like German. As the corpsman removed the last layer of bandage, Luke was able to see again, but everything remained blurry.

"Here's what happened," Bill began. "A German sniper's round hit the wall you were using for cover. It also hit you. We've done some work to rid your face of the stone fragments from that wall you were peeking through.

Your eyes got filled with some of that debris, too, but the doctor believes your wounds will heal, and your eyesight will clear up in time."

Luc could do nothing but listen as the corpsman continued.

"After it blew a little more of that wall away, the bullet also shattered the stock of your Enfield before finding its way into your shoulder. Thankfully, the doctor got the remains of the bullet out, and your wound should heal in time. We've given you some pretty strong pain medicine, so you'll be groggy for a while. That's the end of the good news. The bad news is that we'll have to send you home, soldier. Your right shoulder won't bear a weapon in battle any longer, and we're not sure your eyes will be ready to aim a rifle accurately for some time. Meanwhile, just rest and call for me if you need anything," Bill said.

"Wait," Luc asked, a hint of desperation in his voice. "I need to know. I fired my rifle twice. Can you tell me what happened on the other end?"

"Can I tell you what happened?" Bill asked as a smile grew on his face. "You bet I can. Everyone's been talking about it. Those two Nazi snipers killed six men before they were done, and they wounded four more. But, you, Pvt Boucher, you took them down with only two shots, saving who knows how many lives. They're calling you a hero, Private. I'd wager there will be a medal to reward your bravery."

"But, the two I shot," Luc asked, "what happened to them?"

"Oh," Bill said. "The first was a clean kill. An older fellow about my age, they told me. He didn't suffer - breathing one moment, gone the next."

Luc said nothing. A moment later, he asked quietly, "And the second?"

"That one was different," Bill said. "He's the one you hear screaming from two tents down. From what we can tell, your second shot went straight up his scope, exploding it in his face. It's a miracle he's alive. From what I saw, the bullet never hit him, but they're still picking pieces of the scope and the lenses out of his face and skull. The doctors are doing what they can for him—better than the Nazis would do for one of us, I'd wager. Anyway, I'm afraid he may never see again, and it looks like his face will be permanently disfigured, but he's alive. The two of you are miracles, you know. Snipers don't generally shoot each other and live. This is one for the books," Bill said as he left to treat another wounded soldier.

Five weeks later, Luc was fortunate to have a bed at Queen Alexandra Military Hospital in London. His physical wounds had healed, and his eyesight was only minimally impaired. The wound to his shoulder wouldn't prevent him from shouldering a rifle or a shotgun to hunt at home, and the scars on his face were growing less noticeable every day. When he asked his nurses, they assured him he'd not need to worry about scaring little children away when he returned home.

Sadly, though, Luc's other wounds still lay open. They are the memories that began with an overnight sea voyage to an island called Crete, of waking up in a field hospital on that island, and of hearing about a German soldier, shot dead in a church tower, and another young soldier who will live out the rest of his days blind and disfigured.

Those wounds continue to wake Luc on most nights. Those wounds still bring tears. He dares to hope that someday those wounds, too, will heal.

Chapter 34

When Michael brought the Highfield mail from Charlottetown on that mid-summer day in 1941, he discovered an unusual letter addressed to Susan. It had been posted from a solicitor's office in London. The solicitor, Mr. William Barrows, had written to inquire about Joseph.

"Michael," Susan said as she read the letter, "a solicitor from London has written to me as Joseph's custodian, inquiring about Joseph Fenton's whereabouts. Apparently, Joseph had a grandfather and an uncle who were recently killed in the Blitz in London. It appears that Joseph is the sole remaining heir to their estates."

"I don't believe I've ever heard his surname before," Michael said. "Fenton," he repeated. "I suppose they must have inquired after you at the orphanage," Michael said. "Since the orphanage ceded Joseph to your care as guardian, the solicitor will likely look to you to represent him until he comes of age at twenty-one. What else do they say?"

"They suggest I engage a solicitor here to represent Joseph's interests. It appears that the estate includes a home near London, its contents, an automobile, some securities now in the care of the Crown, the cash balances in several bank accounts, and the unknown contents of two safe deposit boxes in London," she said.

"This sounds like a job for Atty Leighton," Michael said, "but what a surprise for Joseph. Has he ever spoken of an uncle or a grandfather?"

"Never," Susan said. "As I remember, the orphanage records indicated simply that his father died a month before Joseph was born. He was a member of the fire brigade in Ipswich and was killed in the collapse of a burning building. His mother died from consumption about a year after Joseph's birth. That's when the orphanage took Joseph in."

"Let's forward this information to Atty Leighton right away. I could telephone his office to let him know it's coming if you like," Michael said.

"That would be lovely, Michael. Thank you," she said.

A month later, a large, thick envelope from Atty Leighton appeared in Highfield's post office box. Michael knew that Susan would want to see it as soon as he returned home. When he arrived, she was sitting in the shade of a red maple on the west side of the house while the boys napped in their playpen beside her.

"Shh!" she whispered as he approached with the envelope in his hand. "They just fell asleep."

Michael nodded his agreement and handed her the envelope. "I knew you'd be interested in this," he whispered.

It was a half hour before they finished perusing the documents in the envelope.

"Michael," Susan said, "If I am reading this correctly, the estate includes not only the home in Ardingly but also a small parcel of land on the Isle of Wight, an automobile, a sum of cash and securities, with an estimated total value of over 15,000 pounds."

"Yes," Michael said as he made a quick mental computation. "In Canadian currency, that's more than $60,000, which doesn't include the unknown contents of the safe deposit boxes."

"That's a small fortune here, isn't it?" she asked.

"If you consider that a new home for a small family here on Prince Edward Island costs less than $4,000, yes," he answered. "Remember, however, that you are the estate's custodian until Joseph is of age."

"I don't know where to begin," Susan said.

"There's a lot to consider," Michael began. "There's the care of the house near London during wartime, where anything can happen during the Blitz. One might consider selling it now, although the market must be severely depressed. If it is hit during the Blitz, it may become worthless. Cash is one thing, Susan, but property, especially an ocean away during wartime, can be challenging to maintain. Then again, if the house survives the war and Joseph reaches twenty-one, he might want to move to London to live there. It would also be helpful to know something about the value of the land on the Isle of Wight. The island could become a Luftwaffe target, too. A $60,000 inheritance could dissipate very quickly during wartime. There's a lot to consider," Michael repeated.

"I hadn't thought of all that," Susan said quietly. "There will be solicitor's fees, too, of course. I'll need your help, Michael. You'll help me, won't you?"

"Of course, I will," he said, "but let's spend a little more time together before we engage Atty Leighton. Then, after we have his advice, we can tell Joseph everything. Without a plan, I'm afraid he'd be overwhelmed with the news, even though it would seem wonderful at first glance. Agreed?" Michael asked.

"Agreed," Susan answered.

"Until then," Michael said, "let's say nothing to anyone. That's the best and only way to care for his interests. He should be the first to know, but not until we're better organized. Then he can share the news with anyone he pleases."

"I agree wholeheartedly," Susan said with a nod, "but there's one thing more."

"What would that be?" Michael asked.

"The solicitor is asking for Joseph to produce a document, a copy that matches one that his mother sent to the solicitor's office shortly after Joseph was born. It's proof of his identity," she said.

"What kind of document?" he asked.

"A baptismal certificate. Joseph's baptismal certificate," she said. "It seems his mother hid it in a family prayer book that she left for him at the orphanage before she fell too ill to care for him. From what I can gather, Joseph's grandfather was displeased with his son's marriage to Joseph's mother. As a result, he broke off contact with his son. Joseph's mother wrote to her father-in-law to tell him of his son's death in the fire, but she never received a reply. Joseph was born just four weeks later. At his mother's death a little more than a year after that, the orphanage contacted his grandfather concerning Joseph's care, but his grandfather, not knowing he had a grandson, believed they had contacted him in error."

"So, Joseph's grandfather and uncle never knew he existed?" he asked.

"Correct. It seems the vicar at her parish church signed and supplied Joseph's mother with two copies of Joseph's baptismal certificate. She sent one to the solicitor, but another is supposed to exist hidden in a prayerbook she left for Joseph. That is the evidence the solicitor requires for Joseph to retrieve his inheritance."

"That must be the prayerbook Joseph carries to St. Peter's for every service. He's never without it," Michael said.

"I wonder if he knows that his baptismal certificate is hidden there," she said.

"He's not scheduled to be back from Montreal for another three weeks," Michael said. "We'll have to wait to ask him then."

"But if he can't produce that certificate, he has no inheritance. He'll be shattered to know he had an inheritance coming, only to lose it a moment later. How do we ask him to search his prayerbook and not tell him why?" she asked.

"I think we can tell him there's a possibility of an inheritance. We don't have to tell him how much it's worth, at least not at first. Let's pray that the certificate is in the book as his mother left it," Michael said.

Susan nodded her assent, and watching him reach into his attaché a second time, she asked, "What do you have in that other envelope?"

The second envelope had been posted from Atty Leighton's office, too. Michael quickly read through the cover page and extracted the following two pages to share with her.

"Last year," he began, "the United States Quartermasters Corps began soliciting bids from over 130 manufacturers for what they call 'General Purpose' vehicles or GPs, nicknamed 'Jeeps.' At the same time, they requested bids for many much larger trucks suitable for battlefield conditions," he said. "I believe the US is preparing to join the Allies in the war."

"That's good news," Susan said, "but what is it you haven't told me yet?"

Michael continued, "Those larger tactical vehicles are designed to face tremendous challenges in the terrain they encounter on a battlefield. Irregular terrain like foxholes, bomb craters, and the like will present dangers to their vehicle's undercarriages and especially their brake systems," he said as he began to smile. "My point," he said, "is that the patent for the Moreland dual-reservoir master cylinder was issued last month, and already two of those major truck manufacturers appear ready to include the Moreland system on every vehicle they build for the Quartermasters Corps."

"Every vehicle they build?" Susan asked. "Will they be building many of those trucks?"

"Thousands and thousands, Susan," he said.

As she fell into his waiting arms, she said, "You've done it again, haven't you, Michael. These two boys," she whispered, pointing to Case and Reed, "will be so proud when they discover someday how their father's genius has affected the lives of so many people."

Just then, Reed stretched out his little arm, and his fist met Case's chin. With his eyes still closed, Case whimpered his disgust at the poke that woke him, and then both boys were awake. As their whimpers turned to cries, Susan's instant inspection indicated a need for two fresh diapers.

Resigned, Michael said, "I'll take Case."

"Then, I'll take Reed," Susan answered as she lifted him from the playpen.

Michael wrinkled his nose as he reached for Case and performed a preliminary examination of the diaper's contents.

"I wish someone would invent a diaper with a dipstick so we could skip the visual and olfactory inspections," he said. "Better still, I wish someone would invent diapers we use once and just throw away. I hate dealing with these deposits and stinky diaper pails all the time."

"I'm afraid you're dreaming, Mr. Moreland," Susan said, laughing. "No one will ever invent a replacement for a clean, soft diaper that one can use once and throw away. However, when you create a sample in your workshop, I'll be happy to look at it."

Chapter 35

"I can hardly believe everything is as we left it," Deborah Abrams marveled as she followed Daniel through the front entry and past their second-floor staircase.

"We are so fortunate that the bombs left Hyde Park untouched," Daniel said. Deborah nodded and watched as Daniel and Jan Molenaar parted the blackout curtains and let light flow into each room, dispelling the darkness in rooms that began to awaken from a very long sleep. Besides the dust and cobwebs they expected, nothing was awry. The furniture waited silently in the dining room, Deborah and Daniel's studio still smelled of oil paints, and the kitchen and pantry, though void of food, seemed ready to come to life once more.

Neither of the Abrams was eager to mount the stairs that led to the bedrooms on the second floor. Two of those rooms belonged to Jacob and Naomi, and neither Daniel nor Deborah was eager to enter those rooms. There, a flood of memories lay ready to overwhelm them, ready to ignite the grief they had known every moment since they last saw their children in Leiden more than four months ago.

At length, they forced themselves to climb the stairs, open the remaining blackout curtains, and shed their tears together in the children's rooms. Once more, they promised each other that the time when their family would be reunited was not far away. They made that promise to each other every day, sometimes several times a day, unwilling to believe anything could prevent the reunion so vital to both of them.

"Jan," Daniel began, "we need to re-stock the larder. Come with me to meet the greengrocer, the butcher, and the baker. You'll need to deal with them once Deborah and I can secure passage on a ship to Canada. On the way back, we'll stop at the Royal College if you like."

Despite the travel weariness they all felt, Jan smiled broadly.

"I never thought I would live to see London or know a professor who teaches at the Royal College of Art," Jan said. "Now I have a wonderful opportunity to stay in your home while you sail to Canada to reunite with your children. I am a man who is blessed beyond measure and happy to follow you anywhere, Daniel."

Their travels away from the jail cells in Leiden on foot, by train, by boat, and by bus had wearied all three, but it had also sealed a bond among them. While Deborah exercised a broom and a dustmop, Daniel and Jan walked out the door to see how the rest of the city had fared.

As they walked, Daniel said, "Deborah and I need a day or two in London to meet with our banker, explain our situation to our colleagues at the Royal College, and find passage on a ship bound for Canada. As we discussed, Jan, I will introduce you to the admissions representatives at the Royal College and offer my recommendation, but once we have boarded our ship, you will be on your own."

"I understand," Jan said, nodding, "and I am most grateful."

"We owe you our lives, Jan, and we will never forget the risks you took to help us secure our freedom. Our people have long memories, and we will not forget what you have done for us," Daniel said.

"Neither will I forget your generosity," Jan said, "nor that of those who not only cared for Jacob and Naomi in Lowestoft but also paid our fares to travel here."

"Yes," Daniel said. "I learned a great deal from the records they supplied upon our exit. The family in Canada who sponsored Jacob and Naomi's evacuation is from Suffolk. We passed their home as we traveled south from Lowestoft. The name Moncrieff was not unfamiliar to me because the Moncrieffs have long been patrons of the Royal College. I understand from Mrs. Goodwin's notes that they evacuated to Canada years ago for their safety. He, Sir Richard Moncrieff, served among the admiralty during the Great War."

"They seem to be fine people, Daniel. I'm sure Jacob and Naomi will be in good hands once they arrive there," Jan said.

"My heart tells me the same," Daniel agreed, "it tells me the same."

The weather in London on that August day was seasonably warm. However, in the North Atlantic aboard the British merchant ship *Mulbera*, the Abrams children huddled below decks in a cold cabin where they had been remanded with the other evacuees since their journey to Canada began. Now, eleven days later, they were only a few days from landing in Halifax. As best they could tell, the ship was sailing beyond the usual range of German U-boats. The crew's demeanor gave them the primary indication of their safety. After sailing from Liverpool in an ON convoy of more than twenty-five ships, the crew seemed to remain on high alert by day and night. After the eighth day, though, several crew members no longer seemed as reserved and nervous. They occasionally stopped to talk with the passengers. One pleasant young seaman from Sierra Leone began to keep the two informed each day.

"You're lucky to be in a fast convoy, an ON convoy," he told Jacob.

"What is an ON convoy?" Jacob asked.

"It means Outbound North. We sail from Liverpool, and we generally make the crossing in fourteen days or less. We'll be docking in a day or two," he said.

Jacob and Naomi would be glad to be off the ship, where the conditions were usually cold and damp, but they still wondered what awaited them in the next chapter of their journey. Naomi was yet unable to hold back her tears when she thought of her parents, locked in a Nazi cell in Leiden.

At the same time, Daniel and Deborah were saying goodbye to Jan at the dock in Liverpool. They, too, had found passage to Halifax on a merchant ship sailing with an ON convoy of twenty-seven ships. Unlike their children, though, they were about to sail into the most dangerous waters of their voyage, where the Kriegsmarine and its U-boats were waiting.

Their ship, the *Empire Lightning*, was sailing with a skeleton crew. As a result, the captain provided Daniel and Deborah two berths in a crew cabin with three other passengers. Privacy was sorely lacking, which, although difficult for Deborah, was nothing to which she couldn't adapt. On the fourth night of their voyage, however, Daniel was saddened to find her with her face turned toward the bulkhead, sobbing quietly.

"I'm sorry you are so sad, Deborah," he whispered. "I wish I could help you."

As she turned to him with her red nose and eyes, she said, "I'm not sad right now, Daniel," she answered, "I'm ashamed."

"Ashamed? But why?" he asked.

"This letter was waiting for me in London. It's from my cousin, Bertha, in Rotterdam," she said, showing Daniel the pages in her hand. "Her son, Karl, went missing six weeks ago. She wrote to tell me that they found his body along with those of six other young men. They were buried together, hardly covered with earth, beside a road outside the city. Hungry dogs had found them. Their hands were bound behind their backs, and they had been shot. I didn't want to tell you."

"I'm so sorry," Daniel said, his eyes filling with tears, "but why would you feel ashamed, Deborah?"

"Because I am so ungrateful," she said. "We might have died in that jail, but someone came to rescue us. Our children might have been captured, but another angel helped them. And now, while London is being bombed night after night, here we are, following our children to safety across the ocean, far from the dangers behind us. He is rescuing us, Daniel, but still, I worry and live in my fears, accusing him. King David spoke the truth, 'Yahweh Ra'ah - the Lord is my shepherd.' I want my heart to live in fear no longer, Daniel. I want to be grateful."

Daniel could say nothing. As they faced each other in the half-light of their cabin, he gently raised his hands to her temples and leaned forward until their brows met. They were one in their grief, one in their hope, one in their gratitude, and one day soon, he believed for them both, they would also be one in their joy.

Chapter 36

Sitting in his truck at the telegraph office in Charlottetown on a crisp September morning in 1941, Michael held a telegram sent by the Senior Staff Officer at RAF Newmarket Heath, an RAF airfield in England. He couldn't fathom why the Senior Staff Officer would send him a telegram. Grayson was stationed at Kirton in Lindsey, so Michael knew the telegram wouldn't bear news concerning him. That news, of course, would be posted directly to Michelle in New Mills.

Michael knew that only bomber squadrons flew out of Newmarket Heath, and he knew only one man who might be serving there. However, RAF telegrams were sent only to next-of-kin when a serviceman was either killed or missing in action. Michael had no next of kin on the battlefield, at sea, or in the air. Nothing on the envelope hinted at the contents of the telegram, but Michael guessed what must lie within. He waited another minute before taking his penknife from his pocket and slitting the seal to open the telegram. When he unfolded it, he read, "I regret to inform you that Pilot Officer Ernest Duncan is reported missing on Active Service."

Within a week, a letter arrived from Senior Staff Officer Kirkpatrick explaining that after completing a bombing mission that successfully destroyed its target, Duncan's aircraft had been hit by anti-aircraft fire. The bomber was already losing altitude when a Luftwaffe fighter strafed it. Another RAF bomber pilot reported seeing several parachutes in the air before Duncan's aircraft crashed and burned in a field in Germany, not far from the French border. The letter went on to say that those who safely parachuted from the aircraft might have survived and could now be in hiding, hoping to find their way out of Germany, or they might have been taken as prisoners of war. In either case, they were still classified as Missing and not Killed.

Michael was surprised but proud that Duncan must have named him his next of kin. Lacking anyone else who might care for him, Duncan chose Michael, who felt strangely honored. Still, though, as the letter promised, the RAF would consider Duncan missing but not killed. Michael was ready to do the same.

What Michael did not know was that the Senior Staff Officer's letter contained an error. The RAF aircraft that crashed and the men who parachuted to safety landed not in Germany but in France. Before any Nazi ground patrols were able to intercept them, French resistance forces spirited the survivors off to farms, attics, and barns while the Germans continued searching. While Michael read the letter, Ernest Duncan had already begun a new military career with the French resistance.

"Your German, *mon ami*," began Emile Boudreau, the farmer who had rescued Duncan from enemy bullets in an open hay field, "it's much too perfect for us near Strasbourg. How does a British airman speak German like that?" he asked.

In the relative safety of Emile's barn loft, Duncan didn't apologize.

"It's what I have had from childhood, and perhaps perfect for what I need to do next," he said.

"And what is that?" Emile asked as he opened a basket of bread, cheese, and a bottle of red wine.

"I'm hundreds of miles from my base in England," Duncan said, "and I would risk capture every day if I tried to travel there. I believe I can be of more value to the Crown here. You didn't hesitate to rescue and hide me, which leads me to believe you could introduce me to some of the resistance fighters in the region. Am I correct?"

"I could," Emile admitted as he opened the wine, "but what do I tell them you can do for us?"

"With their help to secure a German officer's uniform and some identification documents, I could use my 'too perfect' German, as you say, to impersonate a German officer. As an officer, I could open doors, sow confusion, and help the resistance attack the enemy in all the dark corners around the city," Duncan said.

"Very ambitious," Emile said, "but I cannot consent to take you to meet my cohorts. Instead, I will bring them *here*. If they like what they see, perhaps one could say something very helpful dropped out of the sky today."

"I respect your caution, and I will be happy to meet their every challenge," Duncan said.

Now, weeks later in Sir Richard's study at Highfield, Michael shared his letter with Sir Richard.

"Remarkable," Sir Richard said after reading the RAF letter, "but here's an update I'm sure you'll enjoy." He reached into a bottom drawer to hand Michael a folder.

A few minutes later, Michael finished reading a report from one of Sir Richard's SIS operatives embedded with the French resistance near Strasbourg. It described a rescued RAF navigator who preferred not to provide a name. He came to be known to them only as "Eddy," the name they gave him after discovering the initials E.D. carved into the grip of his Enfield revolver.

The report went on to say that after parachuting from a burning Vickers-Wellington bomber, Eddy was rescued by the farmer who owned the field where he landed. He spent several days hidden on the farm before it was safe for the farmer to introduce him by night to members of the Strasbourg resistance. With his impeccable German and the German uniforms and papers the resistance soon provided, Eddy proved his ability to travel the city unrestrained. In a few short weeks, he was able to guide resistance personnel in and out of several German strongholds, attacking them with impunity.

"Amazing," was all Michael could say.

"My office will have the RAF report amended to report him Killed in Action," Sir Richard said. "Then he'll truly be able to disappear. Ghosts make the best operatives, Michael, ghosts," Sir Richard said with a wink.

"But, how do you know he'll stay there?" Michael asked. "He could disappear at any moment, couldn't he?"

"Correct, Michael, but we've seen this man in action, haven't we? He's fiercely loyal to whatever authority he chooses, and right now, it's us," Sir Richard said. "He redeems his injured conscience every time he does something to obliterate the errors of his past. He's in his glory right now, paying back the Nazis who used him and abandoned him."

"Do you think he suspects that you're watching him now, watching him redeem that past?" Michael asked.

"He doesn't know and won't know," Sir Richard said. "I am insulated from my operatives by at least three degrees and most by more than that. My identity is well hidden and superbly protected."

"It will be interesting to see how well he continues to perform at this level. You'll be watching him, I take it?" Michael asked.

"Like a hawk," Sir Richard answered, "like a hawk."

Chapter 37

The *Lady M* was a perfect boat for a retired man of the sea like Sir Richard. As much as he loved to sail, sailing a craft this size required a crew that his family had provided in his younger days. He dreamed of the day when his children would reunite at Highfield. If the season was right, perhaps they could re-live the old days when the breeze was brisk and the sails were full. Until then, however, during the fine fall days of 1941, the *Lady M's* crew was solely Lady Moncrieff. The sails were not required, as the *Lady M's* engine sufficed for power, and the captain and his crew of one enjoyed the salt air and the occasional spray over the bow together.

Sir Richard enjoyed a full summer of exploration, sailing at one time or another around the entire island. Later in summer, he ventured farther out, exploring the waters to the northeast that U-boats might be tempted to infest if the war brought them this far west. That, of course, would probably depend on the United States' involvement in the war. When the US Navy found its way out of its ports to protect shipping lanes in the North Atlantic, the U-boats would probably remain at a safe distance.

The seas were rougher than usual today as the fall's northeast breezes grew in intensity, rough enough that Lady Moncrieff finally asked her husband to come about and head back to port.

"Richard," she shouted from the deck chair, which had begun to slide on the wet deck beneath her, "let's turn about and strike a heading for port."

At the wheel, Sir Richard was still staring over the bow, unable to see because of the spray. At that moment, a rogue wave hit the starboard bow, causing him to lose his grip on the wheel and casting him onto the deck at Lady Moncrieff's feet.

Although he appeared uninjured, it was clear he was not the same man who could spring back to his feet following such a fall some years ago. Instead, he moved slowly but deliberately and crawled toward the wheel, coming to a standing position with one hand braced on the captain's chair and one on the wheel. Slowing the engine to an idle, he took a moment to recover before raising the engine speed and changing course to the southwest. All the while, Lady Moncrieff looked on, powerless to help.

With the wind at their stern, the seas seemed to calm, and, content to let the *Lady M* drift for a few moments, both retired to the cabin below. Removing their wet slickers, they sat opposite one another at the galley table.

"So," Angela began, "tell me what that was about, Richard."

"I'm sorry," he said, hanging his head. "I'm sorry."

"Sorry for what, Richard," she asked.

"I don't know precisely," he said, "but I feel embarrassed. I should be able to do more, Angela, more to care for you. Instead, I put you in danger."

"Who told you that you should be doing more, Richard?" she asked. "It's not I, is it?"

"No," he answered, "of course not, Angela. You've never asked for more than I could do," he said. "It's just how I've always lived. I know I push myself harder than is necessary," he said, "always striving for something beyond my grasp. It truly is the way I've always lived."

"If it's how you've always lived, Richard," she began, "then let me suggest that you take a good, long look at your father, the only one before whom I've ever seen you shiver," she said.

"My father?" he asked.

"Yes, your father, Richard. None of us sees our parents as the rest of the world sees them. We can't, really. It takes an outside viewpoint. Would you like to know what I saw in your relationship with your father?" she asked.

Though unsure he wanted to hear what his wife had to say, he relied on what years of their marriage had taught him about her wisdom and said, "Say on, Angela."

"You made him into a man of legendary proportions," she began, "a man who, in reality, was very lonely. He was never able to enjoy his sons. He was never able to approve fully of anything you accomplished. I watched you in his shadow for years, Richard. He set an impossible standard for you. But he's gone now. He came by the legend honestly, you know. He learned it from *his* father, who probably learned it from his. But you can end that legacy if you wish," she said.

Sir Richard sat silently while his wife paused.

"Make no mistake," she said, "I loved your father as much as he would let me. I loved him because *you* did. He was always very kind to me, but I fear only because I was your wife. Not owing him the debt that blood requires, I saw him perhaps more clearly. But, Richard, I want more for you than he ever allowed himself. I want you to revel in the joy that our sons and Susan can bring you."

Looking up at her, Sir Richard nodded.

"You made a start with Michael, Richard, and it has made your relationship with him all the richer," she said. "Your sons, however, will never know you and your better side until you leave your relationship with your father behind. It was not ideal. It was distant and dry and cold. It wasn't his fault. Again, he learned it from *his* father, but you can break the pattern, Richard. Don't require your children to live in your shadow, always striving to fulfill an impossible role. Rather, be the light that attracts them as moths to a flame."

Sir Richard nodded again and brightened just a little.

"You've seen Michael with our grandsons, haven't you? He's neither a father like yours nor the one you've been with our sons. No," she said, "he's their *Daddy*, Richard, the man who plays on the floor with them, making funny faces just to see their smiles, doing things you never let yourself do with our children."

Abandoning his silence, Sir Richard said, "No, I didn't. I'm afraid I wanted our sons to be men before they were boys, Angela. It's all I knew. And Susan," he said, "I'm afraid I left her to you."

"Yes, Richard, that was all you knew then. But now we know better. Our grandsons will only have one grandfather and one grandmother. Let us be the ones they remember with joy, not fear. Respect for the aged will always be in fashion," she added, "but let's lose reverence, all right?" she laughed.

Sir Richard nodded and began to smile.

"What do you find funny, Richard?" she asked.

"I'm thinking of Susan and Michael's faces the first time they see me playing on the floor with Case and Reed," he laughed. "They'll wonder who the strange man is playing with their boys."

"Oh, it will be a marvelous day for all of us, Richard. But let's attend to one detail now," she said. "You need a name for the boys to call you. Something simple with no more than two syllables for their young tongues to fashion. Don't hold on to it too closely because children often choose a variation of the one you supply," she laughed.

"Well," he asked, "what have you chosen for yourself?"

"I favor Grammie," she said.

"Hmm," he said after a moment, "I was thinking of 'Grampy,' but that's pretty close to 'Grumpy,'" he laughed. "What do you think of 'Grampy'?"

"Grampy, it is," she agreed as they stood, looked fondly into each other's eyes, and embraced. "Now, let's return to the dock and find our way home to a hot cup of tea. You need to make some time to play with those boys before they're too old to enjoy the funny faces you'll show them."

He had to laugh again but postponed his laugh long enough to kiss the woman who loved him so well.

Chapter 38

Fortunately for Michael, when he arrived at Pier 21 in Halifax to pick up the next group of guest children, Sir Richard accompanied him in the Ford sedan. Phillipe followed them in the second car. The British merchant ship *Mulbera* had arrived overnight and was unloading its cargo after its last passengers had disembarked.

Upon his arrival at Pier 21, two RCN officers met Sir Richard to drive him to a previously scheduled meeting. At the same time, Michael and Phillipe entered the immigration office and prepared to wade through all the required immigration procedures before the evacuees could be released to their care. This time, however, they faced a problem they couldn't solve. Michael was never happier to see Sir Richard when the RCN staff car returned with him.

"You look worried, Michael," Sir Richard said. "Is there a problem?"

"I'm afraid so," Michael answered. "Jacob and Naomi Abrams have been held up in the immigration office. I sent Phillipe back to Highfield with the other children."

"But what is the problem with the Abrams children?" Sir Richard asked.

"I don't know," Michael answered. "The immigration officials won't speak with me. They want to see you or Lady Moncrieff, the Abrams' official sponsors."

"Then, see me, they shall. Lead the way, please, Michael," Sir Richard said.

Michael was never more thankful for Sir Richard's dress uniform. As Michael walked a few steps ahead, Sir Richard, briefcase under his arm, suddenly became Rear-Admiral Moncrieff. He marched erect and somewhat ceremoniously behind Michael to the glass-partitioned office complex that served as the immigration office. An RCN guard stood at the door. As the Admiral approached, the guard came to attention and saluted. Returning the salute, Rear-Admiral Moncrieff, looking at the identification tag on the sailor's breast pocket, said, "Petty Officer Nelson, we meet again. It's been more than a year, as I remember."

"Yes, Admiral, sir," the young man answered. "It is an honor to see you again, sir."

"When we last parted, your rank was Able Seaman. Please accept my congratulations on your rapid advancement," the Admiral said.

"Thank you, sir, but I have you to thank in part for that. Your letter to my commanding officer brought an almost immediate reward. I must thank you," Nelson added.

"A well-deserved advancement in rank, I am sure," the Admiral replied. "Now, if you would, please announce my arrival to the ranking officer within."

"My pleasure, Admiral, sir," Nelson replied as he saluted again.

The gentleman who returned with Petty Officer Nelson was not in uniform. A civil servant wearing a wrinkled and worn blue suit stood dwarfed before the Admiral at his door. Looking somewhat bewildered, he said, "May I help you?"

"Rear-Admiral Sir Richard Moncrieff, here on official business. To whom am I speaking, if you would, please?" the Admiral asked.

"I am Agent Richard Creighton, Chief Immigration Officer here at Pier 21," he said quietly.

"Thank you, Mr. Creighton," the Admiral began. "As I do not customarily conduct Royal Navy business in less than private settings, I must ask if you have somewhere other than this open hallway where we may speak, sir."

Taken aback by the Admiral's request, Creighton replied, "Of course," and turning clumsily and bumping into the door, he said, "Please follow me to my office."

As the Admiral passed through the door, he winked at Petty Officer Nelson, who could not hold back his grin. Michael followed the Admiral close behind. When they arrived at Creighton's office, the Admiral and Michael took seats in front of Creighton's desk while he sat in his chair behind.

"How may I help you?" Creighton asked.

The Admiral opened his briefcase, retrieved a small folder of papers, and began, "My associate here, Michael Moreland, has reported a problem with the immigration status of two children, one Jacob Abrams and his sister, Naomi Abrams. The remaining children traveling on the same ship, arriving here in convoy from Liverpool, from the same evacuee agency, and in the same party, have all had their papers processed and are on their way to Prince Edward Island. Could you explain to me the reason why you are detaining these two children while the others have been released onto Canadian soil?"

It was plain to see that Mr. Creighton was unaccustomed to a confrontation with a man of the Admiral's status. After looking at the clipboard on his desk and swallowing, he looked up again but could not look directly at the Admiral. Eventually, he said, "There were some irregularities in their paperwork."

"Irregularities in their paperwork," the Admiral repeated, but not as a question. He waited a long moment.

Breaking the silence, the Admiral said, "Please describe the irregularities."

Clearing his throat and still not looking at the Admiral, Creighton said, 'I'm afraid I am not at liberty to discuss the nature of the irregularities."

"Not at liberty," the Admiral repeated, "meaning that you have a higher authority who has ordered the Chief Immigration Officer at Pier 21 to disallow the immigration of certain individuals based on a standard which cannot be explained to a common man such as myself?"

Overwhelmed, Creighton stammered, "Not exactly. There is no single person who handles this kind of irregularity. It's simply a policy that everyone understands."

"A policy that everyone understands," the Admiral repeated. Again, it was not a question.

"So, then you, Agent Richard Creighton, Chief Immigration Officer at Pier 21," the Admiral said as he picked up the wood and brass nameplate from the desk and read it, "you are the only one here who has the authority to identify and enforce the irregularity policy at the primary immigration port in Canada, is that correct?"

"Yes," Creighton answered.

"That authority must be a weighty burden," the Admiral said.

Brightening a bit, Creighton said, "Yes, it is. Most people don't understand."

"I must confess, however, that I also do not understand," the Admiral said. "I'll ask again. What is the 'irregularity' that prevents the immigration of the Abrams children?"

"It's so evident," Creighton said. Leaning forward and glancing both left and right, he said, "They're Jews."

"I see," the Admiral said. He handed Creighton one of the papers from the stack before him. "Please examine this document and tell me what you see, Mr. Creighton."

Creighton surveyed the document a moment before he looked up and said, "This document speaks of a Dr. Daniel Abrams, Professor of Art at the Royal College of Art in London."

"Yes, the Admiral said, "a British subject, born in London, and the father of Jacob and Naomi Abrams."

The Admiral handed Creighton another document. "Review this document, if you please, Mr. Creighton."

After examining the letterhead, Creighton reacted almost immediately. He replied, "But this is from 10 Downing Street in London."

"That's correct, Mr. Creighton. Please read the second paragraph," the Admiral said.

Creighton read, "I congratulate you and Lady Moncrieff for making your home in Canada a welcome destination for so many evacuee children from England, especially those from Lowestoft who have been rescued from persecution at Nazi hands."

"And the signature?" the Admiral prompted.

"Prime Minister, Winston Churchill," Creighton mumbled.

"Just one more, Chief Officer Creighton," the Admiral said, handing him an envelope containing a third piece of stationery.

Creighton was visibly humbled. He read the short paragraph and looked up in silence.

"This communication was posted from . . . ?" the Admiral asked.

"Buckingham Palace," Creighton said quietly.

"The last paragraph, if you please, Mr. Creighton," the Admiral requested.

Creighton read, "The Queen and I are happy to share your support for the unfortunate Jewish refugee children in Lowestoft. Thank you for receiving them to your care in Canada."

"Chief Immigration Officer Richard Creighton," the Admiral began, "to my knowledge, Canada remains a member of the British Commonwealth. Would you agree?"

"Yes," Creighton answered.

"And our sovereign, King George VI, is still Britain's king, is that true?" the Admiral asked.

Creighton could only nod.

"Then, as the Chief Immigration Officer of Pier 21, Halifax, Nova Scotia, Canada, a member of the Commonwealth whose monarch remains King George VI, is there any other authority to whom you must apply for permission for the Abrams children, Jacob and Naomi, son and daughter of Dr. and Mrs. Daniel Abrams, to enter Canada?"

Quietly and with a downward glance, Creighton replied, "No."

"Thank you for your thoroughly reasonable acknowledgment of British sovereignty, Mr. Creighton," the Admiral said. "Now, if you would send your kindest representative to guide Jacob and Naomi Abrams to my personal vehicle, which is waiting outside, I would be happy to accompany you when you offer them your own kind welcome."

Creighton nodded, made a short telephone call, and left the office at the Admiral's side while Michael followed.

As they approached the car, the Admiral asked, "Mr. Creighton, may I ask you a question of a personal nature?"

Defeated on every previous count, Creighton could offer no other response except a quiet "Yes."

"Are you a man of faith, Mr. Creighton?" the Admiral asked. "I am, you see," he added, "baptized in the Anglican faith."

"And I, in the Methodist," Creighton replied meekly.

"Then, Mr. Creighton," the Admiral began, "allow me to remind you, if you will, that the Lord we name as our savior, Jesus, the Christ, was a Jew. I believe he still holds a soft spot in his heart for every Jew. I recommend you consider that the next time you encounter an "irregularity" in another worthy immigrant's paperwork."

"I understand," Creighton said.

"Thank you, Mr. Creighton," the Admiral offered. "Please be informed that Jacob and Naomi's parents are scheduled to arrive in Halifax sometime in the next two weeks in another ON convoy aboard the *Empire Lightning*. May I trust that they will receive your personal welcome?" he asked.

"You may, Sir Richard," Creighton replied, "along with my apologies for the harsh treatment their children endured at my hands. I ask your forgiveness as well."

"Granted without condition, Mr. Creighton," the Admiral replied as he offered his hand. "We must remember that we all seek the same forgiveness."

With eyes full to overflowing, Creighton bowed his head to say, "Thank you."

Upon Jacob and Naomi's arrival at the car, Creighton apologized for the delay and welcomed them to Canada. With their meager possessions in the car, Michael took the wheel and drove Sir Richard and the two tired immigrants home to Highfield.

Chapter 39

The letter the Bouchers received reporting that Luc had been wounded on a battlefield on the island of Crete brought them immediately to Highfield's front door. They desperately wanted more information than the terse description that their letter provided. When Michael answered their knock at the door, Jacques had the letter in his hand. In one brief moment, Michael read the letter and looked back at his friends' confused and grieving faces.

"Michael," Jacques said, "this letter tells us nothing more than that Luc was wounded and evacuated from the island. We have no idea how seriously he was hurt or where he is now. We certainly don't want to impose, and we know that Sir Richard is very busy, but we were hoping he might be able to . . . "

"Find out where Luc is and learn the extent of his injuries?" Michael asked. "Yes, Jacques, and yes, Doris," Michael said as he brought them into the parlor. "I know he will be as eager as I am to learn all we can about Luc's condition. I'll take this letter to his study. Please, wait right here until I return."

Michael returned a few minutes later with Sir Richard close behind.

"Jacques and Mrs. Boucher," Sir Richard said as he offered Jacques his hand. "Please know that we share your concern to learn all we can about your son's condition. I have sent queries to all my contacts who have access to the information we seek. I trust we will have a full report by tomorrow morning at the latest."

"Thank you, Sir Richard," Doris said through her tears.

"It is our duty as well as our pleasure to be able to help, Mrs. Boucher," Sir Richard said. "Luc became a member of the Highfield family years ago. Neither you nor he will be ignored in your hour of need."

As the news passed through the house, Lady Moncrieff and Susan appeared to offer all the comfort they could. Phillipe and Alida found their way to the parlor from the hen house and the barn. As a family, they prayed together before Doris and Jacques returned home.

Later that day, Susan was surprised to find Lois at her door with Patrice by her side. Susan was not surprised by Patrice's red eyes but didn't expect to see Lois in tears.

"Miss Susan," Patrice said, "Lois asked to see you if you have a few minutes."

"Of course, Lois," Susan said. "I just put the boys down for their nap. I'll meet you in the parlor in five minutes."

"Thank you, Mrs. Moreland," Lois said as she turned toward the staircase.

"Patrice," Susan said as Patrice turned to follow Lois, "are you going to be all right?"

Patrice said, "Not yet, Miss Susan, but I have sister feelings about my brother. Lois has a different kind. You understand, don't you?"

Susan nodded knowingly and said, "I think I do, Patrice, and thank you for being such a good friend to Lois."

"Yes, ma'am," Patrice said as she disappeared down the staircase.

When Susan appeared at the parlor doors, Lois was seated on one of the sofas. She came to her feet when she heard Susan arrive.

"Please sit, Lois," Susan said as she joined her on the sofa. "You seem upset. How can I help you?"

Lois raised her handkerchief to her eye as she said, "It's about Luc."

Susan nodded and asked, "Can you tell me what it is about Luc?"

"Yes," Lois said, "but I should probably tell you something more about me first."

"All right," Susan said, "please tell me."

"Our home in London is not far from the East End," Lois said. "Do you know about the East End?"

"I've not been there, but I understand the very poor live there under difficult circumstances," Susan answered.

"That is correct," Lois said, "but poverty also brings crime, immorality, and worse. A seventeen-year-old woman living there is in danger of being identified as potential property for any man's use."

"Were you ever accosted there, Lois?" Susan asked.

"No, I wasn't. We lived far enough away from the worst sorts to be in that kind of danger regularly. However, the young men were not always gentlemen, either, at least not like Luc," Lois said.

"I see," Susan said, waiting for Lois to continue.

"Many of them were going off to war while I was there, and all of London appreciated their sacrifice. There would often be parties before they reported for duty, and even long-time friends who had enjoyed too much ale would get much too 'handy' all at once. Holding them off with a laugh was no longer enough when they began demanding 'something to remember you by.' Thankfully, I wasn't a drinker, and I was able to stay ahead of them."

Susan nodded as Lois continued.

"At seventeen, I was much older than the children evacuating from London. My mother sent me here to get me away from the jackals in the streets as much as for my safety from the bombs," Lois said, wiping her eyes again.

"So, tell me, Lois," Susan said, "what has set your tears off today when you are so far away from the troubles you knew in London?"

"It's Luc," she answered quietly.

"What is it about Luc, Lois?" Susan asked.

"Luc is a gentleman, Mrs. Moreland. He always makes me feel like a lady. He appreciates my artwork and even tells me what he sees in it. He looks at my face, my eyes, my hair, and not where the boys in London were always gaping. He asks how I'm doing, and he really wants an answer. He's not like any other boy I've known," she said.

"Are you in love with him, Lois?" Susan asked

"I'm afraid I don't know," she said. "I know I've never been in love before. He's the only one who has ever made me feel this way."

"Have you reason to expect that he feels the same way for you?" Susan asked.

"Perhaps," Lois said. "He noticed that I wore a sterling charm bracelet, and the night before he was to report for duty, he gave me this," she said as she showed Susan a heart-shaped charm among the many on her bracelet.

"It's lovely, Lois," Susan said. "What happened next?"

"Well," she said, "I thanked him—with a kiss."

"And did he kiss you back?" Susan asked.

With a twinkle in her eye, Lois smiled and said, "He did the second time. I think I surprised him with the first," she laughed.

"That's the first smile I've seen on you in some time, Lois," Susan said before adding, "We're all worried about Luc. Most of us are worried about his injuries, as you are. But you are worried about something even more important. You're worried about his heart. When he returns, he will need you, probably more than anyone else. So, in the meantime, don't forget that your soldier needs mail often. Give him lots of reasons to come home to you. He'll have adjustments to make, but I believe you'll find ways to make them easier for him."

"Yes, Mrs. Moreland, I will," Lois said as she stood and stepped toward Susan with open arms. "Thank you."

"This is only our first talk on this subject, Lois," Susan said as they walked to the door. "Let's talk again soon."

With another hug and a smile, Lois was on her way.

It was only an hour later that Sir Richard asked Michael to call Doris and Jacques so that he could share the news he had gathered from London. When they arrived, Sir Richard began.

"I am overjoyed to offer a very optimistic report on Luc's condition. Luc has been transported to Queen Alexandra Military Hospital in London. Although he suffered battle injuries, they were limited to superficial wounds to his face and a shrapnel wound to his right shoulder. All those wounds are healing well and without complications. His eyesight, affected by battle debris, is only marginally impaired and is expected to improve. In its current state, however, his eyesight fails to meet minimum RCA requirements, and, as a result, Luc will soon be granted a berth on a troopship bound for Halifax. When he arrives, he will return to Camp Debert and be granted an honorable discharge within thirty days."

"Then he'll be home by Christmas," Doris said joyfully. "This will be our happiest Christmas ever."

Sir Richard added, "Luc's fellow soldiers and superiors have heartily commended his service. In his first and, thankfully, last battle on the island of Crete, he was able to eliminate two German snipers who were shooting from the towers of a church. They had killed six of Luc's fellow infantrymen and wounded four others. Luc's two shots ended their rain of bullets on our troops huddled behind low stucco walls. With the enemy approaching from both flanks, our men would have been overwhelmed by enemy fire in minutes were it not for Luc's intervention. I am assured that an appropriate commendation will await him upon his discharge."

Jacques and Doris thanked Sir Richard as the rest of the Highfield family, led by Lady Moncrieff, crowded into the parlor. While the women gathered around Doris, the men surrounded Jacques as both parents shared their good news. The room buzzed for a few minutes, but when the conversation eventually grew quiet, Jacques lifted his voice to say, "Our Father . . . ," and Highfield joined him in a prayer of thanksgiving. Their wounded one was coming home.

Chapter 40

Although full of business with Agent Creighton at Pier 21 one moment, Sir Richard amazed Michael by capturing the Abrams children's attention and making them comfortable as they began their drive to Highfield. He was a different man than Michael had ever seen. Ordinarily, he was one to get on the road and proceed in all haste. Today, however, no timetable appeared to rule him. While they were still driving off the pier, he offered a real schedule breaker.

"I'll bet you two are hungry," he said as he turned to look into the back seat. Jacob sat behind Michael as he drove, while Naomi sat behind Sir Richard. "Do you think you could eat something?"

"We haven't eaten yet today," Jacob said. "When the others were excused earlier, no food was provided."

"I am famished," Naomi said, "and a bit thirsty, sir."

"Then I know a fine place to stop where we can find something wonderful to satisfy our appetites," he said. "Do you know the *Green Lantern*, Michael?" he asked.

"I'm afraid I don't. Is it on our way?" Michael asked.

"No, it is not, but that hardly matters today. Naomi and Jacob are hungry, and you and I should eat before the long drive home, so let's stop now. At the next stop light, turn right, if you will," he said, smiling.

The restaurant was more posh than Michael expected, and the menu was extensive. There was no problem finding something to satisfy everyone's palate and diet. The children were amazed that they could order whatever they liked, including dessert, and Sir Richard felt free to encourage them to enjoy the first day of their newfound freedom.

"I'm sure your sea voyage was cold, dark, and damp. Am I correct?" Sir Richard asked.

"Oh, yes, sir," Naomi said. "We were not allowed on deck for the entire journey, and there was so little light below. The food was tiresome, too, but none of that mattered, really. We knew it would be over soon, and we would land in Canada. Of course, we didn't know what Canada would be like either, but so far, it seems delightful," she said as she coaxed the last bit of chocolate frosting onto the last crumb of cake on her plate."

"Mrs. Goodwin said that we would be going first to a place called Highfield. Is that correct?" Jacob asked.

"Yes," Sir Richard said. "I'll let Michael tell you all about it."

Michael took several minutes to describe the guest cottages, the stable, and the barn. Then, he named all the animals the children would see in only a few hours. "Of course," he said, "I should also mention the schoolhouse, the garage, the hen house, and the pastures. We never lack for things to do at Highfield," he said.

"And the boys stay in one of the guest cottages and the girls in the other?" Naomi asked.

"Usually that is true," Sir Richard answered, "but this time, we have to make a big change, bringing me to the best news of all."

"The best news of all?" Jacob asked. "Please tell us."

Sir Richard began, "I met with some naval officers this morning to learn which other ships are landing in Halifax over the next two weeks. One of those ships is named the *Empire Lightning*, sailing from Liverpool."

"We sailed from Liverpool, didn't we, Jacob?" Naomi asked.

"Yes, Naomi, but let's hear the news. Shh!" he chided.

Sir Richard continued, "I had an opportunity to peruse the passenger list, and two passengers are from London. Their names are Daniel and Deborah Abrams."

Jacob and Naomi looked at each other in stunned silence as tears welled up in their eyes. Using their napkins as handkerchiefs, they wiped their eyes before standing and rushed to surround Sir Richard with their arms, hardly able to utter a word. Finally, not releasing his embrace but resting his chin on Sir Richard's shoulder, Jacob asked, "Do you know when they will arrive, sir?"

"Yes, I do, Jacob," he said. "Barring any storms at sea, they will arrive in eleven days. If you would like, you may come back to Halifax with me to greet them when they leave the ship."

"I would like that very much," Naomi said, exchanging her tears for a smile. "Very much."

"Then, you shall have it," Sir Richard laughed. "Now, before we strike a course of west by northwest, how about everyone stopping at the loo before we set off on the next leg of our journey?"

Although the children had begun the drive to Highfield quietly a few hours ago, there wasn't a quiet moment in the Ford sedan for the next hour. They had more questions about Highfield but left those behind regularly to remember that they would soon share every moment with their parents.

"Have Mother and Father ever ridden horses?" Naomi asked.

"I don't know, but won't it be fun to learn together?" Jacob laughed.

"I want to try to milk a cow, too," Naomi said, "a brown and white cow."

"Why does the color matter?" Jacob laughed.

"I don't suppose it does. I need to see it in my mind," she said as she leaned back and closed her eyes. She was asleep in moments, and Jacob was not far behind. Sir Richard tilted his head back and was soon asleep, as well.

Glancing at the back seat in the rearview mirror as he drove, Michael wondered how many other families separated like theirs had ever come together again. He knew he was witnessing something rare and priceless. Inside, he felt a keen grief for the unspeakable pain that too, too many others in Europe were suffering, day after day.

Chapter 41

Eleven days became twelve, and then thirteen as the *Empire Lightning's* convoy suffered through some of the roughest seas of the season. As the wind and sea continued to batter the ship, the days and nights became the same for the Abrams. With the delays they were facing at sea came other doubts and fears.

"I'm sorry to say this, Daniel," Deborah began, "but I fear what may await us when we arrive in Canada."

"What do you mean?" he answered.

"We know that Canada has not welcomed Jews in the past. Instead, they have sent ships seeking refuge away, forcing them to return to the same dangers they fled," she said.

"True," Daniel answered, "but we have something many of them did not have, Deborah," he said, trying to reassure her.

"Our British citizenship?" she asked. "How much did that help us in Leiden? I can still hear the voice of the officer on the train platform. Do you remember what he said?"

"Yes," Daniel answered. "He said, 'I'm afraid there will be a short delay,' "and then they took us to . . . "

"The jail, Daniel," she said, "where we endured more than eight weeks in the cold and the dark before Jan Molenaar rescued us."

It was a moment before Daniel said, "Deborah, the cold and darkness on this ship is only ours to bear for a few more days. Then we shall see our Jacob and Naomi again. Not even the sun will shine as bright for us as their faces. Yes?" he asked.

With a heavy sigh, Deborah turned to reach for Daniel, and as he joined her in their embrace, she said, "My heart will not rest until they are in my arms, Daniel. I will not be able to endure another horror like Leiden."

Twenty-four hours later, the *Empire Lightning* docked at Pier 21 at eight in the morning. After what seemed an interminable two hours, Canadian immigration officials arrived at the ship to guide the passengers to the processing stations. With their meager possessions in their arms, the Abrams found themselves separated from the other passengers. At the same time, two officers spoke in whispers, looking back at them several times as they shared their conversation. Eventually, one officer approached them.

"Daniel Abrams and Deborah Abrams?" he asked as he looked at the clipboard he carried.

"Yes," Daniel answered.

"Professor Daniel Abrams, from the Royal College of Art in London?" he asked again.

"Yes," Daniel answered, "I teach there."

"I hope the bombs have spared your home and the college, Professor," the officer said. "We hear more about the bombings every day."

"Yes, thank you," Daniel said. "Thus far we have been spared."

"Professor, the Chief Immigration Officer, Agent Richard Creighton, is coming here to meet you. He will be with you presently. He asked me to take you to his office while you wait," the officer said.

It was only a few minutes before Agent Creighton arrived. As he entered the office, the Abrams stood, and Agent Creighton offered Daniel his hand.

"Professor Abrams and Mrs. Abrams," he said. "I'm sure you are happy to be here on Pier 21 and no longer aboard ship. As they nodded in agreement, Agent Creighton, looking at their credentials, said, "I believe everything you have provided here is in order. However, before we can release you to Canadian soil, I'm afraid there will be a short delay,"

His words hung in the air like an anvil waiting to fall. Deborah's face turned gray as a wave of terror turned her eyes to meet Daniel's. Both turned to look at Agent Creighton.

The fear in Deborah's eyes was unmistakable, and Creighton was taken aback.

After swallowing slowly, Daniel asked in calm, measured words, "What kind of delay?"

Puzzled, Creighton made his best effort to relieve their fear, saying, "It will be only a few minutes while your driver finishes fueling your car. Rear-Admiral Moncrieff has arranged a car and a driver for you. The

Admiral is waiting outside at this moment," he said. "Shall we go?" he asked, motioning toward the door.

Still haunted by memories of the Leiden jail, Daniel and Deborah followed Agent Creighton as he led them down a series of corridors until they reached a small foyer. The light from the mid-morning sun crept through two sidelights flanking a large windowless oak door. When Creighton opened the door, the light flooded in, causing Daniel and Deborah to close their eyes momentarily. When they opened their eyes, they saw Sir Richard opening the rear door of his car while Jacob and Naomi tumbled out, running to greet their parents. As their eyes adjusted to the sunlight, the couple found themselves immersed in their children's arms. In a mixture of laughter and tears, the four neither saw nor heard anything but each other for several long minutes.

Sir Richard approached and offered his hand to Daniel, who grasped it with both of his.

"Richard Moncrieff," Sir Richard said to Daniel, who replied, "Daniel Abrams, sir. We are in your debt. Please meet my wife, Deborah."

"Mrs. Abrams," Sir Richard said. "We are so happy to have you here, safe at last."

Still teary and with her children clinging to her, Deborah said, "We have no words sufficient to thank you, sir."

"We'll have time to hear your whole story when we are all together at Highfield. I have business here in Halifax for the day, but I have arranged for Petty Officer Nelson to drive you to Prince Edward Island. Since it is a lengthy drive, he is ready to guide you to some worthy stops for refreshment and rest on the way. As my guests, I leave you to enjoy whatever his imagination can provide for your comfort," Sir Richard said.

As Petty Officer Nelson saluted, the Abrams family piled into the RCN staff car. Sir Richard could hear the echoes of the children as Jacob said, "There are two cottages, Father, and because the other children from England found homes with families on the island, we have both, all to ourselves." Not to be outdone, Naomi added, "And there are horses, Mother, two of them." The banter and laughter continued until the doors closed and the car left the pier.

"There's one family, intact," Sir Richard said. "How I wish we could help thousands more."

"Yes," said a voice behind him, "and I regret I didn't do so sooner."

Sir Richard turned to look into the eyes of Agent Creighton.

"And I regret my reticence to be more involved earlier, Agent Creighton, but now that we have begun, may we not lack the courage to continue."

The men shook hands, and as Sir Richard returned to his car, both wondered how much time would pass until they met again.

Chapter 42

When the British steam tanker *Caspia* landed at Halifax on October 9, 1941, she had been at sea with Convoy ON 20 for fourteen days. Pvt Luc Boucher was the only uniformed passenger among the few others aboard. Although his eyes were no longer overly sensitive to light following his injuries on the battlefield in Crete, he often wore dark glasses during daylight hours. He found those glasses a comfort when mixing with others aboard the ship. They tended to limit questions too often asked of soldiers sailing home and leaving the battlefield behind.

Luc rarely told his story except to another soldier who had seen combat. Even then, he offered only a terse account of the battle and the wounds his service had brought him. He learned early that only another wounded soldier could truly comprehend what he endured when he had to leave his comrades behind. Every night, Luc rehearsed the names of the men with whom he had served and prayed that they were still alive and well. And always, he remembered those who had died. Each had a face and a name he would never forget. In his best moments, he knew he hadn't abandoned his comrades, but those few moments lived among the many hours of each day that plagued his mind and stole his peace.

The ship at the dock was wholly different from the ship at sea, though still not as stable as the dry ground his body craved. He had yet to endure another few hours aboard the *Caspia* before his feet would rest on Canadian soil. With his days at sea behind him, his orders required him to wait at Pier 21 for transport to Camp Debert, where he would be processed for discharge and return to civilian life. A bus from Camp Debert arrived in mid-afternoon with several soldiers aboard. By five o'clock, Luc had a bunk in a barracks among another two dozen soldiers.

Two weeks after Doris and Jacques learned that Luc's ship had arrived safely in Halifax, a letter from the Royal Canadian Army arrived, inviting them to visit him at Camp Debert. They made immediate plans to make the three-hour drive, accompanied by Ingrid and Patrice. Doris was not surprised to hear from Lois when they announced their plans at supper. Lois approached her in the kitchen as she helped to dry the last dishes.

"Mrs. Boucher," Lois began, "if it would not be an imposition, I was hoping that I might accompany you and your family when you go to Camp Debert to visit Luc."

"Why would that be an imposition, Lois?" Doris answered.

"Because it's such an important family reunion, ma'am," Lois said, "and especially since you came so close to losing your son in the war."

"You are correct, of course, Lois. Our family has endured many worrisome days while Luc has been away, but we intend to celebrate our good fortune now that he is returning. Our son is safe and will soon be here with us, at home. I'm sure he would be happy to see you. Of course, you are welcome," Doris said.

"Thank you," Lois said. "I don't want to be an imposition, and I hope he will be as happy to see me as he will be to see all of you."

"I'm certain he will be, Lois. Although it may be unknown to you, in every letter he has sent us, he has not failed to mention your name," Doris said.

"Truly?" Lois asked.

"Yes, Lois. No matter how his training and the battlefield may have affected him, he has not forgotten you for a day," she said.

With that hope in her heart, Lois accompanied the Bouchers to Camp Debert on a warm weekend in mid-October. Doris had spoken to Luc by telephone the night before, and after the Boucher car was parked within the camp gates, the Bouchers followed one of the guards who accompanied them to a building not far away. The building had a large meeting room for family visits, a small yard with tables and chairs, and a walking path among a half-acre stand of shrubs and trees. The family didn't have to wait long before Luc arrived to join them.

Luc lacked the uniform he wore when they last saw him. Instead, he wore fatigues, making him look like he was somewhere between two worlds, neither a soldier nor a civilian. In spirit, though, he did his best to assure his family that he was healed and well. The few traces of scarring on his face were almost indiscernible, except for one bit just over his left eyebrow. When they asked to see the surgery scars on his right upper arm, though, his injuries proved more real. Tears appeared on several faces as he rolled up his sleeve.

"Not to worry, now," he said as he rotated his arm to show his full motion and strength. "I was on the firing range this morning and did quite respectably at 100 yards." Then, laughing, he added, "The geese at home will still have something to worry about from this soldier, even with this shoulder. Oh, and now I have these," he said as he took a pair of gold-rimmed eyeglasses from his pocket. "I only need them for reading and fine work, and if you promise not to laugh, I'll try them on for you."

There were a couple of giggles when he did, but Luc laughed with them before he retired the glasses to his pocket.

As his family shared the oatmeal and chocolate chip cookies Doris had packed, Luc and Lois took a few moments outside on the walking path, where they found a bench to sit and talk.

"I didn't expect to see you here today," Luc said, "but I'm glad you came."

"Why would you not expect to see me?" she asked.

"I'm not sure," he began. "It's just that so much has changed in me. I wasn't sure you would want to be here."

"I haven't seen any big change in you, Luc," she said, "and you've just shown us that you've healed well. Have I missed something? Is there something you haven't told us?"

It took a moment before Luc could speak. Then he said, "I spend time on the battlefield each night, and sometimes it comes to find me by day. Those times are hard, and I am alone with them, Lois. No one sees what I see. No one else can."

Lois said nothing but wrapped her arms around him and drew his face to her shoulder, where his tears melted into her sweater. When he raised his face, he saw her tears, too.

"Luc," she said, "you are right. No one else can see those things you see, but if you let me, I want to walk beside you when you see them."

Then, she noticed something hanging around Luc's neck on a fine, dark cord.

"What are you wearing around your neck?" she asked.

"Oh, this?" Luc asked as he reached behind his neck to pull the cord over his head. "It's the remains of the bullet they took out of my shoulder. It shattered the stock of my rifle before it hit me, so it doesn't look much like a bullet anymore, misshapen as it is. The doctor gave me some of the catgut they used to stitch me up so I could wear it."

Lois held the piece of gray metal in her hand, turning it over and over as an idea formed in her head.

"Why do you wear it?" she asked.

"I don't know," he said. "It's just a souvenir. Lots of the other guys were bringing pieces like this home."

"Would you let me wear it for you, Luc?" she asked.

Surprised, he said, "You want to wear this piece of lead?"

"If you'll let me," Lois answered.

"Sure," he said. "If you want it, it's all yours."

Two weeks later, Doris and Jacques returned to Camp Debert and brought Luc home. Luc wasn't ready for a homecoming celebration, though. He wasn't prepared to face a crowd of people or answer questions yet. Late that afternoon, though, Lois persuaded him to take a walk with her. Hand-in-hand, they started up the Highfield's north path to the fire tower. When they arrived and sat together on the bottom step, Luc noticed something hanging around Lois's neck.

"Lois," he asked, "around your neck, is that what I think it is?"

"Perhaps," she said. "What do you think it is?"

"It's the same shape as that battered bullet I gave you the last time we were together, but," he said, looking closer, "it's golden now."

"Yes," she said. "I asked Mrs. Moreland to direct me to the best jeweler in Charlottetown. She sent me to a lovely old family shop on Grafton Street. I was surprised to find that I had met the proprietor at one of my showings at *For Art's Sake*. The jeweler was happy to plate the bullet in gold and place it on this gold chain for the trade of two of my paintings."

"It's lovely, Lois, but why did you do it?" Luc asked.

"Because I don't believe it was an accident that this bullet hit your rifle before it hit you, Luc. I believe someone wants you to remember that your life was saved. Someone has plans for you, Luc Boucher. Your life was spared on the island of Crete. It's no longer your own," she said.

Luc sat speechless for a moment. Then he asked, "Could I see it, please?"

"Certainly," she said as she leaned forward.

"No," he said. "I mean, would you take it off so I can see it?"

She answered, "Why don't you take it off for me?"

"All right," he said, a bit puzzled.

Luc leaned forward to reach under her hair to find the clasp on the chain, but he couldn't find one. Another moment of searching told him that the chain had no clasp.

"Lois," he said, "there's no way to take it off. There's no clasp."

"That's right, Luc," she said. "The jeweler was kind enough to fulfill my request, and he fit the chain to my neck."

"But why?" he asked.

"Your life was spared in that battle, Luc, and this piece of metal brought you back to me. I intend to wear it for the rest of my days, and I want to spend those days with you. You may think the injuries that haunt you by night could prevent us from having a life together. But I believe we were meant for each other, and I will wear this necklace as long as I live or until you decide to take it away from me."

Luc's eyes, full of tears, overflowed, leaving him speechless. When he recovered, he said, "Please, Lois, wear it forever," as he leaned forward to kiss the bullet that spared his life, "and let me kiss it every day."

"Done," she said, "but we have other kisses to share, Luc Boucher, and I'll not be one to let a golden bullet get in the way."

And share they did, again and again and again, amidst laughter, tears, and with full hearts.

Chapter 43

When Joseph Boucher returned from Montreal for a semester break from his classes at the hospital, he was overjoyed to find Luc well and waiting to see him. They took Abe and Billie for a run around the pasture and up the north path, stopping at the stream north of the sawmill to let the horses drink.

"So," Joseph asked, "what are you going to do now? You're not one to sit still, but I don't see you going back to daily chores at Highfield, either. Any plans?"

"Not yet," Luc said. "I need to keep my hands busy, and I've been thinking about finding a carpenter who needs help. The trouble is, there isn't much work to be had, especially with the war on. Folks aren't spending money to build new homes or to make anything more than small repairs. I'd like to find a project to sink my teeth into, but I don't know where to find one."

"I've been away in Montreal most of the last few months, so I can't help much when it comes to building projects close by," Joseph said, "but I got a letter from the Morelands a while back, and I need to stop and see them about something that came from England. I'll go see them after we put the horses up, and while I'm there, I'll ask if Mr. Moreland knows of any building projects nearby."

"That sounds good, Joseph," Luc said, "I'll be waiting to hear what you find out."

With Abe and Billie curried and combed, Luc headed home while Joseph went to find Michael in the kitchen. Susan was there with him, and each of them was holding one of their boys.

"Joseph," Michael said when he heard the voice at the back door. "Come in and see how much Case and Reed have grown."

"They have now, haven't they," Joseph said as Michael placed Case into Joseph's waiting arms. "I see newborns in the hospital on occasion," he said, "but these fellows look like giants!" he laughed.

"They have giant appetites," Susan said, pointing to two empty bowls with baby spoons on the table. "They've just had their second breakfast of the day."

"They like to sleep after they've eaten," Michael said, turning to Susan, "so why don't we put them down upstairs so you and Joseph can talk."

"Perfect," Susan said. "I'll meet you in the library, Joseph, as soon as the boys are settled."

As Joseph walked to the library, he tried to imagine what kind of news from England the Moreland's could have for him. Surely, the orphanage didn't need to contact him. When Susan arrived with a small stack of papers, he began to be concerned.

Susan saw the worry on his face and said, "Joseph, you have nothing to worry about." As she sat opposite him, she said, "The news I have for you, I'm sorry to say, concerns some family members who are recently deceased."

"Family members?" Joseph asked. "But I have no family."

"That's what everyone in Suffolk thought, too. Recently, however, we have learned of an uncle and a grandfather from London who perished in the bombings there," Susan said.

"I had an uncle and a grandfather all these years, and no one knew of them? How could that be?" he asked.

"It appears your grandfather, your father's father, did not approve of his son's marriage to your mother," Susan said. "He ceased contact with your father, and a short time later, your father died fighting a fire in Ipswich. Sadly, he had never informed your grandfather of your birth. Your uncle never knew of you either."

Stunned, Joseph sat back in his chair and asked quietly, "So, why are we learning of this now?"

"Because at the death of your grandfather and uncle, their solicitor was required to search for any living kin qualified to inherit their estates. When they inquired at the orphanage, they learned of you and learned you had come to Highfield. Subsequently, they contacted me as your guardian," Susan said.

"Estates?" Joseph said. "I am the heir to their estates? What does that mean, Mrs. Moreland."

"It means that you may be a very wealthy man, Joseph, but there is one vital condition. To prove your identity, the solicitor requires a document that we hope is in your possession. You will be disqualified from any inheritance without it," she said.

"What document?" he asked.

"A baptismal certificate. They believe it may be hidden behind the inner cover of a prayer book. I understand you have such a prayer book, do you not?" Susan asked.

"Yes," Joseph said, "I have. It's the prayer book my mother left me, the only possession I have that was hers. I brought it home with me from Montreal. Shall I go home and bring it back here now?"

"Right away, if you will, Joseph. Right away, please," she said.

While Joseph ran home, Susan checked on Case and Reed and found them sleeping soundly. Then she called Michael in from the paddock.

"Joseph will be back with his prayer book at any moment," she said. "I hope there's a certificate to be found."

"I hear him coming in now," Michael said. "We'll know soon."

Joseph was breathless when he entered the library, but he smiled when he found Susan and Michael waiting there.

"Here it is," he said as he handed the prayer book to Michael, but I don't see anywhere to hide a certificate."

Michael examined the prayer book carefully. It was a fine leather-bound volume with brass corners and a brass clasp. It bore a copyright date of 1908.

"Everything I see tells me that this book is correct for the period in question," Michael said, "but let's look closer."

Michael found nothing unusual as he examined the front cover and its leather binding. Upon inspecting the back cover, though, something interesting caught his eye.

"Look at this, Joseph," he said, "where the leather folds over and meets the inside cover beneath. Do you see the remnants of a yellow-brown stain?"

"Yes," Joseph said, "here, here, and here," he said as he pointed.

"I believe those are remnants of glue, hide glue, if I'm not mistaken. It's a common glue that every household has kept handy for generations. A little steam will prove helpful in loosening it," Michael said. "We may find the key to a fortune when we loosen the inner cover. Let's take it to the kitchen and put on a kettle."

When the kettle came to boiling, Michael held the prayer book carefully in a towel, directing the steam from the teakettle's spout to the intersection of the rear page and the inside cover. In a moment, the hide glue began to lose its hold on the page, and it started to lift. Michael took the penknife from his pocket and gently persuaded the rear page away from the cover as the steam continued to do its trick. A moment later, he carefully extracted a delicate sheet of fine vellum, the certificate Joseph sought.

"Congratulations, Joseph," Michael said. "I believe we've found everything the London solicitor requires for you to claim your inheritance."

Still gazing at the certificate, Joseph asked, "And what is included in the inheritance?"

"A great deal," Susan answered, reading from one of the several papers in her hands. "A twelve-room home in Ardingly, a small parcel of land on the Isle of Wight, an automobile, a sum of cash and securities, with an estimated total value of over 15,000 pounds."

"Fifteen thousand pounds?" Joseph asked.

"About $60,000 in Canadian funds," Michael said.

"And in two banks, there are safety deposit boxes whose contents are yet to be revealed," Susan added.

"Then am I a wealthy man?" Joseph asked.

"There are many costs associated with settling the estate, Joseph," Michael said, "but, in the end, you will be a relatively wealthy man."

"However," Susan said, "until you reach your twenty-first birthday, it falls to me, as your guardian, to manage your estate. There will be many details to which we must attend, but, in the end, you will enjoy a sizeable fortune."

Ecstatic, Joseph leapt to his feet to embrace Michael and Susan, saying, "Thank you, thank you, thank you! I must tell Ingrid, I must. Thank you!" he said again as he turned toward the door. However, once outside the library, he returned to ask, "Mr. Moreland, could I speak with you for just a few more minutes?"

"Of course," Michael said. "Follow me out to the garage."

Chapter 44

When the Abrams children arrived at Highfield, they brought little but the clothes on their backs. Once they were settled in their cottage, Michael, with Patrice's help, found everything Jacob and Naomi would need for the fall and winter seasons at St. Onge's. Now that Daniel and Deborah had arrived in an even more needy state, Michael stood ready to make a second trip to help outfit them with clothes for the winter. However, Susan had another idea and invited Deborah to her dressing room before Michael could drive Daniel and her to Charlottetown.

"Deborah," Susan said, "I don't know about you, but I find it nearly impossible to shop for clothes without another woman with me. I always need a second pair of eyes to help me see everything I can't see in a mirror."

"I understand completely," Deborah answered. "I've always brought a friend with a good eye to advise me."

"Sadly, I need to be home with our boys. They've come down with the sniffles," Susan said. "I don't believe anything is really concerning, but I don't feel I should leave them right now."

"I understand," Deborah nodded.

"However, I have another idea," Susan said as she opened all six closet doors. "Until we can shop together, some things here might suit your fancy. I think I was very close to your size before these two came along," she said to Deborah with a laugh, putting her hands on her hips before pointing to her sons in their playpen. "Please remember, Deborah," Susan said with a wink, "anything you find here is a boon to me because then I'll have to fill its space with something new. If you see anything you like, it's yours."

Deborah had never seen such fine ladies' clothing, and all in up-to-date styles. Even better, Susan was right; everything Deborah tried on fit her well, except Susan's shoes.

"I'm afraid my feet are somewhat larger than yours, Susan," Deborah said as she put the third pair she tried back in its box.

"Well, that's no matter," Susan said. "I think you and I will be able to shop for shoes and for what the men call 'unmentionables' sometime tomorrow afternoon. I'll be able to leave the boys with Michael by then. We have some fine stores in Charlottetown with wonderful selections of everything you'll need."

Susan also had a trunk large enough to hold everything Deborah had chosen, with room to spare for whatever she might find the next day.

"You and your husband have been so kind and generous with us," Deborah said, "and we, especially Daniel, are not used to receiving such charity. We would like to repay you in a small way if you will receive our gifts," she said.

"Receive your gifts?" Susan asked.

"Yes," Deborah answered. "Daniel is a skilled portrait artist, and I primarily paint landscapes and architectural subjects. We both work in oils, and if you would allow us, we would like to offer you what we have: our talents. Would you accept our gifts while we enjoy your hospitality at your home?"

Susan, overwhelmed, said, "Deborah, we could never refuse such generosity. What we can provide for you will last only briefly, but the artwork you offer will grace our home for many years. Thank you for giving so much of yourselves to us."

"It will be our pleasure," Deborah said. "When our men return, perhaps we can settle on subjects for the paintings."

Daniel and Michael were having a similar conversation while a tailor at St. Onge's was fitting Daniel for a new suit.

"I am overwhelmed at your offer, Daniel," Michael said. "Sir Richard has admired both your work and Deborah's in exhibitions at the Royal College during his years while serving in London. To have your paintings here on Prince Edward Island would be a stunning addition to our home. Thank you, Daniel. We will be delighted to receive the gifts you offer."

"Then let us settle on our subjects soon," Daniel said. "I have written to my uncle, Adolf Abrams, in the United States. He has invited us to stay with his family in Connecticut for the duration of the war. One of his sons, my cousin Herbert, is a budding artist, and his father would like us to offer him the benefits of our expertise. We hope to travel there as soon as they are ready to receive us."

“How wonderful for you, Daniel, to have families on both sides of the Atlantic,” Michael said. Please allow us to help you with your travel itinerary when the time comes. Meanwhile, I will speak with Sir Richard, Lady Moncrieff, and Susan, and we will do our best to choose two subjects for you right away.”

Not surprisingly, Sir Richard and Lady Moncrieff initially favored a family portrait of Susan, Michael, and their sons. In the end, though, they chose a portrait of Lady Moncrieff by a vote of three to one. Daniel promised to limit the time she would have to sit for him by starting his work from a photograph. Lady Moncrieff was overjoyed with the news. “I'm simply not one to sit still that long,” she said. For Deborah's painting, they chose Highfield. A late fall morning, when the trees were yet full of color, was a perfect season for Deborah to capture the house in all of autumn's charm. After a trip to the art supply store in Charlottetown, Daniel and Deborah were equipped to begin their work.

Three days later, as Deborah worked at her easel on Highfield's front lawn, Joseph and Michael stopped to compliment her work. They were just leaving Highfield to look at two much smaller houses not far away on Suffolk Road.

“Luc's waiting for us to pick him up at home,” Joseph said. “Ingrid and Lois are baking today, and wherever Lois is, Luc is usually close by,” Joseph said.

“Well, I've noticed that you've been bit by the same bug when it comes to Ingrid, haven't I?” Michael asked.

“Yes, you have, Mr. Moreland,” he said. “That's why I'm hoping Luc will listen to my idea and partner with me to get the job done.”

“We'll know soon enough,” Michael said as they stopped in the Boucher driveway. “Here he comes.”

Once in the car's back seat, Luc asked, “So, what do you want me to see?”

“It's an opportunity for both of us,” Joseph said. “Something that will take a year or more to complete.”

Confused, Luc asked, “For both of us? But how will that work? You'll be in Montreal, and I'll be here.”

“It'll be clear when we get there,” Joseph said. “You'll see.”

“So, where are we going?” Luc asked.

“Not far,” Michael answered. “A short ride to a place we've passed a thousand times.”

They drove only a half mile down Suffolk Road toward Charlottetown when Michael stopped the car in front of a substantial two-story house known to all as the old Mitchell Farm. Luc squinted to read the small print on the 'For Sale' sign on the front of the house. It was a two-story garrison colonial with a center door flanked by two first-floor windows on the left and right. There were five windows across the second floor. Luc could see part of a first-floor roof at the back of the house, which, he guessed, was probably a kitchen ell.

As the three got out of the car, Michael explained.

"Joseph came to me last week to ask if I knew of any local carpentry work available for a man like you, Luc. I hadn't seen anything in my travels until this sign was posted on the property the other day. I met with the agent in town, asked a few questions, and got a few answers. I asked Joseph to pass the news on to you."

"He hasn't told me anything yet," Luc said. "He said you'd be able to explain it better."

"Well, he's probably right," Michael said, "so here it is. That 'For Sale' sign on the front of the house is a sign of the times. The Mitchells are wealthy folks who live near Halifax. They inherited this place years ago and had great plans to bring it up-to-date as a vacation home. Like Highfield's first owner, though, economic problems kept them from realizing their dreams. One of their sons started to build his own house on the property, but he never finished it. That's the house we passed about four hundred yards back up the road. Their real estate agent described it as a 'Tudor-style cottage.' It's more modern than this old farmhouse. That one looks good on the outside but has never been finished on the inside. The builders got the house tight to the weather, but it's just a shell. Neither the utilities nor the interior have been finished. Now, this old farmhouse is solid, but it needs a lot of repair, and all the utilities need updating. The Mitchells know it's time for them to sell the property, and over the last year, they've lowered the price several times. Still, though, they've had no interested buyers. In my mind, the land alone is worth the asking price."

"All right," Luc said, "but I still don't see what that has to do with Joseph and me."

"Joseph will have to tell you about that part," Michael said as he stepped back.

Luc turned to Joseph, who began, "Luc, by a miracle, I've come into some money. It turns out that I had an uncle and a grandfather in London whom I never knew. They were killed in the bombings recently, and I am their only heir."

Joseph paused as Luc nodded and said, "I'm sorry to hear about your family, Joseph. At the same time, an inheritance means congratulations are in order, too. But, still, tell me, what does that have to do with me?"

"It's just this, Luc," Joseph began. "I need your help. I've got another year at school in Montreal and six months of in-service training in the hospital after that. When that's finished, I want to marry Ingrid. I want to provide a home for her, and there are two on this property. They both need work, a lot of work. Michael looked at them, and he estimated that the total labor cost and the materials needed to finish both houses would equal the purchase price of the entire property."

"I still don't understand," Luc said. "Why do you need my help?"

"Because without much building going on, carpenters all over this island have turned to fishing and farming to make their livings. They take on only small repairs to fill in their schedules. Others have gone to war. There's no one left to take on a project like this. But I know you could do it, Luc, and in the end, we'd both have a house to raise a family in," Joseph said.

"What do you mean, 'we'd both have a house,'" Luc asked.

"Like I said, Luc," Joseph answered, "the total labor and materials costs equal the property's purchase price. So, here's my idea. I'll buy the property and supply the materials. If you'll take on the work to finish the houses, you can take your pick—the cottage or the farmhouse. In the end, we'll split the property in half."

"But the sign says there are seventy acres here," Luc said.

"That's right," Joseph said. We'll each have thirty-five acres; you'll have one house, and I'll take the other. I'll marry Ingrid, and you'll marry Lois, and we'll each have an almost new home, all paid for when we're done. And, best of all, we'll live right down the road from all the people we know and love."

Luc stood silent, unable to believe what he was hearing. He looked up when Michael began to speak.

"I've been through both houses, Luc," Michael said. "Their bones are good, their foundations are solid, and the water in both wells is fresh and sweet. Those seventy acres have some open fields but are well forested with hardwood and softwood on high ground. And just for your thoughts, the woodworking shop at Highfield will be available, and since we're past the harvesting season, we've got a flatbed that sits still most of the time. When you need it, it will be yours to use."

Luc looked at the farmhouse before stepping back and straining his eyes to take in the cottage. He looked down at the ground a moment before looking back at Joseph.

"I've got one problem you don't have, Joseph," he said.

"What's that?" Joseph asked.

"You said you've got another year of school in Montreal and then another six months at the hospital before you marry my sister and I marry Lois," Luc said.

"That's right," Joseph replied.

"Well, I don't want to wait that long to marry Lois," Luc said. "So, I may just have to work day and night to finish the job ahead of schedule. If you can put up with that," he said, "here's my hand with Mr. Moreland as our witness."

With that, Joseph smiled broadly and said, "Done!" He shook Luc's outstretched hand, and the two brothers shared a hearty embrace while Michael smiled and looked on.

Chapter 45

Susan could tell there was something wrong. Patrice, usually a sparkle of life and energy wherever she appeared, had become quiet and pensive over the last several weeks. Though always dutiful and efficient in her work at Highfield, especially when attending Lady Moncrieff, she simply wasn't herself. Susan wanted to find out why. On a Friday afternoon in late November, she invited Patrice to share afternoon tea with her in the west sunroom.

When Patrice appeared with the tea tray, Susan could see she was putting her best foot forward. She'd abandoned her daily work garb for a red plaid kilt, a crisply ironed blouse, and an ivory cardigan sweater. She smiled appropriately, but Susan still didn't see the spirited Patrice she missed.

"With so much happening here with the Abrams family and Luc and Joseph coming home, I realized we haven't had time to talk for weeks, Patrice. You've seemed quiet lately. Tell me, how are you doing?" Susan asked.

"I don't know," Patrice said as she stirred her tea. "I should be happy that Luc and Joseph are safe and at home, but I'm having trouble losing them and being left behind, too."

"Losing them and being left behind?" Susan asked. "I'm not following you, Patrice. Tell me what you mean."

"Well," Patrice began, "Luc and Lois only have eyes for each other, and Ingrid and Joseph are a constant couple. You never see one without the other. Lois, Ingrid, and I used to talk together all the time, but now they're always busy talking to each other about Luc and Joseph. I hear about the houses they'll move into once they're married. They leave me out of everything. It's like I've become a little kid to them, leftover and left behind while they go on with their lives."

"Is there anything else bothering you?" Susan asked.

"Yes," she answered, "I miss Aunt Michelle. It was so much fun when you and she had make-up parties and sleepovers with us. But more than that, she listened to what I had to say, like you do. Do you think she'll ever come back from England?"

"I don't think they'll travel anywhere while the war is still on," Susan said, "and after that, I really don't know."

"It probably doesn't matter anyway because by then, I'll be just an old maid aunt, babysitting Luc and Ingrid's babies," she said.

"Now, what do you mean by that?" Susan asked. "Aren't you getting way ahead of yourself, Patrice? Yes, two young couples seem to be headed for marriage, but Luc is still recovering from his injuries, and Joseph has to complete more than a year's training at the hospital in Montreal. Michael told me those two houses you mentioned will require a year or more of work. Their weddings may be a long way down the road."

"But, I'll still be left behind, Miss Susan," Patrice said. "Luc found Lois, and Ingrid found Joseph, but all the boys my age on Prince Edward Island are lining up to go to war. I don't even know anyone I can imagine marrying. There's no one left in sight for me," she said, "is there?"

"Maybe not yet," Susan answered, "but remember, Joseph and Lois arrived from England. Neither of them had any prospects for wives or husbands there. They found them here, three thousand miles away. Lois was about your age when she arrived. We have more guest children coming soon, you know. Who can say if a young man about your age might be among them?"

"Do you think so?" Patrice asked, her eyes widening.

"I can check the most recent correspondence on my desk and let you know in just a minute. Wait right here," Susan said as she stood and turned toward the stairs.

Patrice freshened her tea and was halfway through the second of her mother's lemon sugar cookies when Susan returned with an envelope in hand.

"So, let's see," she said as she opened the envelope. Turning to the last page, she said, "Ah, here it is," and continued to read on.

Sitting on the edge of her seat, Patrice could hardly contain herself.

"Is there anything there?" she asked.

"Yes," Susan answered. "Here it is. Come sit beside me so you can see for yourself."

Patrice was close beside her when Susan pointed and said, "We have a brother and sister from Highgate, a suburb of London. Their names are Ainsley and Fletcher Ross. Ainsley is twelve, and Fletcher is sixteen.

"Fletcher is sixteen?" Patrice asked. "Does it say anything more about him?"

Only that he is five feet eleven inches tall, has light hair and blue eyes," Susan said.

"Light hair and blue eyes—like me," Patrice confirmed.

Susan nodded and continued, "Then there are two brothers, Chad and Addison Miller," Chad is seventeen, and Addison is fourteen. Their home is on the Isle of Wight."

"And about Chad?" she asked. "What else does it say?"

"That he, too, is five feet eleven inches tall and has dark hair and brown eyes," Susan answered.

"Did you say 'The Isle of Wight?'" Patrice asked. "Isn't that where Joseph inherited some property?" Patrice asked.

"That's correct," Susan said, "but more to your concern about young men, Patrice, two who will be arriving soon, Fletcher and Chad, are very close to your age."

"Yes," Patrice said, smiling, "they are."

"Then, perhaps you could give up those faraway future worries concerning available young men?"

"Perhaps," Patrice said, the twinkle returning to her eye. "But, tell me please, Miss Susan. Fletcher is Miss Michelle's son's middle name, isn't it?"

"Yes," Susan answered. "Fletcher is Grayson's mother's maiden name. A fletcher is a man who makes arrows, you know. So, long ago, Grayson's ancestors were probably known for their skills at making arrows."

"Perhaps they helped Robin Hood," Patrice said with wide eyes. "They could have, couldn't they?"

"Perhaps," Susan smiled. "Robin Hood is a wonderful story, but I need your help organizing a ladies' event this weekend that concerns an equally fantastic story.

Sitting forward, Patrice asked, "A ladies' event? What kind of an event."

"The Capitol Theatre is showing a heart-warming new American film full of fantasy. It's an animated feature about a flying elephant named 'Dumbo,'" Susan said.

"A flying elephant?" Patrice laughed.

"Yes," Susan said, "and ever since it came out in October in New York City, people have been standing in line at theatres to see it. The same man who created Mickey Mouse also produced this film. Michael is willing to purchase our tickets early for the matinee at the Capitol on Saturday, so we won't have to stand in line. Do you think you could persuade Ingrid and Lois to join us?"

Patrice raised her hands as if they were claws and laughed, "I'll do it even if I have to peel them away from Joseph and Luc with my bare hands!"

Susan couldn't contain her smile. Patrice was back.

Chapter 46

It was the thirteenth of November at 3:30 AM when Lt Nigel Moncrieff, unable to sleep aboard the HMS *Ark Royal* sailing north off the coast of Gibraltar, walked among the dozen Fairey Swordfish bound to the flight deck. None were armed with bombs or torpedoes, yet unsure of what the next day might bring them. Since mid-summer, the *Ark Royal* had sailed these waters on convoy duty again and again while ferrying aircraft to Malta in the Mediterranean. A well-supplied Allied force on the island of Malta was vital to foiling Rommel's Afrika Corps as Germany prepared to invade Egypt. Morale had remained high among the pilots and crew of the Fleet Air Arm aboard the *Ark Royal* since the sinking of the *Bismarck*. However, it began to fade when faced with the Royal Navy's opposition in the Mediterranean. On sleepless nights, Nigel's sorties to inspect the aircraft on the flight deck were one way he sought to maintain his focus on the tasks he faced each day.

The explosion came without warning. Thrown into the air and then to the flight deck of the *Ark Royal* on his face in an instant, Nigel lay unconscious. Blood streamed from his right temple where one of the Swordfish that had been loosed from its bindings and thrown into the air had struck him as he fell to the deck. As gravity reclaimed the aircraft and set it back on the flight deck, Nigel lay helpless beneath. There, he began to regain consciousness with his face on the wet deck and salt spray dripping on him from the bi-plane wings above. Strangely, first amidst his thoughts was a girl he had met in Malta. He knew her only as Annette, a French girl who had brought him a glass of red wine at a street café near Grand Harbor. His next thoughts were of his mother's last letter when she had written, "Your father came home to me from Jutland. I'll expect no less of you, my Nigel." Next, he saw Susan's face and the tears on her cheeks when he left home for active service years and years ago. When he could finally raise himself fully conscious to all fours, he surveyed the state of the aircraft before him. He was amazed to find that all but one of the Swordfish had burst its bindings, and several lay entangled with another, bi-plane wings forced among other bi-plane wings. Even in the worst of storms at sea, Nigel had never felt the ship shake so violently that aircraft on the flight deck were thrown into the air and loosed from their bindings. He was also conscious that everything about him lacked sound, as if he was in a dream. Still deafened by the explosion, he stood to make his way toward the bridge.

What Nigel didn't know was that the *Ark Royal* had been hit amidships by a U-boat's torpedo. Below the waterline and centered on the carrier's bridge was a hole in the hull that was more than thirty feet wide and one hundred thirty feet long. By the greatest of fortune, the torpedo had missed the fuel bunkers on one side and the compartments where tons of bombs were stored on the other. However, one of the boiler rooms flooded immediately, communication systems on the ship had been disabled, and all electrical power to the ship's rear half had been lost. Below decks, the crew struggled in utter darkness.

No practice drills could have trained the men aboard the *Ark Royal* to cope with such widespread damage caused in a single moment. Because the explosion had severed communication lines to the engine room, the captain's orders to stop the ship's engines went nowhere. As the *Ark Royal* continued on course, sea waters forced through her gaping wound began to tear her apart. Nothing could save her now.

When Nigel reached the bridge, he was amazed to discover that every pilot in his squadron was uninjured and waiting on the flight deck. Officers were shouting over the noise of the sea, the wind, and the confusion to organize the crew. Eventually, the captain sent damage control crews below decks to re-establish power and communications, but to no avail. With virtually the entire crew on deck and the ship listing severely, there was no opportunity for Nigel and the other pilots to put the Swordfish into the air. Meanwhile, other Swordfish from Gibraltar began circling overhead, ready to defend the *Ark Royal* from further attack.

When the *Ark Royal*'s list to starboard became severe, the HMS *Legion*, a destroyer sailing with the *Ark Royal* in convoy, came alongside, and the crew was ordered to evacuate. By 4:30 PM, all were aboard. Then, the captain and crew learned that of all the men aboard the *Ark Royal*, only one had perished in the attack. Although there were many men injured and in shock, 1,487 had survived. Within hours, all aboard the *Legion* landed at Gibraltar, some silent, some full of bravado, some in grief, but none who would ever be the same.

Confident that his father would soon learn of the miracle of the lives preserved aboard the *Ark Royal*, Nigel felt assured that news of the sinking would not shock his family. Still, a strange mixture of emotions remained for him and every man aboard who had lost nearly all his possessions—only the clothes on their backs remained. Everything else was at the bottom of the sea. Among Nigel's comrades, a strange silence commenced, broken only by moments when one or another tried too hard to make sense of something that remained a sad miracle. Certainly, all the men enjoyed being alive. Still, some felt guilty for the one who perished, others grieved for the loss of trinkets, while all remained incensed at the Nazis and the damnable German U-boats that continuously threatened their lives.

Lacking leave on Malta the following day, Nigel and the comrades in his squadron found an hour of comfort at the Officers' Mess. Though constantly vulnerable to incessant Luftwaffe attacks, the men celebrated life, toasted their comrade who had made the ultimate sacrifice, and swore, once more, their undying oath to defeat Britain's enemies. Nigel, their leader, raised his glass to say, "To Able Seaman Edward Mitchell. May his family remember him with pride for his sacrifice, and may we, his brothers, ever proclaim his honor."

Nigel's toast was answered with a rowdy "Hurrah" as his brothers emptied their glasses.

Chapter 47

Nurse Mary Clark had seen her share of deliveries in the maternity ward in Montreal and several more while in the bush in Cuba, so a routine delivery of a healthy full-term expectant mother at Charlottetown Hospital did not worry her. Her patient had received the best prenatal care possible, enjoyed good health, and, though a little older than most mothers bearing their first child, offered no reason for concern. No, Nurse Clark was not concerned about the expectant mother, but she could do little to keep the expectant father from worrying. Worse still, the father was the Chief of Staff at the hospital.

When Emily arrived at the hospital in labor, her water had not yet broken. However, within twenty minutes of her arrival, it had. Nurse Clark determined that Emily was dilated to eight centimeters, indicating that her baby was well on the way. The nurse went to the waiting room to bring Dr. MacMillan the news.

She found the doctor pacing back and forth in front of the coffee urn, a cup of hot coffee in each hand. He was sweating profusely and mumbling, "She'll be fine, our baby will be fine, there's no need to worry." The doctor repeated this statement each time he crossed the room, again and again. Thankfully, there were no other expectant fathers waiting. Nurse Clark hesitated to interrupt his routine but eventually spoke calmly, "Dr. MacMillan, I have an update for you, sir." She was surprised to find that he hadn't heard her. Neither his pace nor his repeated assertion had changed. She tried again before stepping in front of him and interrupting his pacing. She took one cup of coffee out of his hand before speaking again. His statement ended mid-sentence this time, and he handed Nurse Clark the other cup of coffee.

"I'm sorry, Nurse Clark," he said. "I'm afraid I am a bit nervous. Have you anything to report?"

"Yes, Dr. MacMillan," Nurse Clark began. "The patient's heart rate is elevated but within a normal range during delivery. Respirations are at an expected rate as well. Temperature and blood pressure are fine. We have an eight-centimeter cervical dilation, indicating that the baby is well on its way. Dr. Murray is attending Mrs. MacMillan as we speak. "

"Then she'll be fine, our baby will be fine, there's no need to worry?" he asked.

Recognizing the phrase he used to comfort himself, Nurse Clark said, "That's what we expect, Doctor. I'll be back with a further report soon."

A few minutes later, Nurse Clark returned to say, "The baby is crowning as we speak, Doctor. Mrs. MacMillan is doing well. It should only be another few minutes."

Andrew could only nod as Nurse Clark passed through the double doors on her way to the delivery room. He followed her and pressed his ear to the crack between the doors. A few short moments later, he heard a newborn's first cry, and a relieved smile erased the worry on his face. With his ear still poised at the crack between the doors, he retrieved his handkerchief from his back pocket and mopped his brow. At the same moment, Nurse Clark, happily rushing toward the waiting room, pushed the doors open to bring him the news.

The ensuing thud shocked both doctor and nurse but thankfully resulted more in embarrassment than injury. Andrew eventually arrived at Emily's bedside, where she lay exhausted but smiling. Their daughter, Heloise, was in her arms. As Andrew bent to kiss Emily's cheek, she saw the ice pack he was holding to his ear.

"Here is our daughter, Andrew," she said, "all eight pounds, eight ounces of her. Nurse Clark told me of the collision her news brought you. I wasn't expecting two of us to become patients here today."

"My injuries aren't serious, Darling," he smiled, "more bruised pride than anything else. Look," he said, his eyes on Heloise. "She has your hair. I hope she'll have your blue eyes as well."

"We won't know for a few days," Emily said as Andrew dared to place the softest of kisses on his daughter's brow.

"You'll rest now, won't you?" he asked, offering more of a recommendation than asking a question.

"I'm sure I will, Andrew, but not until you take the photos you promised. We'll need to send copies to your mother and sister and Michelle and Grayson as soon as they are developed," she said.

"Oh, my, I left the camera in my bag in the waiting room," he said. "Of course, I'll retrieve it right away."

While he walked to the waiting room, Nurse Clark returned to report that she had made a telephone call to Highfield as Emily had requested.

"I delivered your message to Mrs. Moreland, Mrs. MacMillan. I can report that she was more than delighted to hear your good news," the nurse said.

"Thank you, Nurse Clark," Emily said. "When Dr. MacMillan returns, could we impose on you to take some photos of our new family with his camera? We have friends waiting to see some evidence of our good fortune."

"It would be my pleasure, ma'am," the nurse replied, "he's arriving as we speak."

With the photo shoot complete, Andrew drove downtown to the Rexall drugstore with two rolls of film. In a week's time, the MacMillans would be able to post a cache of photos to their family and friends.

Chapter 48

Luc and Lois faced each other as they sat on the bottom step of the center staircase in the Mitchell farmhouse. They had spent an hour at the Tudor cottage earlier, but there was nothing to see inside but partition walls of bare studs. It was hard for Lois to imagine how the house would feel when finished. It was a large enough house with eight rooms, but Luc and Lois felt more comfortable in the farmhouse. With ten rooms and higher ceilings, it felt more like home to Lois, who was used to the tall ceilings she knew in her London home.

"Notice the staircase, Luc," she said. "At your parents' home, one often feels the need to duck a bit when approaching the bottom step, but here, one can maintain full height without fear of hitting one's head."

"What else do you see?" Luc asked.

"I see an opportunity for some lovely crown mouldings to define the intersection of the walls and ceilings, the same mouldings you find at Highfield. And perhaps we could add some wainscot paneling, waist high in the dining room," she said as she placed her hand on her hip at waist height and pointed through the adjacent room toward the kitchen. "And having the kitchen in its own ell is so sensible," she added. "It will keep the rest of the house cooler on hot summer days."

Luc marveled that Lois had an eye for things he'd never heard a woman notice before, things that could turn an old farmhouse into a home. She took his hand and, giggling, led him up the stairs.

"This bedroom at the back of the house will be a grand studio for my artwork, Luc. See," she said as she pulled him into the room, "the north light is just perfect."

"And where will we sleep?" Luc asked.

"Oh," she said as she led him down the hall to the front of the house, "definitely here, in the south-east bedroom. The east sun will greet us with its morning light, and the south sun will warm the room all day. By late afternoon the sun will be setting in the west," she said, pointing past the stairway to the opposite bedroom, "so our room will darken early enough for us to get a good night's sleep."

Although Luc smiled as he admired her enthusiasm and wisdom, he stiffened at the words 'good night's sleep.'

He stood silently, holding Lois's hand for a long moment. Lois brought him back with a soft, "Luc?"

As he recovered and returned to the present, he brightened and said, "So it seems we've made our choice then? It's the farmhouse and not the cottage we want to make our own?"

"Where did you go, Luc?" Lois asked.

"Go?" Luc answered, looking at her. "Nowhere. Just thinking."

"About what?" she asked.

"Nothing really," he answered, "just what you said."

"What?" she asked.

"A good night's sleep," he answered.

"What about a good night's sleep?" she asked.

Luc hesitated again before responding. Then, as he turned to look out the cobwebbed window, he said, "I still don't like to sleep. I try to stay awake, but I always fall asleep eventually, and that's when they come."

"When what comes?" she asked.

"The dreams," he said as he looked at the floor.

"Can you tell me about them?" she asked.

"They're not good, Lois. Not good. You don't want to know," he said.

"But I do, Luc," she insisted, standing to face him and taking his hands in hers. "They steal your peace, and when they steal yours, they steal mine. Please tell me, even just a little. Please?" she begged.

After another long moment, Luc hung his head as if speaking to the floor and said, "I see his face."

"The man who tried to kill you?" she asked.

"No, the man I shot," he said.

"But that's the man who shot at *you*, Luc, isn't it?"

"Yes," he said, "but when I see him, his face, his face," he repeated, "is shattered, all blood and flesh and screaming . . . "

"At the field hospital, Luc?" she asked.

"It wasn't a hospital, really," he said. "They called it a hospital, but it was just some tents with a few stretchers."

Luc was silent again for a long moment before saying, "Two days, two days after I shot him, I went to find him. I couldn't see well, but when I looked, his bandages were open, and I could see the wounds to his eyes, and I knew he would never be able to look back. I watched them wrap his face in bandages again. I couldn't see his face anymore, but still, I wake up to it, night after night."

When Luc was silent again, Lois waited before saying, "May I ask you a question, Luc?"

As if from far away, he heard her, and in a small voice, he answered, "Yes."

"Short of letting him kill more of your comrades that day on the island of Crete, what could you have done differently when you saw his scope in yours?" she asked.

Luc said nothing.

"You both fired your rifles," Lois said. "Your bullet stopped him from killing anyone else that day. He lived, but he lost his sight. Don't let that moment take yours, too."

"Take my sight?" Luc asked.

"Yes," Lois answered. "Hold on to it to *see* that your life and your sight were spared, Luc. They were spared for a reason. Every day, you need to rehearse that. You owe no debt to any man, but you do owe your life to another who wants you to live it and live it fully. You have life to live and good to do, Luc Boucher. Hold tight to the vision that will let you answer the call to do it."

Luc stood for a moment longer before Lois saw him begin to tremble and then sob. They sat together on the top step, and with her arms wrapped around him, she held him until his shivers subsided and his tears no longer fell. Her simple words had touched a deep root within, a place that told him he was unworthy. When he raised his head again, he wiped away his tears, took her hands, and looked into her eyes.

"I love you, Lois Wilshire," he said.

As her embrace met his, they sat together for a long moment. Their hearts met anew, found harmony, and began to beat as one.

Suddenly, they heard a knock at the door, and Ingrid's voice called, "Lois? Luc? Anybody home?"

When Lois looked at Luc, he saw her gentle nod and the question in her eyes. When Luc nodded back, she called over her shoulder, "Coming. We're upstairs, coming down now."

They found Ingrid and Joseph waiting at the bottom of the stairs. Both looked happy and excited as Ingrid took Joseph's hand to say, "I hope you two love this farmhouse because we adore the cottage. Everything about it feels right to me, even though we have no walls inside," she laughed. "Joseph told me he thought you two favored this house, and I hope you still do."

Luc looked at Lois and nodded, and she turned to Ingrid and Joseph to say, "We do, Ingrid. Even with all the work it needs to make it our home, this old farmhouse will be perfect when Luc is finished. I've made him promise to leave some details to me, but I know we will make this house ours. I'm so happy that we can agree so wholeheartedly."

"I don't know if you've seen it yet, Luc," Joseph said, "but about a hundred yards past the first stand of locust trees behind us, there's a little spring-fed pond." As Luc shook his head, Joseph said, "Then come with me to see it. We discovered an overgrown path to it from the cottage. I'll wager there's one behind your house, too."

While Lois began to share her ideas for the farmhouse with Ingrid, the men found their way to the pond. Joseph was right; a path was waiting for them. As they pushed the occasional branch out of their way while walking, Luc found the right time to speak.

"Joseph, you've been too generous with us. My family has been happy to live in our little house on three acres all my life. Mom was still paying a mortgage when the old house burned. To own a ten-room house on thirty-five acres free and clear after one year's work feels like theft. Lois is delighted, but I can't help feeling guilty."

"I don't see it that way, Luc," Joseph began. "Please remember, I came here with nothing but a suitcase, a change of clothes, and a prayer book. Highfield welcomed me, but then your family took me in. They gave me their name, Luc, your name. They shared everything they had with me. How can I not give back? When we became brothers, Luc, everything I have became yours, too. And just so you know, our mom and Jacques are not making mortgage payments anymore," he said with a smile. "Everything I have is theirs, too."

"But, don't you want to see the house you own in London and what's yours on the Isle of Wight?" Luc asked.

Shaking his head, Joseph said, "No, Luc, I don't. I've never been to London. It was never my home, and the Isle of Wight is a stranger to me, too. No, my home is here. It always will be. And now that your family is giving me a prize beyond price, Ingrid," he said, "how could I be happy anywhere else? No. Luc, if you're still willing, we'll be neighbors right here for the rest of our days."

"Then I will thank you again, Joseph," Luc said, "and I pledge to use every skill I have to make your home the one you and Ingrid deserve."

When they arrived at the pond, Luc found the spring that fed it. Gurgling out of the ground, spring water trickled over a bed of smooth rocks as it ran to the pond. "Almost sounds like it's laughing," Luc said, lifting a double handful of water to his lips to taste.

"Fresh and sweet," he said. Then, a confused look overcame him, and his brow wrinkled.

Joseph asked, "Something wrong, Luc?"

"Yeah," Luc answered. "I just thought of something. How do I tell people my brother is marrying my sister?"

Joseph grinned, shook his head and said, "And when you introduce me and they hear this British accent, they'll be even more confused!"

"'A British Boucher?' they'll ask," Luc laughed. As another thought hit him, he said, "And then, I'll introduce Lois . . . "

"And," Joseph jumped in, "when they hear her speak, they'll think she's *my* sister!"

"You know," Luc said, clasping an arm around his brother's shoulder, "we'll probably be explaining ourselves for the rest of our lives!"

Two brothers left the pond behind them and laughed their way home.

Chapter 49

It was the third week of November when Luc received orders from the Royal Canadian Army for a final assignment before his discharge. He learned that the Commander-in-Chief in the field during his service in Crete had recommended he receive the Military Medal, a medal awarded to Canadian Expeditionary Force members for acts of bravery during battle. Along with that news was a personal appeal from the Commander-in-Chief. He requested that Luc complete a tour of thirty-six New Brunswick and Nova Scotia venues to tell his story and encourage other young Canadian men to join the Royal Canadian Army.

When Luc received his medal in full dress uniform at Camp Debert in New Brunswick, he told those gathered that day, "I don't feel like a hero. I did only what I was trained to do. Those who provided that training, helped me hone my skills, and refused to send me into battle until I was fully equipped are the men who deserve this medal. Even more, though, those who died before I entered the battlefield that day in Crete will always be the real heroes. To them, we owe our heartfelt thanks." Luc didn't embellish his story but kept it simple and genuine. He shook the hand of every young man he met, most of whom sought an appointment with an enlistment officer before each rally ended. As a result of his tour, Luc was gratified to learn that one hundred sixty-nine men enlisted in the RCA.

Unbeknownst to Luc, officials at each venue had collected an honorarium on his behalf. Each audience member learned that Luc was still recuperating from his wounds and hoping for the full restoration of his eyesight. As a result, the donations had been generous. When the tour ended in the third week of November, Luc received his final paycheck from the Royal Army. Instead of the $39.00 he expected, he discovered a second check for a sum sufficient to meet his needs during the entire year ahead.

During that week, Sir Richard answered a request from Prime Minister Churchill to plan a trip to Washington, DC, to meet with the United States directors of military intelligence. At the same time, the Abrams family secured the visas required for their travel to join Daniel's family in Connecticut. Sir Richard was happy to route his itinerary through Hartford, and with his help, the family successfully made their border crossings and completed their trek to Hartford. Once the Abrams family received them in Connecticut, Sir Richard continued to Washington, arriving on the first day of December 1941.

Away from home and alone in his room at the British Embassy on Massachusetts Avenue in Washington, Sir Richard had the evening hours free to write to Nigel and Boyd. He smiled as he thought of Nigel's exploits on the HMS *Ark Royal* when he and his fellow airmen helped sink the *Bismarck* in early May. However, he remained even more grateful for Nigel's survival during the battle that sank the *Ark Royal* only two weeks ago. Tonight, Nigel was serving aboard the HMS *Formidable* in the Mediterranean. Sir Richard was sure that the next time he met his son, Nigel would have stories to tell.

Security regulations kept Boyd's last letter brief and without detail, but his father was well-informed through his own sources about the escapades of the HMS *Revenge*. Almost a year ago, the *Revenge* had a crucial role in the bombardment of the French port of Cherbourg, where in eighteen minutes, the *Revenge* and her escorts fired over a thousand shells into the harbor. As a result, Germany's fleet of invasion transport ships was destroyed. Once again, Hitler's hopes of invading the UK were foiled. Today, the *Revenge* was with the 3rd Battle Squadron based in Columbo, Ceylon, far from the U-boat hunting grounds.

It was a comfort to Sir Richard to track the whereabouts of his sons, but his knowledge brought him no real peace. One torpedo had sent the *Ark Royal* to the bottom of the sea. He knew it was a miracle that only one life among the crew had been lost. Nonetheless, German U-boats still roamed freely in Atlantic and Mediterranean waters. Thankfully, Boyd was sailing in the Indian Ocean, far from their hunting grounds. Nevertheless, no waters were entirely safe for British ships. Sir Richard returned to his prayers, asking for one more night of safety for Nigel and Boyd.

Over the next several days in Washington, Sir Richard sensed the high tensions American diplomats and the US intelligence community faced. Although he expected to offer some help with their needs in the

European theatre, he found that President Roosevelt was more intent on looking toward the Far East. The President was intimately involved in meetings with the Japanese delegation sent by Emperor Hirohito. Concerned about Japan's aggression in the Pacific theatre, including the invasions of China and French Indochina, Roosevelt sent a telegram to Emperor Hirohito on December 6, urging him to withdraw Japan's warships from Indo-China. Roosevelt included an offer of friendship to Japan in the hope that the conflict between Japan and China could end, but no response from Hirohito had been forthcoming.

The weather in Washington on Sunday morning, December 7, 1941, was seasonably cold. Sir Richard anticipated no pressing business on a Sunday and took time for a brisk walk on Massachusetts Avenue, where he found the temperature was warming each hour. Having skipped breakfast, he returned to have lunch in his room. Sometime after mid-afternoon, an embassy staff member knocked at his door to deliver a message from the Earl of Halifax, the British ambassador.

That message, though brief, told Sir Richard all he needed to know. The Japanese, while still in negotiations for peace with the United States, had launched a surprise air attack on the US Pacific fleet on the island of Oahu in the Hawaiian Islands. With more than 24 US ships sunk, the American death toll was expected to exceed 2,400. Sir Richard also learned that Japan's attack was not limited to Pearl Harbor. The Japanese also attacked the Philippines, Wake Island, Midway, and Guam. Later, he read reports describing Japanese attacks on the British territories of Hong Kong, Singapore, and Malaya. But that was not all. During the same period, Japanese forces also invaded Thailand and the Dutch East Indies.

Listening from the gallery of the House of Representatives the next day, December 8, 1941, Sir Richard applauded with the senators and representatives at the joint session of Congress as President Roosevelt promised, "No matter how long it may take us to overcome this premeditated invasion, the American people in their righteous might will win through to absolute victory." When the applause quieted, Roosevelt continued, "With confidence in our armed forces and with the unbounding determination of our people, we will gain the inevitable triumph, so help us God." Following Roosevelt's speech, both houses of Congress stood ready to affirm Roosevelt's request, and the United States declared war on Japan.

At that moment, Churchill's voice echoed in Sir Richard's ears—"We shall fight on the beaches, we shall fight on the landing grounds, we shall fight in the fields and in the streets, we shall fight in the hills; we shall never surrender . . . "

Sir Richard smiled, for despite the grief that the Japanese attacks had brought to so many nations of the world overnight, he remained confident that the alliance between the British Commonwealth and the United States would not fail to bring peace to the world again.

When he returned to the embassy later that afternoon, Sir Richard found a communiqué from SIS in London. It concerned a Berlin resistance group called *Solf Circle* and its leader, a man known as Beppo Römer. Over the last several years, he, along with a partner, Nikolaus Von Halem, had perpetrated a series of plots to assassinate Adolf Hitler. New information suggested they were ready to launch another attempt, aided by a third associate, a man who had recently joined them from a resistance group in Strasbourg. He was known to them simply as "Eddy."

Sir Richard could wait no longer. He stood at the telephone while the operator at the embassy dialed both Highfield's telephone line and the private line in his study. Susan was passing through the kitchen when the telephone rang. Leaving the receiver dangling, she ran to the bottom of the stairs and called, "Mother, pick up the telephone receiver! Father is calling." At the same time, Michael was passing Sir Richard's office in the study when the secure telephone line rang there. He had just heard Susan calling Lady Moncrieff when he heard Susan desperately calling him, too.

"Michael, please answer Father's telephone in his office."

Holding a telephone receiver in each hand at the operator's station at the British embassy, Sir Richard delivered the news.

"Angela? Susan? Michael? Are you there?"

"Yes," Susan and her mother answered in chorus. "Michael is at your telephone, Father," Susan said.

"Michael," he said, "Are you there, Michael?"

"Yes, Richard," Michael answered, "I'm here."

"Then I ask you to celebrate with me if you please," he said. "I've just come from a joint session of the American Congress, who, answering President Roosevelt's request, have declared war on Japan!"

A cheer from Susan in Highfield's kitchen returned an echo from Lady Moncrieff's bedroom.

"Richard," Michael said. "We read of the Japanese attack in the Pacific earlier today. But, please confirm that the United States will also declare war on Germany."

"Rest easy," Sir Richard said happily. "Neither Germany nor any among their hellish alliance will escape the wrath of the American military might. That Italian dictator and his puny army will endure a fury unlike any the world has known. Finally, the Commonwealth has an ally, one strong enough to make Germany, Italy, and Japan rue the day they woke this sleeping giant."

When the cheering at Highfield subsided, Sir Richard made a polite request.

"Ladies, would you be kind enough to abandon our telephone connection so I may speak with Michael on SIS business?"

"Of course, Richard," Lady Moncrieff acquiesced. "I'm sure you must have a great deal of business to which you must attend."

After the ladies' goodbyes, Sir Richard shared the information he had received from his resistance operatives in Germany.

"Amazing," Michael said, "So, Ernest Duncan lives on, but now in Berlin."

"So it appears, Michael," Sir Richard said. "Perhaps one day soon, we will hear of an attempt on Hitler's life."

"Then I will hope it's more than an attempt, Richard. I will pray that our ambitious Allied sympathizer ends the source of the present evil and that right soon," Michael said.

"In the meantime, however," Sir Richard said quietly, "Duncan's very existence remains our secret. His life depends on it."

"Understood," Michael affirmed, "understood."

With his telephone communications complete, Sir Richard returned to the quiet of his suite at the embassy. A bottle of Dewars and a glass awaited him on the mahogany cocktail table. He poured two fingers before relaxing into the comfort of the blue velour sofa. While enjoying his first sip, he took a final look at the communiqué from the French resistance. A hint of a smile appeared as he slipped the folder into his briefcase next to his Walther PPK. Lifting his glass, he smiled and said, "Now that's a secret worth keeping, Moncrieff. Truly, a secret worth keeping."

Terms and Abbreviations

Allies—those countries who fought against the Axis powers in WW II, chiefly the United Kingdom, the Soviet Union, the United States, and China

Axis—those countries who fought against the Allied powers in WW II: Germany, Italy, and Japan

Blitz—the German bombing campaign against the United Kingdom

Blitzkrieg—"Lightning War," the military offensive strategy used by Germany in WW II

Enigma machine—an encryption device used by Germany to send coded messages

Fleet Air Arm—the Royal Navy's aircraft division operating from Royal Navy ships

Gestapo—the official secret police of Nazi Germany and German-occupied Europe.

Hirohito—the Emperor of Japan during WW II

HMS—His Majesty's Ship

Kindertransport—a rescue effort that helped thousands of Jewish children escape to Great Britain during WW II

Kriegsmarine—Nazi Germany's navy

Low Countries—Belgium, the Netherlands, and Luxembourg

Luftwaffe—the air force of Nazi Germany from 1935-1945

Masefield—John Masefield, Poet Laureate of England from 1930 until 1967

Mussolini—the fascist dictator of Italy during WW II

Nazi—the National Socialist Party led by Adolf Hitler that ruled Germany from 1933-1945

NSB—the fascist National Socialist movement in the Netherlands

Oberleutnant—and Upper Lieutenant, the highest lieutenant rank in the German armed forces

ON convoy—ON (Outbound North) convoys sailed from Liverpool via the North Channel under escort to Halifax Harbor in Canada beginning in July 1941

PEI—Prince Edward Island

Pier 21—Canada's principal military departure point and immigration facility during WW II

RAF—Royal Air Force

RCAF—Royal Canadian Air Force

RCN—Royal Canadian Navy

RN—Royal Navy

SIS—the Secret Intelligence Service in the UK, later commonly known as MI6

SS—Schutzstaffel, a major paramilitary organization under Hitler's Nazi Party Third Reich

U-boat—Unterseeboot (under-sea-boat), German submarines used during WW II

Walther PPK—a small, easily concealed semi-automatic pistol often used by SIS personnel

Wehrmacht—the unified armed forces of Nazi Germany from 1935-1945

www.ingramcontent.com/pod-product-compliance
Lightning Source LLC
Chambersburg PA
CBHW050359030726
47503CB00006B/1932